The Paranoid Thief

*To my sister Alla Deann
My first book in print*

The Paranoid Thief

Danny Estes

Marble, NC USA
2014

Copyright © 2014 Word Branch Publishing

All rights reserved. This book or any portion thereof may not be reproduced or used in any manner whatsoever without the express written permission of the publisher except for the use of brief quotations in a book review.
This is a work of fiction. Names, characters, businesses, places, events and incidents are either the products of the author's imagination or used in a fictitious manner. Any resemblance to actual persons, living or dead, or actual events is purely coincidental.

First Edition 2014
Printed in Charleston, SC USA

Cover illustration © 2014 Julian Norwood

Permission can be obtained for re-use of portions of material by writing to the address below. Some permission requests can be granted free of charge, others carry a fee.

Word Branch Publishing
PO Box 474
Marble, NC 28905

http://wordbranch.com
catherine@wordbranch.com

Library of Congress Control Number: On file

ISBN-13: 978-0615936949 (Custom)
ISBN-10: 0615936946

This novel is dedicated to Patricia O'Reilly.

For without whose love, this book would never have been finished.

Chapter One

Randolph McCann crawled away from the smoldering wreckage of the cross-wired hover bike he'd stolen and shook his dizzy head. With considerable effort, he stood and tried to discern the glow of the stars above, over those swimming around in his eyes. The ride over the tree tops had been one wild scare, with peaks and eddies. *Definitely more excitement than I needed,* he thought to himself, then cleared his head of the obvious.

While his mind and body partly refused to talk to one another, both still living the past ten minutes, Randolph caught a momentary image of a tree amongst the hybrid bushes of Willing's city park and stumbled over to sit his butt down before gravity took over.

I made a tactical error tonight, Randolph needlessly told himself, *one which could have been detrimental to my well-being, if not to my freedom.* With his head laid back against the tree, Randolph tried to focus on the pile of twisted aluminum which once resembled the latest achievement in aerodynamics. *Perhaps it's time for plan D,* he mused as he gathered his wits. *After all, the first three are history now, which means the job is history. Very problematic.*

Randolph looked to one hand, which had balled up into a fist on its own. Mr. Hilden had trapped him into this doomed caper and left very little doubt as to what the results of a failure would bring about. While these thoughts presented themselves vividly before his mind's eye, Randolph's body begin to shake. *A reasonable reaction.* The shakes were not due to Mr. Hilden's threats, but rather from Randolph's heroic efforts to avoid being intertwined in the twisted metal some feet away.

Uncertain how long the shakes would last, Randolph wrapped his arms about his abused self, which at present was encased in a very illegal special-ops night suit he'd acquired for the job. *A rather expensive acquisition,* he reflected with regret, *but as I had no time…* Randolph laid his head back once more and swallowed. He closed his eyes and with some effort reconnected his scrambled thoughts with reality. *Yep, time to cut the umbilical cord and find someplace to lay low,* he told himself, "and I best get a move on." He spoke the last aloud as if that would aid in his recovery. With more effort than he would admit, Randolph opened his eyes and used the tree for support in gaining his full height of five feet and nine inches. *Not a real impressive height,* his mind commented to redirect his thoughts from several painful abrasions, *but one which allows more anonymity, which is useful for blending into crowds.*

Once more on his feet, Randolph used an unsteady hand to pull off the black hood of the suit to better see; for the night vision had been rendered inoperable. As the hot, skin-tight material reluctantly came away from his head, the cool air of mid November rushed over his damp, clean-shaven face, and the scalp covered in closely-cropped hair which Randolph judged neither attractive nor repulsive.

Randolph took in a deep breath of clean, early morning air and exhaled a sigh of gratitude that he was no longer dependant on the suit's chemical air system, an integrated part of the suit's stealth system, which he had no need of. *But then again, one never knows.*

He pushed away from the tree and moved a bit unsteadily in circles until his land lover legs quit wobbling about as if he were a toddler on his first steps of life's adventures. "I've been far more than lucky tonight," he vocalized the blindingly obvious. "With only two weeks to scope out the security measures of that three story mansion, my efforts to pull off this job were far more than epic." Randolph paused in his commentary and searched out the zipper to the suit. *If only I could have backed out of the job. If only Mr. Hilden had listened to me. Now nobody wins,* Randolph argued to no one but himself, while he carefully stripped out of the outfit on steadier legs. *Now the package I'd been sent in for will go to the corporate authorities as forewarned and there's nothing Mr. Hilden can do to stop it.* Randolph's latest target, the Henderson's, lived in the city of Willing, located on the lower tip of what was Arkansas before the inventor of plastic-steel, Mr. Luashess, single-handedly bought Arkansas, Mississippi, and Louisiana, then renamed them as the single state of Luashess. *As Mr. Henderson, an executive officer for the Badding firm and Ms. Henderson, a highly paid lawyer in legal documentation, a pair of very intelligent individuals, will definitely surmise rightly what tonight's failed escapade was all about.*

Now that his wobbly legs were responding reasonably well, Randolph stretched his back muscles to work out any leftover kinks and said firmly to himself, "To hell with it." Without any regrets, Randolph wadded up the lightweight material which had cost over 30,000 credits to acquire and disposed of the suit onto the heap of smoldering aluminum and fiberglass like it were nothing more than a pile of old rags.

"I told that blackmailing, pompous city official I wasn't suited for dirty in-and-out jobs," Randolph argued aloud to the hybrid self-maintaining vegetation, while he extracted a saddle bag from the back of the bike. With contempt for this century's security lock, deemed adequate on all business travel bags, he opened and drew out a white and blue jogging suit and continued to berate Mr. Hilden. "If that self inflated ego had only listened. If he had hired people who do this type of stuff, if, if, if," he told the park's vegetation and miniature inhabitants in anger, now that they had overcome their fright of his unannounced arrival.

After a moment more, Randolph forced himself to stop his unfruitful ranting and took in a deep breath of the earthy incense around him. As fall covered the land, this meant the aromatic scents in the air was not of sweet flowers and new growth, but rather the heady smells of bark and rotting vegetation. A distinct difference some people found objectionable. For Randolph, however, this meant the rebirth of wet weather, a distinct advantage in his chosen profession, as the migration of water molecules helped to dilute any leftover DNA. And as he found a hint of moisture on the air, this helped in his bid for composure. After another breath to reinforce his thoughts of impending rain, Randolph slowed his flustered mind and reasoned his anger was a combination of fear and uncertainty. A knowledge Randolph used to reclaim a calmer state of mind. *Well mostly,* he admitted to himself. A few breaths more and he focused his mind on plan D, outlining its conception in his head. *First, get back to the workshop,* he began to tic them off. *Second, eliminate any equipment that could point fingers at my style of operation. Third, leave the state of Luashess by any means possible. Simple really...perhaps,* he reminded himself. If there was one virtue Randolph had plenty of, it was his grasp on reality. He knew very well Mr. Hilden had a band of muscle men watching his every move, a fact which had not escaped him from the moment Mr. Hilden introduced his right-hand man, Mr. Stanton. The proverbial brick-wall in human form, who walked in Mr. Hilden's office dressed in a top of the line Harmanii business suit. *Geez,* Randolph remembered thinking, *the man's mug alone could stop someone's heart, making his over-large hands rather redundant.*

The Paranoid Thief

A sound in the distance caused Randolph to cock his head. "Sirens," he told himself and searched the skyline above the trees for the direction of the city's air patrol cars.

Whether they were after him or not, Randolph felt he'd rambled on long enough. *Time to get moving.* With a look in the other side of the saddle bag, Randolph removed a small round plastic pouch and discarded the empty bag with the rest of the present evidence to his attempted crime on the aerial-bike. Randolph rotated his head on his shoulders in an effort to work out one last kink before he activated the DNA scrambler's fifteen second timer he'd built from a simple two-credit watch. He walked away, tossing the bag of common household chemicals on the pile. After a short walk, Randolph heard the charge go *poof*, which meant the small explosive sent out a spray of chemicals that would render all surrounding DNA unusable for police labs and dogs alike, a fairly indispensable homemade device for his kind of career.

Uncertain of his current location, Randolph took a look at his compass watch, which showed him via satellite a small rendering of the 20 mile radius park. With an idea of where he stood, Randolph redirected his feet, heading for the jogger's path which he'd used this past week to make him appear as a new regular. *Precautions like this are always necessary to help in any alibi which may be needed if some unforeseen problem should arise, like now for instance.*

Although he was early for his daily run by an hour and twenty minutes, Randolph couldn't wait-out the extra time in the park. Mr. Stanton would awaken shortly, if he hadn't already, and be on the road to intercept him at his base of operations. So a variation of his alibi had to be improvised if he ran into trouble.

When the illuminated jogger's path became easier to discern in the darkness, Randolph stopped his jog through the woods to await a clear gap of early users. This precaution would insure no one saw him enter by the woods, making him just another runner. But as no one could say they had seen him in their run, Randolph forced himself to slow a bit, so as to be seen by others before he continued his run at a normal pace.

As Randolph worked out annoyed muscles, damaged slightly from his sudden unplanned stop, he allowed a small smile to touch his lips, knowing his preparations has covered his tracks. But he wasn't out of the woods yet, *literally,* he told himself as he rounded a hill. For up ahead, a little before the exit to the city's park was a hastily erected police checkpoint.
Man, these people are fast! Randolph thought to himself, but as his run and outfit would aid the officers very little in discerning his involvement in any crime, he felt relatively safe. *Besides,* he told himself to bolster his confidence, *check points are only glorified shows of force, built solely to mollify the mundane city dwellers and no threat to anyone other than the inexperienced thief.*
Randolph allowed these thoughts to trail off as he drew near the post, never even considering any abrupt change in course. *Because something as plainly incriminating as that would have the police chasing you down in no time.* So jogging up on the station like any innocent bystander, Randolph pressed his lips firm to look irritated on the inconvenience to his run. With an eye to normality, he also began a conversation with a fellow runner who had been ahead of him, playing up on his part of just another average citizen. As he questioned the man on the reason for police presence, Randolph paid a token curiosity to the structure's video-cameras, multi-directional microphones, and voice commanded search lights, while inwardly he

The Paranoid Thief

fidgeted on the lost time as the officers worked though the early morning crowd.

When Randolph was finally signaled he was next, he walked up to the decently-built female officer, whose facial structure was greatly mired by her look of constipation. With a quick eye for even the smallest detail, Randolph stopped on the hastily painted white line as directed by an unmistakable large sign on her booth and heard her snap in a no nonsense voice, "Name?"

"Bill Lenton," Randolph lied with practiced ease.

"Occupation?" she asked as she swept him over with an electric detection wand that only beeped on his watch, which she motioned for him to remove so it may be more thoroughly inspected.

"Sales rep for Pro Tip Produce," Randolph said with smoothness, pulling out his wallet to hand her a business card like any pushy business man might have. The woman took the card and his wallet simultaneously, then read the card, checking both sides.

"I see," she said out of boredom to the routine. "Where from?"

"Uh...Lexfunt, south of Portbay City, by the Great Lakes," Randolph added as if out of habit.

"Hmm," she remarked without interest while she pulled out all his fake ID cards and other paraphernalia a traveling sales rep might have. With a non-curious look to each item, she laid each down on her counter so the video-camera could imprint them on file. Once the wallet was empty and the video-camera had its time, she picked up his ID card with a fairly good picture of Randolph's long face, short stubby nose, average chin and hair style. "What are you doing so far from home, and specifically why are you out in the park so early on this particular morning?" She locked her eyes on his.

A pro, Randolph omitted, his opinion of her rising; *definitely a pro,* for the woman was watching his eyes to see which way they rolled up when he told his likely story. But as he had already run through the reason a few times in his brief run, Randolph began his fib with no uncertainty. "I've been visiting the stores nearby, demonstrating our product's differences but today I've a big pitch to give to a larger corporation, so I'm out early for a jog to loosen up before the meeting."

She sat his ID card down and nodded, as if she accepted his lie, then asked with some hardness. "Can you then explain the cut and bruise on your left temple?"

"Wha...?" Randolph reacted in surprise and reached up to touch his forehead. He winced from the light pressure on the damaged skin and his fingers came away with sticky wetness. *Of all the stupidity!* he angrily admonished himself, *I should have known to have given my forehead a 'look see' when my temple began to throb.* A small error like this could delay him even more, if he couldn't come up with a plausible lie in seconds. So he touched the area once more to hide any showing expressions and thought furiously.

"Well?" the woman prompted with impatience, apparently sensing she'd caught him in some illicit act, but whether that was a crime or not remained to be seen.

As Randolph sought out a plausible story, his eyes fell on the two bulges in her shirt which caused his animal instincts to wonder of their true size, shape and firmness. This distraction in the back of his mind brought forward a simple but typical male answer. With a quick mind to seize on such a simple story, Randolph ducked his head to look sheepish and replied, "Well, you see..." he stretched his words to sound embarrassed. "I came up on a nice looking woman, and well..." Randolph gave a hesitant laugh. "When I passed her by, my eyes stayed on her instead the tree I ran into."

"Uh-huh, and you expect me to believe that?" Her face radiated skepticism.

"Honest, Officer McCormick," Randolph added after he caught her name tag and pulled out a handkerchief to mop his temple, just remembering the throb on his forehead before he touched it.

"All right Mr. Lenton, come clean. Tell me the whole story and your lawyer will be able to say you cooperated with the police at your trial."

"Trial? For what? Running into a damn tree because I like women?" Randolph blurted with the knowledge she was only using entrapment tactics.

"Last chance, Mr. Lenton," she warned, signaling her back-up to step closer, an intimidation gambit to get him to bolt for the trees or foul-up his story.

"But I didn't do anything!" Randolph said excitedly, not falling for it, purposely drawing attention from the other joggers, whose faces he surmised held looks in varies degrees of curiosity to insecurity.

"Very well Mr. Lenton," the officer said with hardness. Then she leaned toward him, her body language all about intimidation. "You had your chance. We've got your name and pic ID. Should a woman report being molested and pick out your ID, ten years will be added to your sentence for police evasion." With a motion of her hand for him to pick up his articles, the woman looked down on her screen for any last minute warrants for his arrest. When she found none, the officer motioned Randolph could go, as she held no evidence to hold him on any crime. "You may wish to have a doc look at your forehead before operating any vehicles, Mr. Lenton," she said as he passed.

"Thanks Officer," Randolph responded in ill humor as his act demanded, refilling his wallet, very much pleased with his performance while she fished for the wrong reactions.

In a few steps Randolph exited the park and checked the time under the halo of a sun lamp. "2:47 a.m.," he mumbled. *The skimmerport won't open for another three hours yet. It'll be time enough to tie up loose ends.* With a sigh to resettle his nerves, Randolph tilted his face skywards to feel the moist drizzle in the air. Then after a couple of breathes, he looked down on his wrist watch and tapped its liquid crystal to bring up the avenues of approach to his present office. With one more tap, the watch showed him all the pathways to his office, which revealed one pathway he'd purposely left untraveled, with turns galore that would throw off any unwanted followers. With a causal look about, to make certain of no police surveillance, Randolph set his feet in motion along the near-deserted avenue.

When his first turn came, Randolph ducked into the alleyway with the knowledge no eyes could follow him in without exposing themselves. Now alone from even the regular foot traffic, Randolph jogged to the other end and stopped only momentarily to unzip and zip his jogging suit at key points to change its colors. Clad now in a black over blue jogging suit, Randolph walked out of the darkened shadows and kept track of his location with more scrutiny.

When at last Randolph came within sight of his place of operation, he slowed his hurried steps and watched everything. For now he had to be the paranoid thief he always was, as it was here all his preventive measures would either see him through or...*Hmm.*

Randolph flattened himself on an office wall and reasoned out why he must take this risk. *With the air bike's systems all but fried in my hasty retreat, I held no chance in redirecting the bike to my hidden stash of clothes and hard credits elsewhere in the city.* But as

Randolph was an accomplished pick pocket, this was really not a problem. What in truth was driving him back here was the evidence which could be gleaned from some of his equipment. *Really nothing the police don't already have,* Randolph argued, *but there are one or two items I'd rather not leave for Mr. Hilden. The man was too well connected. And knowing him, he would use them to assassinate my character. This in turn might step up police involvement or deter any others from seeking out my services.* Four or five other reasons were worth the risk of running back into the building. *But are they truly worth risking my life over?* With a turn of his head, Randolph scanned left, right and all directions in-between. But no matter how hard he looked, the stone facing at ground level and the street out front looked unimposing. *But what of the three lit windows?* He didn't even contemplate the hundred or so darkened windows in his inquiry, least he drive himself to distraction. With an eye on the three windows from his concealment, their angle to his office and the front doors seemed too severe for an assassin to attempt this one opportunity. *That is, if I'm worth the price of a competent assassin,* Randolph corrected his reasoning, *but once inside the office building I'd be relatively safe, as no one without an access card could get in, legally. Then again, Mr. Stanton didn't have the look of a man the least bit worried of breaking minor laws.*

With the knowledge of who might be inside, Randolph tried to swallow back the bile fouling his mouth and licked dry lips as he pulled out the building's access card. *If I'd had the time to set up my normal security measures, this trip wouldn't be necessary. If I hadn't left in such a hurry, if,if,if...* Randolph scolded himself. With the knowledge he was only stalling the inevitable, Randolph rubbed his sweaty palms dry on his sweat pants, took a deep breath and dashed across the street shoving the card key home. *Click,* the undeniable sound of the magnetic lock on the plastic-steel door sounded. With a yank on the door the instant the computer registered his office ID number, Randolph rushed in.

Once inside, the feeling of a bright neon target painted on his back by targeting electronics melted away. However, Randolph's elation of this victory evaporated the instant he was a few steps in. *No!* his mind screamed as he stopped in his tracks. With another silent denial to what his eyes were showing him, Randolph tried unsuccessfully to retrace his steps because a bulky body moved in between him and the door, jarring him into an uncomfortable stop. The very next instant before Randolph could side step the human blockage, he felt the unmistakable pressure of a pistol pressed up against his spinal cord.

Randolph's perspiration flew into overdrive as his eyes registered too late the four musclemen resting comfortably in the unadorned lobby couches. *NO! Heaven above no...! They shouldn't be here! I purposely showed off other avenues of escape I could use to sneak in or out of this building!*

Totally at a loss, Randolph looked on the group who by all rights should be elsewhere in the building, spread out to cover three other points of entry, not to mention the roof. So seeing them all gathered in this unadorned lobby meant he had granted them far more intelligence then they held. Or *perhaps I underestimated their numbers!* Randolph removed his eyes from this improbability to turned and look on the wall blocking his way out. He tilted his face up to view the Neanderthal with a uni-brow across both eyes, and upon seeing his menacing grin, knew he held no chance in removing this obstacle. With no need to broadcast his level of intelligence to Randolph, the big fellow motioned with a huge protruding chin that Randolph should walk right on in as he had been doing. Unable to render a justifiable reason why he should not, Randolph tried to swallow, then felt the reason against his side why he should obey the silent command.

For once in his life, while his heart did a double twist nose dive into building stomach acids, Randolph regretted his conviction to never carry a weapon. But even if he had, situations like tonight would still have found him in this same predicament. So even lamenting his choice, he would still be here, slowly raising his hands to inform the row of badly-tailored line backers he held no weapon to endanger their lives.

Unable to influence matters until a change in his favor presented itself, Randolph watched the worst of the lot, the one with more intelligence than the whole group combined, calmly fold up the paper he'd been reading before standing.

Encircled by the five heavies, whose mothers apparently ignored basic nutrition requirements in child care, preferring to raise their sons on beef byproducts and steroids, Randolph watched in mounting dread as Mr. Stanton crossed the badly-polished, dull white floor, dressed smartly in fashionable black dress shoes.

The brick wall dressed in a blue-stripped Harmanii business suit brushed off imaginary lint on the sleeve, before he tugged on a 2,000 credit diamond cuff-link as a signal to his men he wished to speak to his captive. "My dear Mr. McCann," he began with a voice basted in malice, nailing Randolph's wide eyes with his own hard gray ones. "You don't know how relieved I am to see you whole and unhurt. Especially after the all-points bulletin on my police band," he calmly showed off the very illegal card scanner just inside his inner jacket pocket as he switched it off. "Why, by the sound of the chatter, you managed to upset two city precincts, which I must say caused me some misgivings in regards for your safety. But thankfully, here you are." Mr. Stanton smiled then, like the proverbial cat before he devoured the mouse. "But upon my word, you don't look likewise pleased to see me and my associates." The mountain man, whose manicured fingernails looked well out of place, frowned down on Randolph as if he were genuinely aggrieved to learn of this, regardless of what his cold gray eyes said. "This sentiment, of course, could not be from not accomplishing your task this night," Mr. Stanton then announced, "as Mr. Hilden very plainly explained the consequences. So I can only surmise your current state of anxiety could only be derived from being uncomfortable in my presence." Mr. Stanton allowed a false look of sadness to touch his facial muscles before he continued, "I am thusly very hurt, Mr. McCann. I had thought our prior meeting was rather enjoyable. But now I plainly see that you're shaking in my very presence. Very well," he said as if being reasonable, "If you'll but hand over the package you acquired from Mr. Henderson's home office safe, my men and I will depart, and no more need be said or done between us."

Randolph tried to wet dry lips with a dry tongue while he thought furiously. If only he could recalibrate his brain. *If, if, if...* he berated himself, knowing it was futile to render up excuses but he had to say or do something! "Look Mr. Stanton," Randolph began lamely, "I tried! I really did try, but I'm not one of your fly-by-the-seat-of-your-pants sort of thief. I told Mr. Hilden that, you heard me! It takes months for me to setup a properly executable job, not days!"

Mr. Stanton frowned with an evil smile which spoke louder than words he'd never expected Randolph to achieve his task. "So you were unsuccessful?" Mr. Stanton asked needlessly with a shake of his head as if he were even remotely saddened at Randolph's failed attempt.

"Look, please," Randolph threw into the silent moment of false remorse. "I have 50 thousand credits in an island account. I'd be glad to give them to you if you were to simply misplace me. Give me five minutes, just five minutes head start and I'll disappear."

"Tsk tsk, Mr. McCann. Have a little back bone. You failed in your appointed task, pure and simple," Mr. Stanton announced with distaste, taking out a hypo-dart pistol. Randolph's eyes locked on the conceivably deadly weapon that could be supplied with harmless sedatives, or a kaleidoscope of non-traceable poisons. Regardless of whatever Mr. Stanton had chosen to insert into the barrel of his pistol, the consequences would be dire. But before Randolph could fall to the floor to cast aside the remnants of any dignity he may still own, Mr. Stanton pointed the gun and pulled the trigger.

Chapter Two

Randolph became aware of himself sometime later, sitting at his desk. He raised his head, feeling as if he'd had one too many boilermakers and blinked several times. Without any true consciousness of his actions, he took note that his monitor was on and the computer was actively running cheaply-designed intrusion software he'd never use. With a mouth tasting of dry cotton, Randolph smacked his lips and sat slowly up but found he was unable to manipulate his hands properly to acquire a cup of cold tea left on the desk. Still unsure as to why this was, and why he heard the office door slam open, Randolph fought to gather his wits and make sense of the pounding feet attached to bodies attired in Special Forces equipment. Just able to swivel his executive chair a bit Randolph looked blurry-eyed on three laser rifles trained on him before another body passed them by to cast him to the floor face first. Without hesitation the man strapped his arms and legs together in record time as if he were a rodeo bull in an old western video.

"Suspect is down and in custody," was the unnecessary yell above his prone body.

"Fan out and search the rooms," someone else shouted, which added to Randolph's pounding head. The feet about him moved away save one set, which moved one foot to apply weight to the center of his back with the added coldness of a riffle barrel planted to the base of his neck. A precaution which could damaged his spine or takes his life, which ever the officer felt appropriate, should he try and resist. But as Randolph marveled over why he was still alive rather than dead, he gave the armed officer no reason to put him in a wheelchair or incinerate his head.

The Paranoid Thief

"Lieutenant, have a look here," someone called from a closet across the room. His vision clearing, Randolph saw the officer open up a wooden crate he'd never seen before and pull out a strip of plastic explosive he knew with a certainty should not have been here. Randolph would never incriminate himself so easily, nor endanger the lives of any local residents so unnecessarily.

He closed his eyes and moaned in despair. *Mr. Stanton has set me up to take the fall for something. Now the question remains, how bad is it?* To this realization, Randolph sighed. *The court system likes open and shut cases regardless if they are or not. I just hope I get a competent lawyer who will do more than a look-see into where the equipment came from.*

After an hour on the floor while the trained men collected five or six items Randolph never acquired for the Henderson job, the officers gathered around him and applied body restraints. Four men then strapped him to a pole and hefted it up onto their shoulders to carry him out; a standard procedure for any dangerous suspects to restrict any chance of escape while transported through an unsecured area. Next came a short trip to the city jail still suspended within the vehicle; another precaution against any conceivable means of harm to the men present in the vehicle's cabin. Randolph then was carried out and placed in a holding cell where processing could begin.

After only a short time, Randolph was forced into an enclosed booth with half of one side made up of a glass-steel mirror plate, for observation. He was then instructed none too cordially to strip bare before restraint rings were applied to wrists and ankles by a robotic arm. Next came the unpleasant white room, where the magnetic rings were activated, a rather painful experience that resulted in his arms and legs being snapped out like Leonardo Da Vinci's depiction of the human body. Here three different chemicals sprayed over Randolph's body, one to dissolve every strand of body hair, a second to clean his skin of any objectionable germs and finally a third, to disinfect him of any stubborn air borne illnesses or chemicals. Next his arms and legs came together as if he were preparing for a high dive, so a rotating cylinder from the roof could slowly descend to take X-rays and videos of his outer and inner body structure. This unobtrusive technique by the aid of computers could now make a complete rendering of his body to produce his image in any position or outfit to better ID him in any disguise.

After all this humiliation, Randolph finally sat dressed in a bright red coverall, in a gray cell, five feet by five feet, three hours after hitting the jail, as yet without a clue to the charges against him. *But this is normal,* he reminded his overactive imagination. *Criminals should already know why they're here.* However, being set up as a fall guy by Mr. Stanton, Randolph was one of a small minority uncertain of his actual crimes in a system built to process criminals in wholesale fashion.

Given five days to sit on his butt and wonder over the matter, while the charges were tallied and a sentence agreed upon before the kangaroo-court would convene for the public records, Randolph's appointed hour for the public hearing arrived.

With the arrival of grim-faced court deputies, Randolph's restraints activated to a touch of a button, bringing his arms and legs together. Once he was settled on a robotic transport, the group of them, including two city guards as redundancy measure, saw him to the elevator platform. This decadent precaution had been established long before the restraints and robotic transport were incorporated to make certain no prisoners disappeared before the elevator could lift the defendant up into the courtroom.

The Paranoid Thief

Thus, without incident, Randolph was brought up into a glass enclosure, designed specifically so only the selected lawyer could hear the defendant's boisterous complaints. A procedure put in place to protect the sensitive ears of judge and witnesses alike, should an unruly defendant decide to molest those gathered with objectionable profanity.

Once the elevator came to a halt, Randolph looked around the small oak-panel room which included ten witnesses on a pew, a middle aged bailiff, an ambitious looking judge, an old prosecutor, and Randolph's all-too-young, snot-nosed-just-out-of-night-school lawyer. *It appears Mr. Hilden is taking no chances, calling in a favor to make my incarceration a certainty.* Randolph looked skyward, with the knowledge he'd been royally screwed. *The question now of course is how screwed?* And with that thought, his so-called trial started.

The kid outside his inverted containment dome sat down and somehow managed to open his briefcase with trembling fingers. *Possibly because this is his first courtroom appearance,* Randolph surmised.

"Let the video recorders show all court personal and witnesses are present," the bailiff called out. "Case number 37645AD, the city of Willing in the great state of Luashess, for the people. Mr. Prosecutor?" He finished without emotion before he backed away so a fat, balding, older man could activate his monitor which displayed on a liquid screen all charges attached to Randolph's case file.

The prosecutor, who bore the weight of over-indulgent eating habits, stood as customary so all could see the anger instilled in his fat face for the atrocities the defendant committed. "As you can all see," he began in a boisterous voice, "the charges against this unrepentant criminal are substantial. The defendant is accused with fifteen minor and seven major criminal acts which alone would render a life sentence. But those all pale before the willful murder and lack of consciousness for the lives of the whole Henderson family, including their pregnant daughter, five live-in servants, and the rape and murder of a chanced-upon jogger in the city's recreational park only an hour or more after setting up a bomb in the Henderson's three story mansion, causing it to collapse and kill all within." The prosecutor then stroked his black tie with chubby fingers and a cold smirk on his lips as the room of people reacted to his brutal inflection of words on the charges against Randolph. This reasonable reaction of outrage also included Randolph's own disbelief of the charges.

"The Henderson family wasn't even home!" Randolph screamed to the room but the glass enclosure carried his voice only to his lawyer's ear piece, which still lay in its cradle next to the kid's briefcase. "They were over...aw damn-it-all." Randolph exclaimed, as the true folly of his mistake sank in. *They were over at Mr. Hilden's home, per his invitation. Of all the stupidities I could have ever done. There was never any package to retrieve!* Randolph sagged against the restraints. *That was why Mr. Stanton was so smug. The whole thing was a set-up to get my DNA on the grounds and link me to the bomb, thereby killing off the family and leaving me the sole fall guy!* But what he couldn't at first understand was the jogger—why did they kill an innocent bystander? Then it hit him; the bomb had to be set off hours later when Mr. Hilden knew the whole family would be home. The death of the jogger had been the simplest way to get the wheels of corporate justice on the move. Any murder automatically put a person on the top of the list, rating a visit from the city's Special Forces. Once an informant squealed out Randolph's location, the specialized group would have mobilized and entered Randolph's office minutes after Mr. Stanton left. *A truly professional job,* Randolph grudgingly admitted. He turned his face to peer at the snot-

The Paranoid Thief

nosed lawyer whose slack-jawed face gave Randolph every confidence in the court system. With a look skyward for help, Randolph already could feel the imaginary needle of death slide into his arm.

"Mr. Hamming, how does your client plead?" The Judge questioned, his voice colored with loathing to further imprint what the kid's choice of words should render.

"Uh, hmm," the young man stumbled. He opened his collar with a finger and then straightened his tie. With a look to Randolph with fear plainly visible in his eyes, he never even attempted to pick up the ear piece to communicate with Randolph before he said with a squeaky voice, "Guilty as charged Your Honor."

"So entered," the judge declared and slammed his gavel down, totally ignoring that Randolph's lawyer had never spoken to his client. "Mr. McCann," the judge began. "Alias Bill Lenton, John Thornton, and Bob Towner. This court of law has the pleasure of sentencing you to death. As you have pleaded guilty, the sentence will be carried out in three days' time!" With a final drop of his gavel of justice, the judge called out, "Next case," while Randolph, though ranting and raving within his restraints, was lowered out of the courtroom.

Ceremoniously charged with murder meant top security measures were applied to the prisoner to make certain he couldn't deprive the grief-stricken families the pleasure of watching him die. But in Randolph's case, as he had been convicted in the death of a corporate head, the kangaroo court took extra measures to be certain their prisoner didn't off himself before the city could record his death. For executions of his notoriety were a profitable business, one guaranteed to bring in thousands of video sales at twenty credits a pop. This left no opportunity for Randolph to apply his very useful skills as a professional thief and escape artist, which left him, in three days' time, taken to the injection room by the same robotic transportation unit and redundant guards. Unable to control his emotional state, however embarrassing it may have been while moved to the special viewing room, Randolph excitedly implicated Mr. Hilden in the deaths of the Henderson family and the park jogger. Even so, while he cited over and over he'd never take a human life, Randolph knew it would only be seen as a slanderous gesture.

The robotic device of cold steel rolled without judgment of Randolph's disgraceful display of self preservation moved into a sterile room of white and rotated its passenger so that he faced a closed curtain. This curtain hid the faces of those possibly victimized by his criminal deeds. And although Randolph knew he had been judged rightly on most of the minor and major crimes, it wrenched asunder his soul to die for another man's crime! Indifferent to how it might look on video, Randolph fought his restraints, regardless of its futility, and pleaded his innocence at the top of his lungs unto deaf ears even after a neck ring had been forcibly applied to help immobilize his head and press his jaw closed.

"Please..." Randolph begged through pressed lips. "I didn't do it! I've never killed anyone! Please!" He begged on without any conscious thoughts on how history would view his apparent cowardly cry. While he continued to strain every muscle to regain his freedom, Randolph saw through teary eyes the change of staff, which meant the standard deaf medical attendant now oversaw his demise so no one need-be offended by his last words, save those who chose to behind the curtain and those who paid out the credits for the court's recorded video.

Now with the inconceivable last chance of a reprieve gone, Randolph let out a stream of obscenities and vows of retribution while the deaf attendant administered several drops on his lips of a foul-tasting liquid, which burned like fire once it worked its way onto his tongue. Several more drops were then added to the first from another dispenser which cooled Randolph's tongue but also caused it to swell up in his mouth like a dried-out sponge, so he could no longer voice any complaints. Once these measures were taken, the curtain before his eyes was pulled aside. Still whimpering his innocence, Randolph looked on the witnesses and blinked in disbelief as Mr. Hilden's face came into focus among the six present. The sight of Mr. Hilden's old face and appropriately disdaining look caused Randolph's heart to turn black as night and overflow with his first ever wish to kill a living person.

To sit there so smugly in my last moments of life! Randolph raged within his mind. If ever there was such a thing as hell, Randolph would have turned over his soul to give him the strength and time to break his bonds and smash that face back to hell with him!

Not able to look to his arm as his sleeve was cut open and the needle of death bit into his body, Randolph closed his eyes and tried to banish from his sight the slight up-curve grin of Mr. Hilden's lips. But as the cool liquid crawled up his vein in search of his heart, Randolph's imagination showed Mr. Hilden break out in hideous laughter, knowing only moments of Randolph's life remained. The insanity to bear such an image to his grave caused Randolph to rant violently within him; to vow whatever remained of his soul into death would descend onto Mr. Hilden like a merciless corporate giant engaged in a hostile take-over.

Chapter Three

What Randolph supposed the afterlife to feel like was anything but groggy. However, that's how he felt. And to add to his bewilderment, Randolph found he could barely pull a thought together till the last image of Mr. Hilden comfortably seated behind the window floated up into his irises. With a start, Randolph jerked fully awake and for a second or two he blinked before he sat up on a plastic-steel bed, covered with an allergenic non-cotton fiber cushion. In his next thoughts, Randolph realized this wasn't the execution chamber, nor was he back in the city's cell. The next surprise superseded all this when Randolph understood, *I'm alive?* Beyond astonished to find this realization true, Randolph rolled his eyes in his head and over his new seven-by-ten steel enclosure, with its single entry door and stainless steel toilet under a folding sink. *I am alive, but alive where?* Randolph probed ever corner within view. *Is this more of Mr. Hilden's surprises? Perhaps some sort of torture for implicating him in the Henderson's deaths instead of going to my grave in silence?* Questions as these Randolph knew to be a waste of time till some interactions was done to give clues or answers. As Randolph cataloged the obvious questions, his trained eyes automatically picked out the video camera and audiphones mounted in the ceiling, disguised as mere rivets. *Typical...* he mused as he wiped his face with both hands, only then realizing the restraint rings were gone and his face held four days of stubble growth. With this revelation, Randolph stood and did some stretching movements to A. work out some kinks in his bones, as the previous cell allowed little movement, B. check out the elasticity of his new orange coveralls, and C. to better have a look around without appearing to do so.

The Paranoid Thief

To all appearances, after Randolph's examination, he was indeed in a normal maximum containment cell meant for dangerous inmates. And as the security people would be watching him for the fight or flight need in all humans, Randolph moved to the rectangle hole in the door like a good boy, so all would nod their overpaid heads in approval. *Besides, I could use some idea as to what lies outside the cell.* The first thing Randolph took note of was that the designers held some level of education. For the cell doors had been placed so no guard would have his back turned directly behind another cell door. Next Randolph figured his new quarters resided in a small prison, for he counted only five doors on the other wall, which meant the total cells on his block was around nine or eleven. This he confirmed with the presence of a single doorway in the end wall with the all-important red EXIT sign above its frame. Further examination placed his cell three doors away from the opposite wall.

Randolph next bent an ear to the ambient sounds of the air circulation unit, the steady drip, drip of a leaky water pipe, and the unmistakable sound of a florescent light tube in need of replacement. These rather mundane sounds informed Randolph his cell held the only occupant. *Strange that, unless everyone is in the exercise yard, which is mandatory for inmates in normal city prisons,* however, unheard of in corporate-owned federal prisons, where Randolph felt certain he must now reside. After all, he was supposed to be dead. "Hmm..."

Randolph disliked the notion of what this might mean and turned away from the hole to straighten out his spine on the cell door. By all accounts everything looks normal but yet not. Randolph then absently rubbed his face before he checked his eye brows and hair stubble. *A good month will have to pass before any plans of escape could be seriously considered, that is unless I shave my head.* But as Randolph objected to the bald look, awaiting his hair to grow out would gave him time to get the pattern of the guards, food delivery, and identify the magnetic key circuitry in the wall by the door. All important preliminaries regardless of his hair preference, though totally useless until some knowledge of what lay beyond the door at the corridor's end presented itself.

While Randolph considered, he ran a hand over the back of his neck and winced in pain. "What the hell?" he exclaimed to the sudden explosion of angry nerve endings. Why he had not noticed the damaged skin before now was irrelevant; however, what was relevant after he gently explored the bruise located on his spinal column was the suture layer approximately one inch in diameter. *This is not a good sign.* Randolph removed his hand to lay his head back on the cool door. *To the best of my knowledge I've been in no accident to warrant spinal exploration. Conclusion,* Randolph surmised, closing his eyes in apprehension, *a controlling chip has been inserted.*

By force of will Randolph refrained from scowling up at the video camera while he considered this all-important discovery. As he remembered it, the news video implied such devices were still in the experimental phase and had yet to yield up all their capabilities. *However, if I remember rightly, the chips have been deemed illegal to be used on humans, as the Mental Health Institute, about the only governmental organization that could over rule the cooperate world, has vetoed the project.* This far-sighted ruling had been decided so corporations couldn't make it mandatory for their employees to have one installed. A logical outcome of the chip to further manipulate their workers as the corporations owned and ruled everything else, including most of the government agencies. *Though that knowledge is kept on the hush hush. Which bring to mind why I'm still alive.* By manipulating certain drugs, a presumed executed criminal could be removed to such a facility as a perfect guinea pig for further testing. "Hmm..." Regardless of the reason for the suture, Randolph had to admit he had jumped to an unverifiable conclusion. There could be a dozen reasons for the surgery to his neck, all possibly just as distasteful. With a look skyward, Randolph pushed off the door, filled a small metal cup with warm water from the sink and sat down relaxed-like, legs crossed, back to the wall, and took small sips from the cup. He'd found out everything he could without any interaction with his captors, so now was not a time to panic on conjecture, now was the time of recon.

Five days of observation set the pattern for meal delivery and the unwillingness of the guard to say words other than "meal time" or "hand over your plate." However disappointing this was, Randolph was still able to discern an elevator some distance past the door to the prison block. Another confirmation his new home was no normal prison, for most placed a sound barrier in between elevators and cells to limit outbursts from echoing through the shafts. This bit was cataloged along with no other prisoners present on his cell block. Add this to no yard time and no showers meant he would have to use a wash cloth for personal hygiene and make up an exercise program to keep in shape. Of course an entire week had yet to pass, so it was still plausible yard and shower time was given once a week. As Randolph debated on waiting out the time or simply stripping down and wiping himself off, the unexpected sound of the corridor door opening, followed prominently by the voice of a pleading woman, caused him to delay a bit longer on his decision.

"Let go! Please...you can't do this! No, no, no, stop it!" The panic-filled voice echoed down the hall, mingled with the sounds of someone struggling against one or two stronger people. "It's all just a mistake!" she wailed as Randolph bent to look through the meal slot. "I was only dong research!"

Randolph focused on a slender woman with short brown hair who struggled against two brutes while she cried. "You've got it all wrong; I can show you!" As she continued to plead, her long oval face showed cosmetic stains of tears, a sign she'd been crying for about an hour, depending on how much make-up she applied.

The two muscle men in unremarkable standard corporate uniforms held tightly to her upper arms and ignored her pleas like well-trained goons. Upon halting at a cell near Randolph's in the other wall, they turned and slammed the woman face first into the wall, so one could open the door to his left by inserting his card key. "No, no, no, you don't understand, I'm claustrophobic!" she then screamed.

From his angle, the woman was no corporate looker, but rather built like an athlete with braless breasts barely showing through the white ruffled blouse and small hips under the black mini-skirt which just covered her fanny. Randolph lowered his eyes beyond the new fashion black mini-briefs, meant solely by their designer to catch male eyes when women bent over, and noted tanned, strong-looking legs which if used right could be very detrimental to any man's family jewels. At a guess when they shoved her in the cell, Randolph figured her to be around 31, and around five-seven. *Quick too,* he observed, as she bounced off the cell floor quick as you please trying to make the door before it closed.

Randolph eyed the two impassionate men as they walked out of the cell block while the new captive rapidly pounded her fists on her door. But as this pair allowed the steel door to slide back on its own, instead of closing it themselves, it afforded Randolph the chance to count out their footsteps to the far elevator, even over the hysterical woman who for several minutes reacted like a wild animal, before she wore herself out and slid to the floor in frustrated sobs.

Randolph rubbed his growing beard and stood. The addition of this woman gave him new information to his growing list and possibly an invaluable source to more in the woman herself. That is, if he could get her talking. "Hmm..." With a shrug, presently indifferent to her obvious distress, Randolph knew now was not the time to explore this new avenue of possibilities. But later, when she calmed and stopped sobbing, she might open up and fill in the gaps. So he walked away from the door, refilled his cup with warm water and settled in to wait.

Sometime later Randolph awoke from a light doze to the sound of the woman pitifully calling out, "Hello, is anyone here? Please, if anyone is, say something. Please, I can't take this seclusion."

Still unmoved from his position on the bed, Randolph pondered the benefits of silence while her mental state broke down. That would make her easier for extracting information however, Randolph had to admit his own humanity wouldn't permit it, at least not until he knew why she was here, for some people deserved such treatment. "Hmm..." *Oh hell, I'm just a softy.*

"Please talk to me. I'll go insane if I don't talk to someone. I can't take this loneliness."

"So, what are you in for?" Randolph broke in while she was in a fit of crying.

Her first words were not understandable, but finally she calmed enough for them to be understood. "Jill! My name's Jill, Jill Wander. Who are you?"

"John," he lied simply.

"John?" she asked in a quivering voice that began to steady. "John who? Do I know you?"

"I rather doubt it," Randolph replied as he changed positions to relax against the wall with hands clasped behind his head. "I normally don't work west of the Eastern time zone." Which was true, but his last successful job had led him into the state of Luashess after a rich corporate CEO whose bank credits needed removal after screwing over his employees when he rewrote their pension and pocketed seventeen million credits in the process. Randolph gave a rueful smile of remembrance on that job. Hired by the employees to recoup their hard-earned retirement funds, Randolph had transferred equal funds to over seven-hundred bank accounts, minus his commission and expenses, leaving the CEO 2.23 credits in his personal account, which was just enough to buy a cheap cup of coffee. Randolph's smile broadened slightly further as he recalled the two secret accounts he'd stumbled on, buried deep in the bureaucracy of the corporate finances, where the CEO had his two girlfriends' monthly expenses and apartments included in the company's house cleaning finances. This bit of information was the coup-de-grâce when he unlocked the security code so any competent accounting clerk would find it easily in the monthly book balancing.

"John, are you still there?" Jill's voice broke into his reminiscing.

"Yeah sure, it'd be rather hard for me to be anyplace else right now." Randolph turned his head toward the door in a normal bid to make himself better heard and inquired, "So tell me, what corporation is this?"

"Seriously, you don't know?"

"I was rather unconscious when I was brought here, wherever here is." Hopefully she'd tell him.

"No kidding, who do you work for?" Jill asked back without answering his question.

"I am but a lowly business man, in finances really, when men like those two brutes who brought you here busted into my office and knocked me out."

"You work alone, then?"

"I find it better to do so, or so I thought till I wound up here with no one to wonder where I am. So tell me, where am I?" Randolph tried again as plainly as possible.

"The city of Calaway," Jill finally answered. "Do you know it?"

Randolph shook his head. "No, never heard of it. What state is it in?"

"Yanncy, some miles in the Hopeless Desert," she supplied.

Yanncy, he mused, picturing the continent. Yanncy was the redefined lower half of California and Arizona borders when the Yanncy Corporation bought all mineral rights to land and air quality. Definitely out of his operational range as he preferred the East Coast, where the buildings were built to withstand hurricanes and therefore much easier to break into for a competent thief.

"Do you know it now?" Jill questioned, her voice sounding more even and controlled.

"Only as a place on the map," Randolph answered truthfully, then he faced forward and asked, "So tell me, do you work here?"

"Yes, no. Well I did but I guess I just got fired." She sniffed. "Ten years down the drain because I tried to help out a friend."

"Ten years, huh, so you would know a great deal about this place, such as the roads and the nearest skimmer-port?"

"Yeah sure, but what good is that? These cells are five levels underground. And if you're thinking of overpowering the guards, forget it. Their passkeys are coded to their current height and weight when they log in each shift, so when the passkeys are used, any change will alert the security system," Jill freely supplied that rather useful information and then caught on to his question. "Wait a minute—you're planning an escape aren't you?" Jill became quiet for a moment, then her voice perked up. "John, take me with you, please. I don't want to go to jail. I've heard what it's like there."

"Hold it, girl, who said anything about escaping? I was just trying to figure out where I am."

"I maybe a lowly secretary, John, but I'm not stupid. You've figured a way out. Well, if you don't take me with you I'll tell you nothing else of use."

Okay, so I hadn't been subtle enough, Randolph admonished himself, *a mistake that.*

"I mean it, John," Jill stressed. "You either take me with you or I swear I'll tell the guards."

Randolph rolled his eyes skyward on her threat and enlightened her on the realities of their situation. "As these cells are most likely bugged, that admission is rather redundant, for you already have."

"Oh," Jill answered lamely.

"So tell me, with a figure like yours, do you work out?" Randolph needed to get a better feel of her capabilities, as she appeared to be a necessary factor in his escape plans.

"My figure? I thought you didn't know me?"

"I saw you though the meal slot," Randolph enlighten her.

"Oh..." Jill answered slowly before she asked. "So, did you like what you saw?"

"I like a little more meat on the bones, but yeah, you're not bad looking."

"You mean my breasts aren't large enough, don't you? The story of my life." Jill sniffed. "All my girlfriends kept telling me if I wanted to get anywhere in this corporate world, I'd need to enlarge them and the size of my butt." Jill then slammed her hand on the door in anger and complained, "But surgery is so expensive and on a secretary's salary a bit out of reach unless I slept my way into a better pay-scale."

"Is that why you're wearing the latest mini-skirt and panties?" Randolph asked to try and understand her mental stability as he had only one shot at this.

"Yeah sort of," Jill admitted. "I mean, I've seen those women on the top floors with the D-cups and matching hips, and knowing I'm smarter than them doesn't help." Jill paused a moment before she asked, "John? What is it about breasts you men are so fascinated with? I mean, all they do is hang there. Why is it a woman with small breasts will be over looked for those who have larger?"

"I think it's more of a primitive desire in our psyche," Randolph supplied with a shrug.

"Well, why do you like them, then?"

Not able to truly answer that question, Randolph changed the subject. "Never mind that, do you know what time it might be?"

"Maybe," she answered hesitantly. "Are you taking me with you?"

"In truth, I have no choice. Now then, what time is it?"

"Well, it was 6:20 when I was caught. I think that would make it around 8:40 now."

"Morning or night?"

"Oh, sorry," she giggled. "8:40 p.m. Not much later, I'm sure."

Randolph reset his internal clock.

"So when do we go?"

"Probably never, if you keep asking stupid questions like that," Randolph snapped in irritation.

"Oh, sorry. It's that I'm a bit claustrophobic, but I can control it for a short time."

"Good." Randolph sighed and rubbed his eyes in annoyance to this whole business, for he really despised being dependent on anyone other than himself. "Now then, when do the most people get about in the hallways upstairs?"

"I'd say at the change of shifts, about 4:30 in the afternoon."

"Okay, get some rest if you can."

"Are we going tomorrow?" Jill asked in surprise.

"Don't be stupid. I'll need more information before I commit myself. Besides, I need to get to know you better."

"What, something other than my bra size?" Jill asked, her sarcasm thick.

"Jill, if you'll remember, you were the one that brought that up. I asked if you worked out."

"Oh yeah. Um, so tell me, did you like my butt? I've spent half a month's salary on a body tan to wear these panties." When Randolph didn't answer right away, Jill asked, "Or are you a leg man?"

Randolph shook his head and lay down; it sounded as if Jill was self-conscious of her figure. *Oh well, we all have our idiosyncrasies.* Out loud he told her, "Your legs and fanny looked pretty cute to me."

Without interruptions that night, Randolph's mind wandered about and came up with an unanswerable question. *Why did she assume I could get us out of here? And why would she risk it? She's only going to suffer the loss of her job and a fine, or at most a year in a city prison, that's not much. Granted, prisons are not a cushy place, but while inside, those still showing prospects have their pick of training and of course with a body like hers, she could always choose military service instead of jail.* Randolph mulled over his question, then conceded he held no time for answers. If he guessed right, the corporation would scare the wits out of her a few days before the city police picked her up. So if he were to get out of here, this afternoon would be his best chance. *Well, with her help,* he corrected. So around three in the morning, by his internal clock, Randolph lay back in bed and made certain his blanket kept him covered. With the knowledge of what was to come next, Randolph gritted his teeth and took a strong hold of his left arm. Next he took in three quick breaths before he pushed and turned the arm. With a wish to let out a scream of agony, Randolph bit back a cry of pain as scar tissue tore and the arm popped out of joint. As tears engulfed his eyes, Randolph let go of his arm to push on a button in the long bone. This action activated a precisely-calibrated spring to slice an exit in his skin for a slender tube to eject halfway out. With trembling fingers, Randolph removed the water-repellent tube from the cavity in the bone and unscrewed a cap on the cylinder with teeth and fingers. Once the threads disengaged, Randolph allowed the lid to fall in his mouth so a pain capsule nestled within could fall out. Once Randolph spit out the lid, he chewed the capsule to pulp and allowed the pain reliever to slide down his throat to hit his empty stomach like prime seasoned steak hitting battery acid. After ten long minutes had passed, Randolph sighed in some relief. Five more and all the pain was gone. Now able to breathe normally, Randolph worked to reattach his arm and applied a skin-colored patch from the tube to the damaged area. *I bet whoever invented this molding material never conceived it could be mistaken as a human bone by X-ray film.*

"John?" Jill called out. "John are you all right? You sounded as if you were in some pain."

"I'm fine..." Randolph smiled, now that the painkiller was working to its fullest effect. "I just stubbed my toe while sleep walking," he improvised.

"Sleepwalking? Do people really do that?" Jill asked with curiosity, not sounding like she did earlier in the evening.

Now able to move without the annoyance of pain, Randolph popped the arm back in place and moved it about to make certain all seemed well. This had been the second time he'd suffer through such action since the surgical procedure seven years back replaced the real bone with the molding material. "Well, apparently so, if I'd just told you I was doing it."

"You don't have to get all huffy about it. It's not as if we know each other intimately," Jill accused.

"Jill, um, why don't you go back to sleep?" Randolph tried with less annoyance in his voice.

"Humph, I can see why you worked alone. You have no tolerance for someone trying to get to know you."

"The middle of the night is hardly the time to divulge deep dark secrets, now, is it?" Randolph reasoned.

"What does that have to do with anything in this place? Night or day, we're not going anywhere, at least not until you're ready. And as I'm dependent on you, you'd think you'd have some compassion for my feelings, especially as I'm your ticket out of here," Jill huffed.

"Listen, we have plenty of time to get to know each other later, so will you please go back to sleep?" Randolph insisted with some exasperation, rolling to his side so he could pour out the contents of the cylinder next to his chest.

"Boy, you sure are surly at night. Are you always so rude when you don't get eight hours sleep?"

Randolph took in a breath but decided to keep his mouth shut. *She's so full of questions,* his mind threw before his thoughts. *Well, you can't really blame her,* he then told himself, *soon she'll be fully dependent on my capabilities and speaking of which...* Randolph decided to let her ramble as he concentrated on the small items from the tube. With total familiarity of the parts, it was a simple task for Randolph to assemble the two electronic devices he'd specifically designed to snap together without the use of solder.

"John, are you still awake?" Jill asked with a slight catch in her throat. "I only wish to talk a little. It would better help me with my problem."

"Yes, Jill I'm still awake." Randolph sighed, with a wish she'd shut-up. With one component complete, he started in on the other. "How can I not be with your voice echoing in my cell?"

"I was just thinking, once we get out of here, where do we go?"

"You're talking as if I've done this before," he butted in, feeling around for a very small resister and closing his eyes with a sigh once he found it.

"Well, haven't you?" she asked. "Remember, I'm not one of those D-cup-size toys upstairs whose pay out matches their IQ by several digits. I can add one and one, and you're too calm for a simple businessman."

"Perhaps I'm calm because I've been trying to meditate," he shot back, screwing the cap back on after he finished the small but powerful laser pen.

"I doubt that seriously. Within our conversation you've sounded angry, annoyed, bored, bothered and not all in that order."

"What are you, some kind of psychiatrist?"

"I've told you I'm a secretary. I have to know my boss's moods to keep from getting on his bad side every day or worse yet, fired. Of course that's all redundant now, as I've used his computer once in two years and—and here I am."

"I thought you said you worked for him ten years now?" Randolph probed the inconsistency in her story while he check to make certain he'd not missed any components.

"No, I said I worked here for ten years. I've worked for my cold-hearted boss for two of those years." After a moment of silence she asked, "Do you think if I'd screwed him a few times he would have over looked my slip up?"

Still on his side, Randolph opened his coveralls and pushed the laser pen up into his rectum. He used this uncomfortable precaution in case his cell and person was searched once he activated the frequency disruptor he still held in his hand. The small device, shaped like a large pill, made it easier to swallow once activated and harder to find. So with a touch, Randolph triggered the timer and swallowed without water, knowing in about four hours it would emit an ever-increasing electronic disruption till around noon, when it would stop. Then four hours later it would restart, but this time the disruption would be complete for half an hour, time enough he hoped to be on his way out of here.

"John, did you hear me?"

"Yes, Jill, and no, I doubt it. You don't have the body for it. Besides, by handing you over it shows he's loyal to the corporation, a plus in any-one's jacket."

"You sound as if you were a company man once."

"Far from it, but I've known people who are and how screwed they got. Corporations live only for the top executive's credit accounts. If you can't make them richer, then you're dead weight and very replaceable by someone who'll give up life and family. Now, please, I would like to get some sleep." Making himself comfortable, Randolph ignored her next few questions and closed his eyes.

Chapter Four

After his morning meal of grits, Randolph used the washcloth provided and stripped completely to give himself the best possible bath as could be had. As he had of yet not done so, Randolph knew this would stir the interest of the guard on duty while they tried to track down their system problem. But since he showed no other signs of knowledge to their visual problem, Randolph felt fairly assured the guard would settle back and await the electronic team. Once done, Randolph put his plate on the small ledge in the door slot and did the best he could with his hair after redressing.

Before noon, a team of electronic repair men ventured up and down the hall trying to discern the problem with their standard equipment. When the noon hour came, the team left as the problem stopped. *Good,* Randolph thought, *now a problem will be registered with no expectant reactions from the prisoners. The team will logically attach no hurry when next the problem flares up. However, as for maintaining the routine I've set up these past days, they were understandably interrupted with Jill's arrival. Not to mention her constant talking. But could I really blame her?* "Hmm..." That very question did unsettle Randolph, as Jill sounded too much like an inquisitor, though subtler; then again, he could be just paranoid. After a moment of thought, Randolph shrugged and gave in to answer another of her questions. "No, I've never been married. I move around too much."

"I thought by the sound of it you had a permanent office?"

"Nope, I travel from client to client."

When the disruptor vibrated amidst his bowls, Randolph jumped out of bed and fished out the laser pen from his rectum, giving it a wipe down on the bed covers. Next came a wash down of both hands and pen to break down the smell before Randolph vaulted to the wall next to the door. Then with his left hand fingers spread out, Randolph located the spot he suspected the main magnetic wires and circuitry were located behind the wall.

"So who were you working for when, well, when they busted down your door? Do you suppose you uncovered something someone didn't want known?"

"His name is Mr. Hilden, and yes, something like that," Randolph answered with a flick of his thumb to activate the pen. With the use of his other hand to hold the pen a finger thickness from the wall, Randolph squinted against the sparks as the laser pen drilled a small hole in which he could see in-between the walls. Another flick turned off the laser and activated a light to aid in finding the circuit board and wiring.

"John, you seem a bit distracted. Did I hit a nerve?"

"Again yes and no," Randolph answered with a heavy sigh and a shake of his head. "I've something on my mind I'm trying to work out and your constant babble is not helping."

"So you think I babble, do you?" Jill huffed, "I thought we were trying to get to know one another. Isn't that what you wanted?"

"Yes, of course," Randolph answered, wanting desperately to tell her to shut-up, "but all you've been doing is asking about me. Why don't you tell me more about yourself? Like your family, friends, likes or dislikes? Hmm?" He moved up a hand span plus two fingers over then reactivated the laser and cut a larger hole in the metal wall right beside the circuit board while holding his breath. When no alarm went off, Randolph let out his breath and looked inside; now came the tricky part. If there wasn't enough loose wiring inside, he'd never rewire the current to kill the magnetic lock and still fool the board into believing nothing was wrong, thereby making it reluctant to set off the alarms.

"Well, to be truthful, I don't like talking about myself, at least not to strangers."

"Fine then, you pick a subject. Any subject other than me," Randolph snapped and looked skyward for patience. *The damn woman is not catching my flagrant hint to leave me alone!* he fussed within himself. But as time was at a premium, Randolph discarded his wish to vent freely and tried to concentrate. For even though the video-cameras were out, it in no way guaranteed the sound system was out, though it should be.

"Okay, as sex is always on the mind of men, why don't you tell me why that is? Why can't a woman do a simple task like bend over without your eyes glued to our breasts or our butts?"

Randolph let out a sigh of frustration and shook his head; he tried once more to steer her off from asking him questions. "Besides the obvious, like all the advertising by the commercial world and women themselves, you tell me?" After only a moment to evaluate the circuit board, Randolph selected the needed wires and melted off the casings to jump the wires and bypass the alarm. Once the new junction of wires cooled, Randolph allowed the laser pen to melt the remaining wire and heard the satisfying click of the magnet disengage. To this sound Randolph's lips curved upward in pleasure, for now it was an easy thing to reach in and rotate the three deadbolts out of place, thus allowing the door to swing open with but a touch of his hand. He then secured the pen to his collar and peeked out the food slot, just to be sure of no uninvited surprises.

"You're copping out, John," Jill spoke up, sounding miffed, "the corporate world only makes available what consumers are willing to pay for. If men didn't want sex twenty-four hours a day, seven days a week, then marketing wouldn't package men's products using a woman's body. And as for women," Jill continued as he moved to her door unrolling a slim magnetic key-card, designed with a simple trace program to acquire and resend the last key-card codes. "As men show no interest in women unless we wave our breasts or butts in their faces, you can't blame us!" This last she said with a bit of heat in her voice, like she was remembering an experience she once had.

Randolph rolled his eyes on her chosen topic, for it is true men had sex on their minds most of the day. *But why not? With all the garbage we deal with everyday, why can't we daydream about something that gives us pleasure?* But as the program ran its course, Randolph pushed aside the argument to tell her in a quieter voice, "Look, if you wish to discuss this another time we'll do so but at the present, you should be readying yourself to move as I'm about to open your door." The mechanism gave off a satisfying *click*. Randolph slipped out his card to swing her door open and found Jill staring up at him with the strangest, puzzled look, as if she truly didn't believe he'd just side-stepped fifteen security steps and a sophisticated alarm system, while having a conversation.

"Look," Randolph began in a no nonsense voice, "we've no time for familiarities, so listen up."

Jill's brown eyes changed from disbelief to something more calculating, while she remained seated on her bed.

A very bad sign if you ask me, Randolph thought, *but as she's my only hope of getting out, I'll have to catalog it for a later review.*

Then all of a sudden her eyes went misty and she bolted up to him, flinging her arms around his neck.

"Oh, Jonathan, I can't believe you really came for me," Jill cried.

Randolph reached up and with a bit of effort pulled her arms apart so he could push her back and say plainly, "The name is John. No adaptations." Then he looked her square in the eyes and added, brutally frank, "And if I had no need of your knowledge of this building and surrounding area, I would not be taking you along. Got it?"

Randolph saw her lip quiver to his bluntness and felt like a heel, *But I'm not out to win any popularity contest,* he told himself when she nodded. He then pushed his feelings aside. "Good! Now then, you're to do as I say, when I say it with no questions asked. When I move, you glue yourself to my shadow. When I ask, you give me the shortest answer. Up, down, right, left or straight. If I need to know something, tap my shoulder and whisper. Got it?"

"I believe so," Jill answered softly, her eyes holding hurt within.

"No!" Randolph stressed in a harsh whisper. "You either do or don't. One slip up and it's back in the cell for the both of us, and the next trip I do on my own!" he added to emphasize she was a luxury he really didn't need, which of course was a lie, but he had to make certain she was in the right frame of mind.

Nodding, she answered, "Yes, John, I get it."

"Good! Now there are bound to be surveillance videos in the hallways. However, I've activated a scrambler which should take care of them, but we've only half an hour and we've wasted ten minutes of it. So let's move."

Like a couple of mice, the pair moved along the wall to the first door while Randolph looked for trip lasers. Once there, Randolph inserted the magnetic card while Jill whispered the information he'd need for the next hall. When he pulled the door open an inch, he signaled Jill to squat and inverted his pen to open the end and allow a single ball bearing to roll out into his hand. This he rolled down the center to check the hall for strong currents which were tell-tale signs of other security measures. Not until after the ball's straight path to the far door next to a plastic-steel window and security entrance door twenty feet in, did Randolph point out the three trip beams at ankle height along the wall to Jill. Once she nodded understanding, he moved them past the security booth to the secured door before the elevator.

Now comes the tricky part, Randolph considered. *With the key-card port on the other wall, opposite the security window, I'll have to watch the room and slide the card in at the same time. Of course with the video down, the guard might be rather busy with the equipment or if luck is with me, he'll be kicked back reading, waiting for the techs to arrive.* So risking a peek, Randolph inched up under the window and saw the single guard being overzealous by way of checking his equipment AND the wiring. This meant he would need good timing. For the guard's eyes could spot Randolph's bright orange jumper over the gray hallway fairly easily. Randolph squatted and checked his mental clock. If he were right, fifteen minutes had gone, not leaving much time for the perfect opportune to move. So with a quick rundown of possible scenarios, Randolph decided a slightly tan skin texture was far less eye attracting than his bright orange jump suit. So disregarding his present company, Randolph shucked off his jumper and took his chances. Low to the floor, Randolph inched up to the panel and while watching the window, out of the corner of his eye he caught an unexpected appraising look on Jill's face. Distracted by the expression, Randolph risked a fuller inspection and found Jill's eyes roving over his body with a hungry look before giving him a quirky smile and shrug of her shoulders. *So much for sex only in the minds of men,* Randolph thought with a roll of his eyes before he went back to work.

With a slow hand Randolph slid the card in and after only a moment, he heard the hall door *click.* The sound also drew Jill's attention whereby she flattened herself into the corner. An act he himself might have done. *But for an amateur? Hmm...* Unable to waste any time on conversation, Randolph pulled his card and backed up next to her and opened the door. He then ushered Jill in the hallway with the elevator and retrieved his coveralls. But while buttoning up the front, Randolph filed Jill's behavior along with that slight eye change he thought he saw, reasoning, *I best keep a closer tab on her, because she should be more nervous, scared and jumpy, nothing like she is acting.* And then it hit him. *Could she be acting? Could I be some sort of lab experiment? Perhaps a test on their security measures?* Randolph looked her up and down covertly and had to admit she wasn't a typical secretary. She held confidence, an athletic build but then... *But then what?* Troubled by such a possibility, Randolph looked her in the eyes and swore he noted her irises fluctuating again, and this time it was not from the change of lighting. When her eyes steadied and she saw the look on his face, Jill returned a look of puzzlement. As Randolph held no choice in her company, he rolled his eyes skyward, pushed his uncertainty aside and asked her about the elevator and the floors above.

"I'm sorry, but I don't know," Jill whispered, "I was a bit tied up trying to reason with the two bull dogs."

"Okay I'll give you that, so which floor would we get off on?" Randolph activated his pen and began to work on cutting around the button touch key pad.

"Oh, sorry, I thought you wanted to know how to operate the elevator," Jill apologized. "Uh, this one doesn't open on any floor except at the security desk. But once past that, it's a simple walk down the corridor to an intersection where the main one is."

"So where's the guard's desk and is it behind a window?" Randolph asked next, tilting the panel out of the wall to examine the wiring.

"It's in the open, a few feet away," Jill answered, trying to see over his shoulder at what he was doing.

Randolph nodded he understood and found the override security wire and jumped it to the power wire long enough to activate the doors. Then he repositioned the panel so to the casual observer it would look normal before following her into the elevator. Even a second or two added to their escape time could make the difference. Now of course came the iffy part which Randolph held no control over. *With the video cameras coming back up in our vacant cells, will the guard settle back in his chair and believe the two lumps under the blankets are us, or will he check the cells out? And what of the guard watching the elevator feeds? Will he believe it's the same problem just jumping about or will he consider alerting someone, especially after it starts moving? Questions, questions… this is the very reason I'm so highly priced to hire—research, research.* However there were times, like now, when Randolph had to leave things to chance. So touching one of the only two directional buttons, he found out from Jill where the desk was in relation to the elevator and moved her so they wouldn't automatically be seen.

Though the pair were close to making good an escape, Randolph took note his accomplice was far too relaxed. By all rights she should be jumpier than the only woman at a cheek pinching bachelor party. But regardless of how Jill should be, Randolph had to quiet his anxieties and concentrate on the moment at hand as the elevator came to a stop. After the count of three the pair watched in silence as the doors slowly opened. When no guard appeared at the opening, Randolph stilled Jill's move with a hand, knowing a seated guard could trip the alarm faster than he could move. So with a finger to his lips, he allowed the twin doors to slide closed. This reinstated a puzzled look on Jill, which he answered with a motion of his hand to stay put. When she gave acknowledgment to his desire, he pushed the up button again, whereby the circuitry registered its location and reopened the doors. Twice more Randolph selected his floor in an effort to entice the guard's curiosity over that of his natural laziness to get off his keister and have a look. The fact Randolph knew what this would entail did not mean he would be truly ready when the time came. So for each time the doors slid open, he found his heart pounding like a panting rabbit. By the fourth rotation, Randolph found his heart on its way out of his chest when the opening doors finally revealed the average-looking guard stepping into view. When the guard saw the pair of them, the shock on his face gave Randolph that micro second of time to reach out and grab the man's fashionable tie, which to criminals was nothing more than a convenient neck handle. With a jerk and shove, Randolph sent the surprised guard right into the back wall. Then a couple of quick blows to the head as the doors closed sent the dazed guard to the floor, unconscious. His veins bouncing with adrenaline, Randolph locked the doors closed and took a few steadying breaths before he began to strip the man.

"Is he dead?" Jill asked, having moved not one muscle in the violent activity.

"No, just unconscious," Randolph answered, wishing his voice didn't betray his edginess.

"Wouldn't it be better for us if he were dead?"

Randolph had the man's pants off when he picked up on the unfeeling tone in her words. He spared a glance up at her leaning on the wall with her arms crossed and watching him with calculating brown eyes. Warning bells went off in his mind at the ease in which she was standing there but as yet he couldn't reason out what he should be doing about them. As yet she hadn't hindered him in any way, nor has she given any false intelligence. Thus far the only alarming thing about her was her changing moods and uncaring belief in a human life. So with an edge in his voice he told her, "I haven't the right to take his life."

"John, you don't need any-one's permission. Just snap his neck, and we needn't worry about him setting off any alarms."

Randolph stepped into the man's pants and secured his gun, making certain its beam setting was on 'non-lethal' before holstering the weapon, and told her sharply, "His handcuffs will do that for us."

"Yeah? So he can't reach the alarm with his hands, he has a set of legs to use you know."

Randolph's ire rose as he buttoned up his new shirt. Then he set his face in stone and told Jill, "I've never taken a human life and I'm not about to start now, so zip it!" When it appeared she understood his declaration, Randolph used his coveralls to tie up the guards head and shoulders to keep him quite when he did awaken. Next Randolph opened the doors and hurried to the desk, shoving Jill ahead of him so she wouldn't get any ideas. Once at the desk, he rifled through the drawers, pulling out any card keys and also discovering a few spare credits on a petty cash card, which he pocketed, as it wouldn't require any identification to use, like the man's main credit account in the wallet now resting comfortably in his back pocket. "All right," Randolph began, "we'll play it this way. You're a secretary in the wrong corridor and I'm showing you to the other one. So act the part."

"Fine, you're the boss, but what if we end up in a fire fight?" she asked, sounding as if she was little concerned about it.

"If we're lucky it won't come to that. Now follow me."

Randolph took her over to the exit and swiped the security badge, but when the door slid open, it revealed two burly security guards with guns already leveled and an upper management businessman behind them. "Hold it, fellows," Randolph held up a hand, thinking fast, "she's just…" He got no further as Jill swiped his feet out from under him. As Randolph's eyes filled in panic, his arms wind-milled in an effort to reduce the damage he could sustain in a backward fall or at the very least minimize the painful event by landing on Jill. But she had already cleared Randolph's reach and once he crashed to the floor, she grabbed and twisted his arm, forcing Randolph to roll on to his stomach or have it broken. "Oww!" he exclaimed in disbelief, feeling the holster relieved of its weapon.

Once she had him disarmed, Jill let Randolph go just as quickly as she had dropped him and backed away, pointing the gun, and announced, "It's okay guys. He's harmless."

"Uh?" Randolph exclaimed as he rolled carefully to his side and looked about the group.

"So, Major, how'd our boy do?" the businessman in the 3,000-credit blue and gray suit asked Jill.

"Up until Larry in the elevator, he did quite well," Jill answered, motioning with the point of the gun that Randolph should slowly get up.

Randolph did as directed with an eye on the four of them. The two guards, however, waited till he stood before they holster their guns and seized Randolph's arms while Jill and the suit watch him. *I've been snookered,* Randolph acknowledged. *And a right good job of it. But why?* He then took note of Jill's nonchalant attitude with the gun as she aimlessly patted the barrel against her thigh.

"Okay, men," the businessman said as he stepped up to Jill's side. "Take care of Larry and make certain his jacket reflects his poor abilities before firing him and also fire Pete down in the cells with some remarks reflecting his ineptitude."

"Yes, Mr. Bennett," one of the two said while both let go to carry out their orders.

With a look of uncertainty on his face, Randolph looked to Mr. Bennett, who talked in a tone of superiority. "Be of ease, Mr. McCann. If you'll precede Jill to my office, I'll see about clearing up some of your understandable confusion."

Randolph looked over to Jill, who motioned with her easily-acquired gun to take the lead, but also gave him a no non-sense look which spoke louder than words she'd use it without hesitation. So walking in silence, Randolph entered an elevator, then stepped off on the thirtieth floor into a world of cubical people, phones, computers and the countless other activities any thriving business depended upon. Reminded of the gun which Randolph had seen readjusted to lethal by a flick of Jill's thumb, Randolph walked besides a glass wall which separated them form the corporate activity till the suit in front came to a mahogany door which read *Mel Bennett, Senior Floor Executive of Research and Development.*

Chapter Five

You can always tell how important a man is by his office, Randolph quoted to himself as he walked into Mr. Bennett's outer office, which was complete with stylish metal and plastic-glass waiting chairs. Wall hangings and cool bluish-white walls told of a modern thinker who was more interested with the future than the owners who always used earth tones. Passing a true secretary instead of the eye candy the codgers and dead-end managers used, Randolph, Bennett and Jill stepped into Mr. Bennett's private office, decorated in the same manner.

"If you'll take a seat, Mr. McCann, I've a few questions before we begin to enlighten you." Mr. Bennett motioned, rounding his smoky-glass desk.

Randolph did as told, while he noted Jill took the chair next to the wall as if out of habit.

"So tell me," Mr. Bennett asked with curiosity in his voice as he settled himself, "why didn't you kill the guard?"

"Uh, come again?" Randolph asked, bewildered.

"I'm certain the major made it quite clear he was a threat to your escape, so why didn't you kill him?" Mr. Bennett folded his hands on the fire-hardened glass desk, watching Randolph's eyes.

Randolph stared at him in disbelief for a second. "Wait a minute, you mean to tell me you wanted me to murder the man?"

"It would've proven you're capable of close end work. We already know you can murder at a distance."

"Now hold it right there—you have your facts wrong. I've never killed anyone in my life," Randolph explained with a hard edge to his voice.

"Come, come, Mr. McCann," Mr. Bennett began, sitting back in his chair with a glance at Jill. "Your trial is a matter of public records. That explosive you left killed nine people."

Randolph folded his arms over his own chest and told the unfeeling man in matter of fact tones, "Don't believe everything you read. I was framed and done so with considerable skill."

Jill got up to open a mini-bar cabinet and offered Randolph a glass. Randolph eyed the chilled glasses within and the hundred-credit Wild Boar bottle of bourbon but waved off the offer as he liked to keep his reflexes at their peak, even in situations he had no idea how to handle. Jill caught his negative and shrugged before she poured herself a tall one. Mr. Bennett eyed Jill's antics and her free use of his bar but made no comment and instead asked Randolph, "So you're maintaining in all the jobs you've ever done, you've never killed anyone?"

"Absolutely not!" Randolph declared with some force.

Mr. Bennett pulled out a thick file from a desk drawer and flipped the hard copies till he stopped at a page and asked, "Are you opposed to killing, or is it more of a religion?"

"I don't believe in murder, which in no way means there are not people I'd like to see dead." *Namely, one Mr. Hilden,* Randolph said silently to himself.

Jotting a note, Mr. Bennett pushed the file aside and asked Jill, "What do you think, Major?"

"He's got the skills; there's no denying. And he's not helpless in a fight." Then Jill shrugged and finished with, "I've seen better."

Randolph decided it was time to become the aggressor and demanded, "Now I've answered your questions, how about filling me in on what the hell's this all about?"

The Paranoid Thief

"I'm sorry, Mr. McCann, but for now I'll have to leave you in the dark." Mr. Bennett pressed a button under the edge of the desk, where after two guards stepped in from the outer office who must have arrived a little after they did. "If you'll be so kind as to follow these men, they'll take you to your apartment."

Apartment? Randolph looked over the very able duo.

Mr. Bennett pulled out a card key from a drawer and tossed it to one, telling Randolph, "Now don't get any ideas on the way. That item in your skull has other uses then tracking." With that threat plainly aired, Randolph was excused and taken to the elevator.

When the elevator stopped on the forty-eighth floor, Randolph walked out onto dark green carpet along a light green and white hall to room 17. Here one of the two men stopped their casual stroll as the other guard produced the card key.

"This is your pass card, Mr. McCann. It has your room number and a color code. The color code allows you access to any rooms with the same color. Dining hall, weight room, entertaining center and such but a word of warning, using your pass on doors without your color lets Mr. Bennett know within an instant, and that can be very painful, if not detrimental to your health." He tapped the back of Randolph's neck to emphasize his warning before he handed over the card.

Randolph watched the two men walk away without a backward glance before he took note of a sister door right across from his. Somewhat perplexed, Randolph flipped the card about in his hand before he swiped it over the reader to his door. With a glance down the now empty corridor, Randolph pushed open the fake oak door to reveal a thinly furnished apartment, complete with kitchen, living area, bedroom and bath. Though still uneasy with matters, Randolph stepped in and looked over the brown rug, light wood-tone wall panels, and Navajo white walls which showed signs of two wall hangings recently removed. He walked to the back wall-window to pull open the floor-to-ceiling drapes. As expected, the lightly shaded plastic-steel widow looked out onto another corporate building. *So much for figuring out where I am,* Randolph commented to himself, heading next for the bathroom.

Once his physical needs were met and a modest time spent under the shower, Randolph left the basic bathroom and shower combination and ignored the queen-size bed outfitted with brown quilt and matching pillows to check out the kitchen and its cupboards. Here Randolph found a moderately stocked kitchen, as well as a refrigerator of fresh meats and vegetables. He then ran the selection over in his mind. Setting a few things out on the glass top dining table along with the standard spices, Randolph took note nothing was out of date and all were unopened, confirming in his mind someone expected this room to be occupied fairly soon.

He looked over the stove and rubbed his freshly shaven face, feeling worlds better after the hot and cleansing shower. Now that he had time to think, Randolph rolled his eyes to the obvious questions running across his mind and decided to distract his understandable confusion by making himself a meal with a bit more taste then he'd been getting these last few weeks.

Randolph sighed in some pleasure as he laid down the last plate of a well-rounded meal, which consisted of a chicken casserole, potato salad, fresh green beans and a real orange, sliced in eighths. He was just settling down to say grace when a pleasant voice spoke out.

"Mr. McCann, Mr. Bennett and Major Wander are here to see you."

Randolph's face took on the disgust he felt before he sighed in regret and pushed up from his meal to approach the door. Once the door opened to those outside, Jill was first in, now wearing comfortable jeans, a yellow/pink long-sleeve ruffle-collar blouse and light red vest. As Mr. Bennett walked in, Randolph saw Jill sniffing the air with a sub-vocal "mmm" while walking unerringly over to his untouched meal.

"What'cha been cooking?" Jill asked as she looked over the bowls.

"Nothing special, just a simple meal," Randolph commented, taking note no bodyguards were with Mr. Bennett this time. *But then again, why should they be?* Randolph rubbed his neck as a reminder of what could very well be planted in his brain. Mr. Bennett obviously took note of the gesture as he passed but made no outward remark or smirk of superiority.

"Simple?" Jill inquired, glancing his way. "This looks like you've put some time in it."

By the time Randolph closed the door, Mr. Bennett had made himself comfortable on the couch-chair and said mildly, before Randolph could answer, "It looks as if you've made yourself at home, Mr. McCann. Good; I like a reasonable man."

Jill picked up a fork and tried the casserole, smacking her lips with delight. "Hey, Mel, you've got to try this! Oh, I'm sorry," she said, looking back up at Randolph. "May I?"

"As you already are, go ahead," Randolph answered, discounting the meal, as it would be cold by the time their meeting was over. He waved at the plate with a sigh.

Jill took a seat in the only other chair in the room with a delighted smile on her face and began dishing out a good portion for herself. While she did so, Mr. Bennett crossed his legs and motioned Randolph he should sit down on the other end of the couch-chair. "The long and short of it, Mr. McCann, is that I run a task force dedicated to the betterment of our way of living. The projects we perform are solely financed by this corporation, with no outside funding or contributions, to make certain of no outside influences." Mr. Bennett gestured at Jill and continued. "Major Wander and seven other teams, specially matched up, are my field operatives who help insure no corporations or foreign governments step on our rights of fair trade. This sometimes puts our teams in very dangerous situations; thusly my predecessor chose to enlist the aid of condemned criminals so no attachments could be traced back to us."

Randolph caught the meaning of his speech and remarked, "So in other words, I've been invited to the party and the implant is in place to adjust my attitude."

"Very perceptive, Mr. McCann. But let us simply call it a safety measure to protect us all."

"So that whole bit down stairs was my interview into your group?" Randolph received a smile from the executive. "So what would've happened if I'd failed? Would you have killed me?" The question was rather self-evident, but he had to ask.

"No, Mr. McCann, you'd have killed yourself. There were three traps you could have activated, or let the major trip, which would've set off the chip in your head."

Randolph glanced at Jill.

Mr. Bennett denied, "No, Mr. McCann, the major knew nothing about them, save you could be killed if you screwed up."

"Sorry, Randolph," Jill said over a mouthful of potato salad, "but I've my own chip and therefore couldn't warn you."

"I take it all the agents are equipped in the same way?" Randolph once more couldn't help but ask the obvious.

"Naturally. How else can we make sure of your loyalty? Besides, all save you are confessed killers. That, I'm afraid, was my slip up,

The Paranoid Thief

but Jill assures me she can deal with the mistake." Mr. Bennett stood, as if that should explain everything Randolph wanted to know, but then he added as an afterthought, "Regardless of the mistake, I'm dying to find out how you got those wonderful tools past the prison system and my own people. They look home made."

"They are," Randolph remarked with some pride, though he'd be dammed before he showed these people his hiding place.

"Well, business calls, so I'll leave the pair of you to get acquainted. Let me know how things work out, Major. Till later, Mr. McCann." With that said, Randolph's new warden took his leave.

As for Jill, she turned in the swivel chair, calling after Mr. Bennett, "Sure, Mel." Then, downing a glass of wine she'd found already poured out in a crystal wine glass, she began, "So then, by what name do you prefer I call you, Randolph? Your file showed ten to twelve aliases."

Randolph shrugged. "Take your pick. I've worked under so many names, I've tried to keep from becoming attached to any."

"You're also not much for partners either, just a lonesome dove in a world of ducks."

"That's an analogy of my character I've never heard, but yes, I found out early in my career partnering up is the fastest way to get caught."

Jill stood. "Mmm, well, you'll have to change that attitude, for you're my new partner." Randolph watched as Jill sat on the couch-chair and crossed her legs while she stretched out her arm on the headrest. *Just as relaxed as you please.* Then as Randolph digested her bit of news, Jill changed the subject by asking, "Do you cook other meals as good as this one?"

"Mmm? Oh sure, my mother's a chef for a trendy high-class restaurant."

"That good, uh? Wonderful, because I can't cook." Jill uncrossed her legs and slapped both knees in getting up. "Well, I've a few things to catch up on. So why don't you have dinner ready around, what, seven?" Jill looked at the time on her watch. "And we'll discuss our partnership after the meal." Randolph eyed her and her easy way of handing out orders but decided to restrain himself from making any comments, at least not yet. He was about to say he'd need to visit the local store when she reached across the table and turned on the video screen he hadn't looked over yet and punched up a cooking supply book.

Jill pointed. "Just tell the screen what you need, and if it's available, it'll be here in an hour, at least so I'm told," she admitted, indicating she'd never used the time-saving tool in the manner it was made for. Though Randolph was still swarming with questions, Jill headed for the door but called over her shoulder in warning. "Oh, and Mel wasn't kidding about the chip. If you go outside your key card color, your head will feel like exploding or something far worse."

"Well, this has been a real fun day!" Randolph commented to no one save himself, as Jill had already closed the door behind her. With a roll of his eyes, Randolph sent a glare skyward, knowing he had to reorganize his mind. *Like, for starters, am I really better off alive? Normally I'd have said yes.* But with a touch to his neck, feeling the surgery scar he wasn't so sure. *I've dealt with electronics most of my life,* he reasoned, *I'll just have to deal with this as I do all my other obstacles.* For if it had circuitry, given time and equipment he could manipulate it, at least he hoped. Next in the plus column, Randolph understood this nice clean apartment was his to live in, including access to basic computing for ordering anything he wished to cook. *In the minus column, I'm still a prisoner, and so far no one's mentioned maid-service,* he added after looking on the dirty dishes. *However,* *weighing the plus and minuses on a scale makes no true sense till I fully understand my roll. As for what I'm going to do with Jill...*Randolph considered, rubbing his chin before dishing out what was left of his meal and inserting it in a warming unit. *That brings up another matter entirely. Looking at her tells me she visits the gym once a day, which means she wouldn't be a pushover come the time I'm ready to disappear. And as for being my partner, I learned early on women are too damn fickle. One minute you're working with one, and the next, you're in bed with her moments before her husband walks in.* Randolph rubbed his arm, remembering that experience, before he withdrew his meal and went over the food selection while eating. *Since working for Mr. Hilden, I really haven't had a well-prepared meal in a long while.*

Randolph put the steaks on "keep warm," then tasted the meat sauce, deciding it needed a little more red pepper, when the nice voice told him Jill was at the door. With an unconscious wipe of his hands on the apron he ordered with the ingredients of the meal, Randolph made certain all was ready by a mental check list in his head before he removed the apron and crossed to open the door.

The first thing Randolph noticed, as Jill walked in with a light smile and a twitching nose to the aroma of his cooking, was she'd changed clothes yet again. Now she wore an old-fashion long, pleated yellow skirt, an off-white short-sleeved blouse complete with ruffles, a delicate silver necklace and a set of ear rings bearing the universal female symbol of her sex. In her hands, which she held together in front, was a matching yellow purse, accented in silver. The whole outfit, right down to her two-inch yellow pumps, showed off to best advantage—that her athletic figure would allow—her small breasts and thin waist. Taking up the skirt in one hand, she moved it side to side, commenting. "I love these simple, free flowing outfits—they allow one total movement." Jill stopped a few steps within so Randolph could close the door without thought before she turned to him and asked, "So what do you think? I'm a bit self-conscious about my short hair in this type of outfit, but since it'll be only you and I for the evening, I thought it would be okay."

Randolph looked at her, speechless; it was as if he were meeting Jill's twin sister! *Hell, even her voice seems timid and vulnerable, a total reversal to her act in the cells!* "Uh, you look fine, Jill," he decided to answer, keeping his voice even.

"Thank you, kind sir," she replied with an old fashioned curtsy. "Would you mind inviting me in?"

"Uh, sure, but you're already in," Randolph said, wondering what the hell was going on.

Jill seemed to ignore that fact. "I know the pocket book is over-accessorizing, but I haven't had the chance to try it out with this outfit." Then she gave into her interest of the meal he'd prepared and smiled. "Mmm, that smells delicious. Do you mind escorting me to my seat?"

For Randolph, the ensuing evening carried on in the same manner, just as if they were in a fancy restaurant, making him feel severely under-dressed in the gray sweat clothes he'd found in the bathroom earlier.

Around 9 p.m., Randolph took away the dishes as their conversation of normality seemed to wind down and their meal was digesting very nicely. Once at the washbasin, Randolph heard Jill get up and sit on the couch-chair where he'd eaten his dinner. As he set the dishwasher, Jill composed herself like earlier in the day when Mr. Bennett was here. She began a new conversation with an air of disbelief in her hard-edged voice. "Well, I'll say one thing. You have manners and can function reasonably well in polite society. I take it you learned this from your mother?"

"Up until I was eleven," Randolph answered, leaning back on the counter, trying to figure her out.

"So what changed to make you take up your current occupation, if I may ask?"

"The restaurant owner," Randolph answered bitterly, remembering the guy and still finding the memory a raw wound.

"Somewhat of a sore spot, I gather. What happened?" she asked with some interest.

Randolph put away some of the supplies he'd left for the meal and considered shrugging her question off, then he sighed and figured, *why not tell her.* "The owner made my mother give him sexual favors to further her skills. But when he discovered she'd become pregnant with his child, whether intentional or not, he dismissed her like yesterday's garbage and put her on the Blackball list for disreputable chefs. A death sentence for any aspiring chefs, as no respectable outfit would touch anyone on it with a ten foot pole. And as she never reported him to the ethics board in favor of learning her craft to better our future, all he need do was pay her a small amount of child support and she couldn't touch him. So needing to help support our growing family, I started stealing." At this point in his story, Randolph decided he needed a drink to wash out a bad taste in his mouth. So he pulled out of the refrigerator a bottle of vintage wine he'd ordered for the meal but had forgotten when Jill walked in, and poured her a glass as well. "About four years ago, after finding my skills were far better at this job then helping in the kitchen, I broke into his home, and using his own computer, made up transfer of ownership documents to his son by my mother and sent it though the court system with his signature." Randolph set the bottle down and handed Jill her glass before he sat and remarked, with a slight curve of his lip, "I dearly wished I could've been there when my half-brother, sixteen at the time, walked in with my mother and claimed ownership of the place and the three other spin-offs he'd sold franchises to."

"But why didn't you make your mother owner of the place? She has the experience," Jill asked with honest curiosity.

"True, but other than birthing my half-brother, my mother isn't related to the bastard which would've stood out like a red beacon when he took the matter through the court system. But since the documents were in my brother's name, and any blood test would confirm Mick to be his son, the man hadn't a leg to stand on."

"So did you tell your mother what you did?" Jill asked.

"No, but I think she suspects it. Regardless," Randolph said as an afterthought, "I couldn't tell her. If he managed to get her in court, the knowledge I'd done the deed would've come out, giving him grounds to revoke the ownership." Randolph took another sip of the wine, liking the way the bouquet smelled and the delicate taste added to its overall character. "You now know a little of my story," Randolph said in a decision to learn more, "so how is it you found yourself on death row, if I'm not mistaking Mr. Bennett's favored recruitment method?"

Jill eyed Randolph like she was put-off by his question, but in standing, she swirled the wine in her glass, heading over to the curtained window to look out for a moment before answering in a low and meaningful voice. "I was in charge of 129 raw recruits, given the task to toughen them up for combat duty inside 3 months, when my commanding officer gave me orders midway in their training to take them out for a reconnaissance mission. Having just come back from a forced two-day march through a quite zone, I argued the mission on two facts. One, they were not combat ready and two, I wore them out deliberately to weed out the ones who couldn't cut the mustard." Jill downed the wine in one swallow, as if trying to wash away a bad taste in her mouth similar to his own before she went on. "Refusing his orders as was my right being they'd not finished training and I didn't consider them ready for combat. He stepped out of regs and had me arrested for disobeying a direct order from a superior officer. Later that day, he assigned a desk jockey my unit, who foolishly volunteered, as he needed the combat time for a political career." Jill let go of the curtains, leaned into the corner of the wall and crossed her arms a bit tightly in remembrance of that incident.

"By the time I landed at H.Q. to await trial, I'd learned my entire unit had been wiped out, save for five men. After my court marshal and stance of five months in the brig for cowardice in the face of the enemy, a friend of mine in the correspondence center gave me a hard copy of something he had been ordered by top brass to file away without inquiry. Reading the documentation, it showed my unit had been wiped out due to a tragic clerical error. Reading further, the report went on about how a routine search and destroy mission had been given out to the air-boys along the same coordinates as I'd been ordered to scout." Jill wiped away a stray tear then tried to square up her chin. "Anyway, the scuttle butt around H.Q. as I was packing told of my commander's wife, having been insulted by one of the raw recruit's parents at some function, had demanded my CO give her satisfaction. With minimal research on my part, it became quite clear my CO knew of the fly-boys' orders. This fact was denied by my CO in court, under oath, who then gave testimony on the stand that the very major who took over my unit and lead my troops on the ill fated mission, had misfiled the information. Thus he held no knowledge of the mission.

"So dressing in my finest military uniform, I drove my car to my CO's, two-story home on base and informed his house servant that

I'd been asked to come over. Without permission for entry, I followed her into the living room, ignoring her request to wait on the front porch. Upon the sight of my entrance, my former CO stood in anger, demanding, 'What's the meaning of this?' Without the need of words to explain myself, I pulled my laser pistol and swept his legs off with the maximum setting. He yelled to the sudden lost of legs and fell to the floor. His servant, a step to my left screamed and ran from the room. With gun still at the ready, I eyed her antics in little concern as I held no animosity towards her. However, I held an entirely different feeling towards my CO's shocked and alarmed wife. Her, I holed in the chest and beheaded before her body slid from the chair to the floor." Jill's eyes took on a gleam of angry memory as she stared past Randolph in finishing her tale. "Before cutting him into little pieces for the med boys to try and put together like a jig-saw puzzle, I told the son-of-a-cowardly-dog he should've had the balls to confront the parents instead of wiping out my men!"

Jill let out a breath of tension at this point, having realized she was tightening up. She then looked over on Randolph and shrugged off the ugly memories. "The next thing I knew I was here," Jill commented, rolling her eyes about the place. Jill pushed off the wall and walked over to the couch-chair then looked at her watch. "Well, with that bit of unpleasantness behind us, I think we've made a good start." Jill picked up her handbag and started for the door. "Get some sleep tonight. We start training at six in the morning, and I've a full day planned to ferret out your abilities."

Before Randolph could comment on her early morning activities and where she could shove them, Jill was out the door, leaving him bemused, wondering why she'd divulged such powerful emotions to a complete stranger.

Chapter Six

The next two months of Randolph's life were a living hell of exercising, endurance tests, and even physical games of coordination and speed. *I tell ya, I thought I was in pretty good shape,* he commented to himself one day, holding his sides, standing beside Jill, who was merely breathing fast, *but to hear the tale from her, I was a blob of useless muscle masquerading as human.* Also during this time of forced endurance-building exercises, Randolph was introduced to two other two-man teams who took up exercising with them, whereby he learned Hendrix was a downright bully, Joe was a shifty-eyed weasel, Mitch was a personable fellow on his good days and Patrick was just plain fun, for Patrick would have them all splitting their sides with just the right look at the right time. However, Jill made certain they never stuck together long, always laying down a reason for some other activity.

When Randolph approached the subject, Jill answered matter-of-factly, "I've been on three missions and lost two partners. Joe and Hendrix were recruited before you and not one of the teams have been here longer than five years. So it's been decided, unannounced, we should stay aloof."

The next morning, Jill took Randolph to the elevator which led down to the cell block he'd escaped from; however, when the doors slid open she pushed a button which had not been present during his initiation. This lowered the elevator beyond the cell block level by at least four floors or more. Opening up, Jill took the lead without comment to Randolph and led them along an echoing twenty-foot hallway that ended in darkness. Not a darkness for lack of light, Randolph could tell, but rather darkness emitted by a great expanse of openness. Turning to a panel, Jill touched a LED, turning on a lighting system which revealed five floors of openness filled with small buildings and scaffolding to some sort of theater.

"This," Jill said, motioning with her hand at the open area, "is our training facility. Every so often the buildings are shifted around and a new scenario is presented for us to solve. Nothing elaborate, mind you, but just enough to keep our wits sharp."

Randolph followed Jill down the two-story ladder and found her holding a clip board when he touched the ground floor.

Jill showed Randolph the board and read aloud, "You are at a convention center of two political parties. Somewhere, there is a bomb, or bombs, set to explode in five hours. Find the bomb, or bombs, and disarm it or them." Jill returned the board to a hook, rubbed her hands, and set her watch. "Well, let's get to it."

"Why?" Randolph remarked, looking sideways at her. "We could always use a few less of those cretins." To his statement of dislike for the men and women governing the continent, Jill looked sternly on Randolph, but he only shrugged, indicating he couldn't help it if he was so cynical about those people.

"Get serious, Randolph. We've less than five hours, so put your thinking cap on," she snapped.

"All right," he answered with a grimace and started walking out, only to have her pull him back.

"As I've said," Jill began scolding him, "this is an exercise. Everything in here, the bomb and dummies, represents real people, real life—and that includes security alarms and video cameras." Jill pointed at the both of them as she explained. "As we're not supposed to be alive, every pair of eyes in the dummies will be registering our movements. If we're seen too many times, or we trip an alarm, red lights will flash over head, giving us just five minutes to get on solid

The Paranoid Thief

ground before a debilitating migraine sends us to the floor for half an hour or more. After which your equilibrium will be shot for twelve hours."

"You're serious?"

"Damn straight I'm serious," Jill glared at him. "I've had it happen once, and I'll not go through that again. If I do, I'm going to pulverize you up one wall and down the other—you understand me?"

Even though Jill was much thinner than Randolph, he took her threat to heart. Raising his hands in surrender, Randolph acknowledged her threat. "Okay, okay. You get a headache, I get beat to shit. Got it."

Jill nodded, folded her arms and leaned back on the wall. "Bombs are messy and often times non-directional if made by amateurs. Thus a good number of people could be killed just to get the one he/they/she is after." She rubbed her chin, thinking aloud, reasoning still further, "Conventions are notorious for changing schedules and shifting personnel around. A time-set bomb can conclude the object is not a certain person but a statement. Video cameras would be all around so he/they/she could be miles away watching the results." Jill eyed the scaffolding around the theater and pointed. "That would be our best bet."

"You're forgetting under the stage," Randolph remarked.

"Not so," Jill reasoned. "The blast would be restricted to a small area, while an overhead blast would put forth a concussion, stunning the crowd, sending down debris of the scaffolding into their midst."

"That's supposing the intention is a statement and not a person," Randolph injected.

"It's nice to see you're thinking, but you're missing the wording of our mission. Our job is to disarm a bomb or bombs. For someone to apply a bomb in a public place, they would be looking for exposure, so it stands to reason the more people killed or injured the more exposure given on the videos."

Unable to fault her in such reasoning, Randolph shrugged assent. So taking the lead, avoiding the eye path of the dummies as was possible, even though in real life, if a well-trained thief looked as if he belonged there, the average person would never take notice save for a mild curious glance, including most security guards. In this way the pair made the scaffolding and began their search.

They weaved themselves among the metal beams, ever watchful for the eye in the sky, and were moving up to the fourth layer of beams when Randolph put out a hand to Jill. "Hold it. I may have found something." Randolph took out a piece of paper he'd picked up in the dirt, tore and folded it till satisfied with its size, and inserted only the tip into what he thought was a low-wattage beam of light. His action confirmed the near-invisible beam and he discovered two more like it radiating out of a small black box before he looked a little closer.

"What'cha find?" Jill asked, shifting to see, nearly pushing him into one of the beams.

Randolph caught his movement and push Jill back with a hiss of warning. "If you must move, don't do it crowding me!"

"Okay, sorry. But tell me, what'cha found?"

"A trip beam, three to be precise, and of such low wattage, they're housed in a box with an amplifier, which was why I saw it. Very professional," he added, "far too complicated for standard security measures."

"Then we're getting close." Jill smiled, looking at her watch. "And about time, we've less than three and a half hours to work."

"Which in no way suggests we speed things up," Randolph warned her, looking back on the box, sighting in on the three

The Paranoid Thief

directions and taking note of another box attached to a cross beam some distance away. Randolph got the impression this other box also spread into three beams. This small bit of information told him the whole area could be spider-webbed with them. *Neat, very neat. Send out one beam and make them breed with beam splitters and amplifiers. Very time-consuming to install, but guaranteed to waste one's time in tracking them down to their source.* Randolph sat back on his haunches with a sigh and said, more to himself, "We're in deep kimchee."

"What's that?" Jill asked with concern.

"It's a pickled vegetable dish, seasoned with different spices, sealed up in a jar, and buried in the ground for a span of weeks. At least so I'm told. Either way, I've never liked the stuff," he answered off-handedly, trying to reason out the best approach to their problem.

"So what's it got to do with this?"

"It's my polite way of saying were in deep shit," Randolph explained, wishing she'd let him think.

"Well, why didn't you just say so?" Jill admonished, slapping his shoulder.

Randolph turned his head and glared at Jill as he reminded her, "Look, I've worked alone for eighteen years and only three years with a partner. I've my own way of doing things and I tend to talk to myself on occasion. So cut me some slack!"

Jill looked about to fire a group of selected words at him, but swallowed them back, having read his facial expression. Randolph nodded acceptance of her silence and set his mind back to work.

The problem with this setup, he considered while looking about, is that scaffolding are never built to remain perfectly steady, thus a plus and minus factor had to be installed into the triggering device. Regardless, though, not knowing the parameters of the program would necessitate our assent to a time-consuming crawl and as for turning it off? Yeah right. For a moment more Randolph traced the lines in case the builder slipped up. But even if he did spot its origins, Randolph conceded without the proper tools the task would take longer than Jill would permit to deactivate, if her sigh of irritation and impatience behind him was any indication. *And then again, it stands to reason if the maker is of any intelligence, the bomb will go off if the beam is cut, assuring the maker of the same results.* Randolph sighed and told Jill the bad news. "To break or turn off the beam will probably set off the bomb. We've no choice but to ascend. You're going to have to follow me, do as I do, and put feet and hands where I do." With a look skyward for guidance, Randolph admitted, "Even if we are careful as the best acrobats, it may still do us no good. All it will take is for one of those bars to shift out of position half an inch. Got it?"

After a second of consideration, Jill reasoned, "As I'm lighter than you, it'll be best for me to climb up alone."

"What about disarming the bomb?" Randolph asked, watching her face.

"I'm trained in such matters. As I see it, I've the military mind and know how on weaponry. Your job was to get me by the security blanket which you've done."

"Jill, this might not be the only kind of device," Randolph injected into her reasoning.

"If it's not, we were doomed to fail at the start, and Mel doesn't work that way."

Randolph looked sideways at her for such flawed reasoning, but decided it was her head, and only reminded her, "It's your headache."

"Just show me what to look for and shut up," She snapped.

The Paranoid Thief

Randolph did as asked, then remained still and watched as Jill inched her way up into the web of poles, moving ever so slowly to keep from shifting any out of place while not breaking the light beams. Although Jill needed only to cover two floors, at four sets of railing per floor, the forced pace took her a good half hour to make six sections of railings. From his place, Randolph observed Jill as she nosed around for fifteen minutes at a single place before motioning he should climb up and join her. At her beckoning, Randolph rolled his eyes and shook his head in disgust before he moved on up a bit faster than her, knowing what to expect but still slower than his usual, as he did weigh more.

Once Randolph came abreast of Jill, she pointed out a lattice work of very exposed red beams and admitted. "I'm a fool, Randolph. I should've learned by now Mel likes teamwork."

To Randolph, Jill appeared to be out of sorts. *Most likely berating herself on the need for my help and loss of time.* Instead of stating the obvious, Randolph sought a way around their lattice work of beams, a task which after a few minutes of looking did indeed require the both of them. "Do you think you can support my weight for a short while?" he asked.

"You're kidding, right?" Jill answered with narrowed eyes, telling Randolph he had asked a really dumb question.

"Okay. Fine. I had to ask," Randolph answered without apology. After he showed her what he wanted, Jill positioned herself on an outside pole in a squat. With her balance set and her arms holding tightly to a pole, Randolph climbed up onto her shoulders, whereby she pushed him up to the top level with her leg muscles. Not having any room for swinging about, Randolph took a hold of the upper pole, pulling himself up with practiced ease, before locking his legs around the same pole and stretching back down for her. Jill then reached as high as she could, where Randolph caught her wrist and pulled her full weight up. She grabbed Randolph's arm. He shifted his hold to her elbow and continued lifting till she latched onto his belt. But as using her legs to help herself up was out of the question, Jill remained little more than dead weight in Randolph's grip, save for her hold on his belt. As for helping Jill up, Randolph could only think of one sure place which would give her the support she needed to reach the pole above him. Randolph hesitated. *But believe me if this were a true job, I wouldn't hesitate.*

"What are you waiting for? Help me up!"

"I uh, I only know of one way, and—"

"Randolph, my sex shouldn't be an issue here. Now do what's necessary and get me up!" Jill hissed.

"Okay..." Randolph answered, reaching a hand between her legs and taking a firm grip of her crotch. Releasing her elbow, Randolph grabbed her sweats and pulled and pushed Jill up his body till she had a firm grip of the pole he hung from. Once Jill was stable, Randolph got himself up and found her glaring at him.

"You and I are going to have a talk!" Jill scolded.

"I told you, you wouldn't like it," Randolph defended himself.

"Not about that," Jill corrected. "About hesitating because of my sex. That could get us killed."

Randolph wanted nothing more than to argue he would not have hesitated in the field, but Jill stopped him with a raised hand and indicated the time.

"We've work to do, and because of me, less of it."

Well, at least she admits her mistakes. Randolph half smiled, looking about.

After only a couple minutes, Jill found the bomb, or rather one of eight bombs, all lined up in a row, spaced twenty feet apart. "This,"

The Paranoid Thief

Jill indicated the first of the lot, "is a shape charge, and it's set to spread out this clay mold of ball bearings, a cheap but effective version of the outdated claymore." Jill pulled up her sweats from around her calf and removed a small tool kit strapped around her ankle. "Always be prepared, Randolph. It's not a motto; it's a living." With the use of a mini-screwdriver, Jill undid the top of the box and eyed the working within, then mumbled. "Damn, the things are linked by this small antenna," Jill said, indicating the device, "which means I'll have to figure out which of the two end devices has the controlling card."

"Not necessarily," Randolph advised, pointing out the wires. "You see how these wires have a curve in them?" When he received Jill's nod, he explained further, "That means these wires were close to the core of a spool, and most professionals buy their spools to the job. So if this one was wired up last, that means—"

"The far one is our controller!" Jill caught on, smiling. Then becoming more serious, she instructed, "While I go to the far bomb to disable them in sequence, why don't you see what you can do with the trip beams down below?"

"You're the boss," Randolph commented with a touch of sarcasm, selecting a mini-driver from her tool kit before Jill could comment on his attitude. Randolph then moved away to the outer poles where he began the job of tracing the beams from an upside down view. After some careful twenty minutes, Randolph discovered the main box and another problem. *Whoever set up this scenario wasn't playing by any street rules!* he complained to himself. *The first set of trip beams were rather clever but not unheard of, a basic test of agility skills, since I wasn't given time to research the job. This set of beams are rather redundant but again not unheard of in paranoid people trying to make certain thieves like myself can't get to the prize; however, this!*

Randolph thought angrily, *goes way beyond any real-life applications.* Randolph pulled himself back up and worked his way over to Jill to give her the bad news. "Whoever this Mel fellow of yours is, he's not playing by any set of real street rules."

"How so?" Jill questioned, her dislike of the interruption plain in her tone.

"Because the trip-beam starts from that window across the way," Randolph accused. "And any idiot would know all it would take is a single bird in flight to set these bombs off prematurely."

"Okay, so file a grievance with the committee of fair-play later," Jill snapped, "In the meantime, leave me alone, I've almost got this one disarmed." She placed a spare jump wire into the circuit and cut the detonator switch out of the loop. "Now that I know the wiring sequence, the others won't take so long," Jill announced in satisfaction.

Randolph looked down on the internal workings and Jill's handiwork as she prepared to move on. "Hold it, Jill, I wouldn't go celebrating yet," he piped in. "That battery's ground wire is far too thick to be just one wire."

"What do you mean?" Jill looked back on the inner working.

"I mean there's a second battery under this one."

Jill looked up at Randolph and made a face of annoyance. She inspected the battery a moment before she shifted it out of the way and found Randolph was right. "How would you even know to look for that?"

"In my line of work, you expect redundancy. Most alarm systems have some sort of backup system; however, the richer you are, the more elaborate the redundancy. That's why the city jails are full of criminals."

The Paranoid Thief

"Hmm all right. Go on ahead and start pulling off the covers. I have to recheck the wiring for this second battery. With the covers off, it'll save us some time."

Randolph nodded he understood. If Jill had informed him of these exercises, he would have had his own tools, but as Jill had decided to withhold such valuable information, this necessitated their limited course of action. A critical flaw in any partnership, which was why he worked alone; Randolph learned most people tended to do so just so they would look valuable at times of need.

Once Jill held the correct sequence, she moved about the devices till all were disabled with ten minutes to spare. She stood and rotated her back about to loosen up.

"Do we discount the beams now that the bombs are disarmed?" Randolph asked.

"Unfortunately, no," Jill said replying her tool kit. "Although we can take our time now, we're still in the test till we reach the ladder."

At the top of the ladder, the duo leaned on the walls, soaked to the skin in sweat and quite relieved the trial was over. "So how many times a year do we have to do this?" Randolph asked as the lights in the large chamber went out one by one.

"Six." Jill pulled off her passkey before she inserted it in a slot in the wall. To the left of her hand, a blue screen turned on to revealed a set of numbers in red and green.

Randolph looked on the readout of two lines as Jill smiled. The first line indicated the human dummies while the other listed videocams. To the right each followed a percentage. At the very bottom, an average had been tallied and presented. "So what's that supposed to represent?"

"It's a readout of all the cameras that spotted me and for how long. Anything under ten percent is acceptable. Now let's see how well you did," Jill said with a bit of a smirk in her voice, and removed her card to motion Randolph to insert his own. But when Randolph's readout displayed on the blue screen, his numbers were a quarter less than hers. While Randolph looked over his score without smugness, as in truth the test was unsuitable to be associated to the real world, Jill asked him, a bit testy, "How could you have been spotted less than I? I was right on your heels the entire time."

Randolph shrugged. "Blending in is near on second nature to me. The military, I'm sure," he went on to say, for Jill looked about to argue, "taught you to move and move fast. For hesitation is death to a combat unit, where as in my field, fluidness, along with using the natural cover of the city is learned or you wind up in jail."

Jill leaned back on the wall with its screen now flashing a comparison of their scores, and commented, "I'm sorry, Randolph. I haven't been giving you the respect you deserve. I hadn't considered what it really took for you to have escaped arrest this long."

Randolph shrugged acceptance of her apology as she pushed off the wall.

"Come on, let's grab a shower. Mel doesn't like us walking through the office all smelly." Jill headed off for the elevator, but stopped prior to the keypad to push open a door bearing the universal sign of her female sex. Noting the same universal sign for men on the opposite wall, Randolph turned for the men's shower room when Jill grabbed his arm. "No, Randolph, this way."

"Uh, Jill? The men's room's on this side," Randolph explained.

"That's true, but you and I need to get acquainted, so the next time my sex won't be an issue," Jill said evenly.

"In real life, it wouldn't have been an issue," Randolph remarked with frankness. "Hesitation can get you caught."

"Yeah, well, I've heard that a thousand times in the Corps. And 99 percent of them were wrong. So get your fanny in here, because you and I are going to get well acquainted with each other so you won't slip up and get me killed."

"But what about the other women?" Randolph stammered, forgetting where he was.

With a strong grip, Jill pulled Randolph into the women's bathroom and asked as they walked into the changing area, "You're not still a virgin, are you?"

"Of course not!" Randolph blurted a bit hurriedly, as she opened a locker with her name on it; in fact, the only locker with a name on it.

"Good! Now strip," she ordered, tossing Randolph a bar of soap.

Just catching the bar, Randolph watched as Jill pulled off her sweatshirt, then the athletic bra, allowing her white A-size breasts to bounce free of their restraints. A *bit on the smallish side for my tastes.* Randolph couldn't help sizing her up in his mind, but then he wasn't about to pass up a chance to ogle a woman's body so freely displayed for his eyes, not even one that didn't take advantage of today's best bronzing creams. Next off, to Randolph's delight were her shoes and sweat pants, which revealed lacy, pink, see-through panties and very firm buttocks.

Jill dropped her sweatpants and caught Randolph's look of adulation, which she rolled her eyes at before she put her fist on her hip, turning, allowing him to see she even shaved before she commented dryly, "Yes, Randolph, I'm a woman, with all the parts you men can't get enough of. So if you'll get out of your sweats, I promise you'll get to do more then look at them."

Randolph looked up into Jill's brown eyes and caught the meaning of her words. But when he walked into the shower room moments after her, Randolph found he'd had some time to consider the ramifications this little dalliance could install. And with that time, an insurgence of nervousness, which he then shook off. *After all, I'd been with my share of women, but then Jill isn't a one night stand. She is by circumstances my new partner, and getting involved with one's partner could get a guy caught. My last fiasco with a woman client proved that.* Now that he understood where his reluctance came from, Randolph decided for their own safety it would be best if he left their relationship platonic. *Sure, I wouldn't mind seeing her naked from time to time, but for my own self-preservation, that's as far as it should go.* With this mindset firmly in place, Randolph took the shower next to hers, and lathered up, paying her only a neighborly token of attention.

When Randolph reached up to turn off the water flow, Jill stole up from behind and put her arms around his chest, fingers spread. "I haven't had sex in six months," she whispered, pressing her cheek into his lightly tanned back. Jill gave Randolph a passionate squeeze before allowing herself to let go to move around so he could look down into her desire filled eyes. "So why don't you quit pretending I don't exist and prove to me you're a man?"

Up until this point, Randolph had been true to his decision, but now with her arms placed around his neck and the way her eyes looked up at him, desire over ruled practicality. Unable to stop himself, Randolph laid a hand to her oval face and felt her nuzzle his palm, vanquishing any residuals of restraints still lurking within his soul. With inhibition scattered to the winds, Randolph leaned over and took her lips in lustful hunger as he moved his hands down her sides, so he could lift her off the floor. Once Jill's feet left the tiles, he felt her powerfully athletic legs wrap around his torso. With her held so in place, Randolph pushed her up against the wall while Jill's mouth gave as good as she got. After a time of only their mouths and tongues in play, Jill's needs pushed up against Randolph and she reached down between them, learning he was far more than ready to explore the depths of her womanhood.

With the aid of Jill's other hand, Randolph grabbed her buttocks in anticipation of her move and let go of Jill's mouth to raise her face up into the spray as she guided him in. With a moan of pleasure escaping Jill's lips, she lowered her face to the side of his and nuzzled Randolph's ear, as he flexed his muscles in prelude to their private dance.

Once into a wonderful rhythm, with Jill aiding their movements, Randolph felt himself reaching the point of no-return far sooner than he'd have wished. So he dredged up an old problem he'd yet to solve and set his mind on a quest for an answer in an attempt to distract his mind and body in an effort to enjoy their physical activities just a bit longer. However, as Jill's strong legs squeezed him like a grape in her own cry of release, Randolph could not retain his thoughts and climaxed as well.

After their delightful moment of attaining paradise had sailed into history, Randolph reluctantly allowed Jill's smaller feet to find the floor but found in her eyes she, too, wasn't ready to rejoin the world. So amidst the warm spray of water, he sat down and drew her onto his lap, whereupon Randolph soon discovered a softer Jill, a woman who kissed and touched him gently, one who showed timidity, now that their urgency of mutual hunger had been satiated.

After he'd found heaven a second time, Randolph rolled off Jill's slimmer frame and lay stretched out, panting, only partly within the spray of water where Jill relaxed. As Randolph had done most of the work in propelling them into the heights of ecstasy, her more times than himself, Randolph continued to work air down into his lungs.

Jill sat up. "Not bad. Not bad at all, Randolph." Jill approved of his performance all business-like, in-between her own intakes of breath.

Randolph rolled his eyes onto her from his place on the floor, wondering how she could act so vulnerable and shy one moment, then tough as nails the next. "Now that I've worked out the shyness in you," Jill commented, "I'll tell you this. I enjoy sex. And I wouldn't mind sessions like this twice a week." With that admission of her needs laid out before her new partner, Jill got her legs under her and stood up off the floor, adding, "Besides, Mel will probably send us off as a married couple, or corporate executives, with you as my personal secretary. So being familiar with each other's bodies will only aid in this dissipation."

Randolph watched her begin to stretch in all directions from his place on the floor and decided to ask, "If you like sex that much, why'd you wait six months?" He watched as Jill's eyes slid his way, then moved elsewhere. When Jill doubled over and touched her knees with her forehead, Randolph followed up his question and added, "I mean, don't you have someone special to spend time with?"

"I did," Jill answered, somewhat reluctantly. "He was an ensign in the Corps. He became possessive and accused me of sleeping with the men. It was my mistake really, believing he could handle my taking showers with my unit." Jill stepped away from the spray so she could shake the water out of her hair, and continued her story. "He was so possessive, one night he believed I was out screwing one of the men on guard duty when I didn't answer my page. So to catch me at it, he snuck out to the guard post. Unfortunately for him, an alert sentry saw his behavior, and acting on base orders to shoot first, did so." Jill looked down on Randolph with remembrance in her eyes then finished her story with little emotion. "Because of this, I've sworn off relationships. A good thing too, considering where I ended up. Now I only screw my partners to keep my basic needs in check, and as Jessup was killed six months back, well..." She tilted her head back and stared at the white ceiling a moment to regain her composure, then squared her shoulders. "Now come on, I'm starving."

Chapter Seven

Randolph found during his limited time off, his green badge let him explore only a few places with-in the building. His warden, Mr. Bennett, evidently not trusting his pet project of abducted criminals the room to venture into the everyday workings of the corporation. *A good thing too,* he thought, *with so many computers busy in everyday corporate America, I could get myself in a lot of trouble.* As for the up keep on Mr. Bennett's master criminals, the smart executive satisfied his pets' restrictive world with food and socializing, some of which was attained by lunchroom privileges with all the daily workers, just as long as they dressed the part and behaved themselves. Of course there is one other way Mr. Bennett can and does use in controlling his band of thieves: companionship. For although the threat of being killed by the touch of a button kept his pets relatively contained, the ability to order in companionship took the edge off the prisoners' boredom. But for Randolph, he held very little opportunity to order up this kind of entertainment, as Jill kept him well-occupied with her own needs.

A few days later, Randolph opened his door for Jill and heard Mitch and Patrick coming down the hall, announcing, "Morning, Jill, Randolph. Looks as if our boredom's over. Mel just called Mitch and me into his office."

Jill turned as they walked past her. "Has he given you any hint as to what's it about?"

To this Mitch snorted, while Patrick answered, "You know better than that."

"Yeah I know," Jill replied. "Just wanted to check to see if he's slipping up."

"But you know yourself," Patrick added over his shoulder, "that's not the worst of it. Mel loves to sit there all stately in his executive's chair, giving you only half the answers to the job he wishes done, just to see you squirm till he's ready to fill in the gaps."

"Keeps you sharp!" Mitch said through his nose without turning his head.

The two made the elevator by then, so Jill cut the conversation off and walked into Randolph's room looking peevish.

"Why the face?" Randolph asked.

"Mmm, oh, just tired I guess. As much as it scares me to take on a mission, I envy those two and their chance to get out and see the world." Then her nose got a whiff of the eggs and sausage aromas, and her face relaxed. "At least if you get bored, you could work in the cafeteria, and I dare say improve the food in this place."

"Thanks, but no thanks. I've worked the mind-numbing world of a daily job, and you can have it. That's why I've stuck to thieving. Every job is different, every home or business presents new challenges to keep my mind sharp and invigorated. Besides," Randolph continued, as she took her first bite of his homemade omelet, "I don't ever want to catch myself asking, 'you want fries with that?'"

Jill snorted at his quip and made a grab for her napkin, making Randolph smile in return. To give her a moment to regain her composure, Randolph removed the chilled glasses of orange juice from the refrigerator and sat next to her in the new chair he ordered. But as he set them down, Jill made a statement which almost made him spill the drinks. "It's about time we started sleeping together."

"Uh, isn't that what we've been doing?" Randolph asked in some puzzlement.

Jill eyed Randolph in annoyance before she turned back to her plate and used her fork to cut another piece of the omelet before she clarified herself, a bit sarcastically. "No, dummy. I mean sharing a bed for the night. We need to deal with each other's idiosyncrasies so as not to fight with each other over something as stupid as a night's rest." After that statement, Jill gave Randolph a little time to digest her words before she washed down her eggs and announced, "I'll move some of my stuff in today." She placed her glass down and tapped her lip in thought. "I'll need two shelves behind the mirror in the bathroom, half the closet, two drawers in your dresser for underwear and one for folded clothes. Oh yeah." She snapped her fingers in remembrance. "If you haven't got one, I'll need a trashcan by the head, with disposable bags. I can be a bit messy for a few days each month." Jill turned to look at Randolph after this and found him staring at her as if she were a bug-eyed creature from a distant world. But rather than comment on his insult, she continued to tick off items or things he'd need to get or do, as she finished off her meal. With the aid of a napkin, Jill regrettably ended her meal and told him, "Well, times a-wasting. We've a full day ahead of us. First the gym then a long run. Lunch after a shower, and then we need to spend some time getting reacquainted with the world news. After which I'll move my stuff in while you make us dinner."

Randolph remained motionless for a second or so after Jill stood, digesting her incredible announcement, and wondered in whose universe he had signaled she should move in with him! But before he could stabilize a comment on how intrusive he felt her suggestion to be, Jill eyed him with a look that spoke louder than words what she would do if he even tried to weasel out of her move.

Later, Randolph found Jill wasn't kidding about reading up on the news. He'd never thought he'd have to spend so much time watching back issues of the world events just to understand today's reports. *I guess, as I've always kept myself abreast of the daily world, I never considered how much information is splashed out at the common man.* When she patted his head in reward for his thoroughness before leaving to gather her things, Randolph refrained from telling her his true curiosity was to see who was suing who and what corporate owner was screwing over his or her employees. For these were the people who gave him his next challenging job. *At least they used to,* he amended. Then after dinner and an explanation into the origins of their historic plates from Mexico, before it sold out to the unified corporation Vinco, a Greek and Italian conglomerate looking for cheaper labor, Jill headed for the shower while Randolph cleaned up the kitchen. After which Randolph sat down with his adventures in a spicy tea concoction and took a sip, turning on the video-screen, he looked down into the dark brown liquid. *It still needs something, but what?*

"Randolph," Jill called his name from the doorway. When Randolph didn't answer her right away, as he was absorbed in his thoughts of what he could use, Jill called out more impatiently, "Randolph!"

Shocked into the moment, Randolph turned, "Uh, what?"

"I said I'm going to bed now, and I sleep on the right side," Jill repeated.

Randolph moved his eyes from her face to the lacy, see-through, dark blue night gown with matching black thong, then heard an annoyed sound come up out of her throat before she backed into the room and slammed the door as if he'd offended her in some way. Randolph focused on the door and puzzled over Jill's reaction. *If she doesn't want my eyes traveling to places other than her face, then why wear such...* Randolph stopped his thoughts and shrugged it off as one of life's mysteries of women. He then settled back in the couch-chair, forging the unanswerable questions, and finished off the video on the new ways the FoConning Corporation had of rendering plastic into any kind of wood, with all its smells and texture.

If Randolph dreamt at all, he hoped it was of little interest, for it scurried away into non-memories when someone hit him over the head with something soft, backed with a bit of force. Shocked awake by such a rude gesture, Randolph's mind scrambled, which forced him upright in order to fend off another attack as a familiar voice angrily reminded him where he was, while she accused, "I didn't volunteer to sleep over in an empty bed. Now get your butt up, your clothes off and in bed, Mister, and I mean now!"
With the use of his hands, Randolph protected his head from further abuse, then yawned and asked, "What time is it?"
"Its 1:00 in the frigging morning!" a very enraged Jill informed him.
"Okay, okay, give me a minute." Randolph let his guard down to stretch and yawn yet again.
In answer to his request, Jill hit him even harder with the pillow. "You've had three hours of moments mister, now move it!" Not in any mood to await his pleasure, Jill threw her pillow at him and grabbed his arm, hauling Randolph off the couch and into the bedroom. "We'll dispense with a shower, as we only have four hours left of this night," she declared, and shoved Randolph to the bed to strip him. Once Randolph quit his constant complaints and stood to step out of his pants, Jill threw over the covers and pointed forcefully he was to get in first. Once this was accomplished, Jill crawled in and spooned up to Randolph's chest and promptly fell back asleep. Randolph spent an hour of the time remaining trying to figure out

where to put his hands, as he'd never truly "slept" with a woman before, nor was he sure she wouldn't bite off his head if he laid them in places anatomically different from his own.

The next morning's activities, after a simple ham and cheese omelet, found the pair down in the scenario room, where Jill, still pissed with his antics from last night, informed Randolph, "We're to secure files from a twenty-story building."

A rather impossible task, Randolph thought, as the room is only four levels high. But Jill pointed out the seven structures which represented the buildings and how they were connected to each other. Not at all thrilled with this farce of a scenario, nor Jill's attitude one bit, Randolph spoke his mind. "Jill, I'm not a fly-by-the-seat-of-your-pants thief. A job like this takes me weeks, if not months, to set up. Every building has so many unknowns, I spend—"

"We've thirteen hours, Randolph," Jill cut him off shortly, "which started the moment I picked up this clipboard." She emphasized the board by waving it in Randolph's face. "So quit bellyaching, and get me in the building."

"Okay, fine. But tell me, what's your role in this?" Randolph asked. "This is my territory. I specialize in getting in and out of places like this. What's your bit in this caper?"

"In as much as I know, nothing, but we're a team and as such we work together, so do your job and we'll see what comes up."

What came up was Randolph's ever increasing temper. *Buildings are not meant to be waltzed around in if you wish to remain free and breathing,* he growled mentally. *Specific tools are needed on each job. Hence I never render a time frame as I always design and construct my own, given one tool has to accomplish many tasks.*

Some long hours later, Randolph shook his head while working on a problem he would have had a tool for, and hissed at Jill out of frustration, "If you don't get off my back, I'm going to make a mistake!"

"You've had thirty minutes to figure this one out, what's the delay?" Jill asked irritably.

"I don't work like this," Randolph argued just above a whisper, for he knew sound alarms were common in any building as a first defense.

"You do now, so quit stalling. We've eight hours and seven floors to go," she hissed back, slapping his head in frustration. Jill's action caused Randolph's hand to jerk and the pen laser he held sliced a wire he was tracing. Jerking his arm back in belated reaction, Randolph inadvertently jabbed Jill in the thigh which caused her to lose balance and step into a proximity alarm he was trying to disable. The combination of mistakes set off two alarms.

Once Jill regained her balance, she registered the loud bells and red lights. This meant Randolph had slipped-up, in her steamed mind. "How could you? Now I'm five minutes away from a migraine that makes an anti-personal mine feel like a few ant bites!"

When Randolph stood up to yell at Jill for her stupidity, he instead backed away from her murderous eyes and declared with an accusing finger, "Don't you dare look at me that way!" But he got no further in that accusation, as Jill kicked him solidly in the balls and proceeded without hesitation to whale on him like he was a favorite punching bag. When at last semi-consciousness returned him to the world, Randolph found Jill on his chest with his hands locked in a death grip on her slender arms, trying like hell to keep her from smashing his brains out all over the floor.

The Paranoid Thief

Jill continued to scream obscenities at Randolph's clumsiness, till the moment the chips went off in their heads.

Randolph instantly released his hold of Jill in an anguished cry, as excruciating agony cascaded up and down his body, fraying every nerve, every muscle, while every ounce of material not connected to his bones ejected out of every orifice.

~~~

Lying in a hospital bed for some hours before he even chanced opening his eyes, Randolph heard footsteps approaching before he forced his eyes open and saw Mr. Bennett had the nerve to show up by his bedside. The executive looked Randolph over. Glancing at the chart over his head, Mr. Bennett said, "Now that you know how it feels to slip up, I suspect you'll take our little exercises a bit more seriously." He did a bit of preening with his sapphire cuff links then looked to Jill's bed without emotion and then turned to walk away without a word more.

If Randolph had had a gun at hand, he just might, even against all his principles, have used it. *But not to kill him,* he assured himself, *oh no, that would have been far too quick for what I went through. No, I'd have laid into his corporate butt so he'd have to stand from now on to achieve his daily routines, and that would have been just the beginning!*

Chapter Eight

Randolph came out of his state of incapacitation a little sooner than Jill, even with the brutal beating Jill had rendered on his body, which meant he was able to defend himself slightly when she stormed into his apartment and reinstated her objections with her fists about the chip going off in her head. After which, she ignored Randolph for a couple of days, allowing him time to heal from both her beatings and the residual debilitation of the brain chip. This bit of generosity allowed Randolph to use an ice pack against his eyes and cheeks as needed while he worked on plans to, "inform the son-of-a-bitch that being brained fucked was not going to be tolerated." *Not by words of course,* he thought angrily, *as they would be useless. No, but by other means. Means I'm well equipped to achieve with time and research, and best of all, it will be accomplished with their very own credits and equipment!*

Randolph sat at his dinner table with a lovely array of confections scattered about its surface, finalizing a mini circuit board, when Jill walked in unannounced.

"Randolph, we've got to talk."

The abruptness of her entrance caused Randolph to nearly jump out of his skin, whereby the board went flying. *If I've ruined that board,* he grumbled, *it'll be three days of work down the proverbial tubes.*

"Listen, I have to apologize…" Jill began, stopping at the table where he sat, taking note of all the jumbled parts on the table and hearing Randolph's sigh of annoyance. This broke off what she was saying to ask, "What's all this?"

When Jill refrained from resuming her actions of earlier days, he took a calming breath, which didn't work very well, and told her, "What all this is, is none of your business. Now how the hell did you get in without the room telling me?"

"With my passkey, of course," Jill said without thought as Randolph started looking for the board. "This looks as if you're building something for a job," she stated the obvious, accusingly.

"No, I'm not building something for a job," Randolph lied. "Haven't you ever sat down and experimented with your ideas?" Randolph found the board intact, saying over his shoulder as he stood, to distract her, "Can I get into your room as well?"

"Not as yet, but maybe later," Jill answered as he laid the board down, settled back down in his chair and pulled the micro magnifier over for a more thorough examination of the board. With a motion of her hand over the table, Jill commented. "One of the others is a thief as well, but I've never heard of him starting from scratch when all you need do is place an order."

"Then he's far too stupid for this business!" Randolph snapped, irritated, and added after wiping his face, "Probably what got him caught. Now what the hell is it that you want?" Randolph flipped the board over to inspect the back as Jill stammered a couple of words before angrily slapping the top of his head with something hard. "Ow, what's that for?" He glared up at her.

"To get your damn attention while I try to apologize," Jill said with heat.

Randolph lowered his head in disgust, then sat back up in the chair and crossed his arms, noting Jill was wearing one of those out dated dresses yet again, this one polka dotted white over yellow, belted at the waist with the skirt hanging a good foot above her matching high heels. She then took the seat next to him and using a hand to keep the skirt from bunching up under her as she sat, Jill became all feminine-like, ducking her head shyly. "I'm sorry. I know you've told me time and again you work at a slower pace, I've just never considered your job that difficult. That's why I was pushing and I shouldn't have, nor should I have taken it out on you when it was I who slipped up." Jill raised her head just enough so he could barely see her eyes, before she asked in all humility, "Can you forgive me?"

Randolph heard the emotions in those few words, which caused a lead weight of guilt to high dive into the pit of his stomach. And taking note how contrite she look while fidgeting in her chair awaiting his response, Randolph unfolded his arms and put a small gentle smile on his lips before saying. "You know, I've never been apologized to, and even if I had and can't remember, yours was the most heartfelt delivery I've ever heard. So yes, Jill, I accept your apology."

Jill raised her head with a bright smile, causing her face to brighten, then said in true honesty, "Thank you." She moved a stray hair out of her eyes. "Now if you'll take a shower and dress nicely, I'll treat you to a night of dancing and dinner."

Randolph cocked his head and looked puzzled at her. "I thought we couldn't leave the building?"

"Oh, we can't. The big shots are having their yearly ball, and anyone with our clearance may arrive as long as we behave." Jill glanced about in search of something. "Didn't you receive the invitation?"

"Uh, not that I know of, I've been rather busy."

"Well, forget about that tonight." Jill stood, and twirling her skirt so it flared out, she said happily, "For we are going dancing till our feet fall off tonight!"

"Uh, I hate to burst your bubble Jill, but I never learned to dance."

The Paranoid Thief

"Pay no mind to that," Jill said, pulling him out of the chair. "You just get cleaned up, and I'll do the rest on the dance floor." As Jill prodded him toward the shower, Randolph protested he had no dress clothes suitable for an event like this, but she playfully patted his face, explaining she'd already taken care of that.

They were both a bit tipsy as they managed the moving hallway to Randolph's door later that morning. Finally Randolph pulled his card out to access his door, which was a bit hard, as Jill held tightly to his other arm to keep her balance. Still laughing, swaying some to keep her balance, she attempted an intoxicated speech. "Oooh, Johnny, you were won-der-ful. And you said you couldn't dance."

Randolph got the door open and managed to get Jill to the back of the couch-chair without falling.

Still giggling after their stumble-walk, Jill caught her breath as Randolph made for the door to close it. "And the muuusic, ahhh the music, it was—" Jill tried a twirl in her knee-length dress but her feet refused to handle the full circle. Just closing the door, Randolph saw the obvious result about to happen and reached out in time to catch her up before her bottom hit the floor, staggering with her unaided weight in his own mildly drunk state as she tilted her head back to announce, "Every-thing was perfect."

"Yeah, it was nice," Randolph agreed, getting her to her feet and into the bedroom.

Jill sat heavily on the bed and dropped her purse as Randolph stepped away, undoing the useless silk tie which had come with his 1,000-credit suit. But before he could get it fully off, Jill leaned forward to take off her high heels, only to lose her balance. Randolph saw this and reacted, catching her up, but lost his own balance when Jill grabbed and jerked his tie, whereby they both ended up on the bed together with a startled laugh.

Jill slapped at Randolph playfully when he moved off her. She then grabbed his arm in aid of sitting up, saying with a smile, "Hold your horses, lover boy. I want some fore-play before loving you."

"Love?" Randolph exclaimed. Laying a hand on her shoulder, he told her, "Jill, I think we best wait till you're more sober."

Putting a finger to her lips, Jill shushed him. "Not a-nother word John-ny my boy, to-night is not for talking, but for love making. Now be a good boy and pucker up, as I'm still very huungry."

"Jill, you're drunk." Randolph stood to get out of her reach, feeling uncomfortable in how she was talking.

"Huush, dammit, I don't care. I'm in the mood to make passionate love, and youu're spoiling it," Jill argued, throwing a shoe at him.

Randolph backed into the door. "Jill, I may have been sleeping with you, but I don't want to take advantage of you while you're drunk."

Jill stood, using the bed for support, and reached up under her dress to pull off her white lace panties. "I say you're not. Now get those tight buns over here and fondle me!"

Randolph remained where he was and took note of the look in Jill's eyes; even though they were heavily dilated, he could still see the storm clouds forming within, ready to strike if he disobeyed her. *But if I give in, I'm also sure she'll be pissed later today, believing I took advantage of her condition.*

Now that she had her panties off, Jill tossed them up at Randolph playfully as she sat. She patted the bed next to her and undid her belt, saying coyly, "I've two lone-ly breasts wish-ing for a couple of strong hands. Do youu have a pair of hands wish-ing to play?"

Regretfully, for his well-being he had to pass up on her offer. He crossed to her as she smiled, playfully leaning back on her hands.

The Paranoid Thief

"They're uunder my dress wait-ing to see you, but youu'll have to help them get out." Randolph sighed and rolled his eyes skyward, hating himself for this, but gave Jill a right cross anyway, quick and fast.

Around five in the morning, the bedroom door opened and Jill called out, "Randolph, are you out here?"

Randolph blinked a second or so before he felt Jill sit on the couch-chair.

She nudged his shoulder. "What are you doing out here? You should be sleeping with me."

With a bit of effort, Randolph pulled his thoughts together and answered with a yawn and stretch, "I didn't think it was appropriate."

"Why not?" Jill asked massaging her cheekbone.

"Because you were drunk, and I didn't want you accusing me that I helped you get so, so I'd get laid last night."

"Is that why my cheek hurts? Did I fall or something?"

"Or something is about right," Randolph said. She was wearing nothing but a towel, "You were throwing yourself at me, telling me you wished to make love of all things, love mind you, not sex." Now that his mind was working up to semi-speed, Randolph couldn't help but ask, "Jill, is…do…I mean, do you love me?"

Jill sobered some and bit her lip, then shook her head, denying. "Of course not. That was just the alcohol talking." Still rubbing her cheek, she began, "Now then, do you have any—"

"Aspirin?" Randolph finished for her, and in gaining a slow nod he answered, "Sure, third shelf up in the bathroom."

"Thanks. Oh, why don't you get undressed and come to bed?" Jill stood.

"Why bother?" Randolph yawned, causing her to yawn as well, putting a hand to her mouth. "It's nearly time to get up anyway."

Jill glanced at the clock over the stove and seemed to consider for a moment. "No, we deserve a day off. Besides, the big shots will be wandering around acting important today and I'd rather not be pressed into being an escort." Jill turned her head to reach behind in an effort to scratch her calf, where by her towel slipped, exposing her uncovered skin. Once the itch was taken care of, Jill caught up only the portion in front as she turned to walk back into the bedroom, which left her lovely cheeks exposed. As Randolph watched them disappear in the darker room, he reminded himself. *Rolling under the sheets while she was tipsy was out, but now that she's somewhat sober, that body of hers is fair game.*

Jill rolled out from under the covers a little past 10:00 a.m. and put her feet on the floor, stretching. Randolph remained where he was and watched as Jill's honed muscles flowed under her skin and marveled that he could enjoy the sight of a well-toned woman when he'd always gone for the ones with more meat on their bones. "Where you going?" Randolph asked, propping himself up as she stood.

Jill got clear of the bed and spread her legs, bent double to stretch, and answered without looking at him, "I've put off my morning run for far too long." She rose back up and twisted her body to lay her head on first one knee then the other. "And my body's telling me about it." After two of these Jill straightened back up and headed for the bathroom, offhandedly commenting, "You needn't get up on my account, though."

Randolph sat up, stretching, as Jill closed the door. He glanced at his pillow, wondering if he should, but hearing the stool, he looked over as she emerged and pointed out to her searching eyes, "Your panties are on the floor there and your shoes and dress are in the closet."

"Thanks," Jill said pulling out her dress and slipping it on with a look on her face as if she disliked the outfit.

Randolph watched Jill retrieve her panties and shoes without putting them on and decided to ask her. "Jill, after all this time I'm still puzzling over some of your actions. I know this may sound stupid but it's—it's like I'm dealing with two people? One moment you're as timid and vulnerable as a flighty bird, and the next you're as tough as nails."

"Oh that," Jill said, looking for her purse, which he pointed out to her. Jill nodded thanks then explained, "I've a multi-personality complex derived from a childhood accident in a pool." Not looking at Randolph, Jill opened her purse and removed her card key. "In other words, I am two different people. However, unlike most people with such, I'm aware of my other side, and we've worked out a suitable compromise, so it's under control." Jill looked over, and seeing Randolph's face, she smiled, reassuring him. "Don't worry about it. When it's time to be serious, I'm in total control. Any other time it's a toss-up who wishes to be out."

Randolph's mouth hung ajar.

She walked over to the bed where she patted his face. "And as we don't take any medications to render one or the other incapable of emerging, so there are no lapses in our memories, unless we've had too much to drink. Like last night." Jill left the bedroom after exposing that nest of wires, and picked up her shawl lying on the floor just in sight of the doorway, and headed for the front door calling out, "Oh, uh, do you mind making dinner tonight?"

"If you don't mind eating on the couch," Randolph called back, reminded of his work scattered about the table.

He put on a robe and moved out of the bedroom in time to see Jill looking on the cluttered table. "You couldn't shove all that into a box?"

"I'd rather not. I've a system in where I place things so I can put my fingers on something without looking up."

Jill made a face to his reluctance then looked at the door, apparently thinking before she made up her mind. "All right, I'll have your card keyed into my door. But I don't want you rummaging around in my room. And I'll not have you making any smart-alack remarks, either. My room is my sanctuary." With that said, Jill was out the door and across to hers. "I just remembered, I've things I need to get done today, so I'll be tied up till seven or eight."

Randolph closed his door after hers closed, straight across from his. With a shake of his head in wonder, Randolph headed for the bathroom. *I've heard of such cases, but of course I've never had to deal with one.* He took a shower and reaffixed his mind on the matter of Mr. Bennett's payback.

Chapter Nine

Randolph examined a half-made tool which he wouldn't finish out in the open like this, in case of hidden video-cameras in the walls he had yet to find, and looked up to blink his eyes a few times, seeing the time above the stove. "Seven?" Randolph exclaimed in disbelief, "Rats, I should have started dinner an hour ago!" he berated himself. Now having no time to order up supplies, Randolph rummaged about his kitchen and improvised with what was on hand.

Later, stirring up a steak sauce on a low burner, Randolph heard his door open and Jill's voice calling out to him.

"Randolph, what are you doing in here? Couldn't you get in my room?"

Randolph looked over and saw Jill, nose in the air, enjoying the mingling smells like they were aromatic scents from a candle.

"Sorry, I lost track of time, and knowing you don't cook, I just started it up here."

Jill approached, now wearing a gray on dark gray business suit, and took a big whiff over the stove, asking with a smile, "Mmm, do I smell real apple pie?"

"That, among other things. Come on—every-thing's ready so if you'll help me carry this lot and get the doors, we can move to your room."

Jill did as asked and opened her door, but then glanced hesitantly sideways at Randolph before allowing him in. If he ever had any doubts about her being female, they were dispelled at once. For while Randolph's apartment was dull browns and white, Jill's apartment had bright yellow walls overlooking a medium green rug under a light green couch and chair set. Still adjusting his eyes to the color change,

Randolph saw old-fashioned frilly white dollies over every armchair and one draped on top an oval mirror and wooden counter top that stood near the front door. With a quick eye for wealth out of habit, Randolph estimated this room alone would fetch 50,000 credits easily from an antique dealer, for it was like he'd stepped into a time capsule of the twenty-first century, all save her holographic videos on the walls and her very modern but unused kitchen appliances.

"Where in the world did you get all these antiques?" Randolph couldn't help but ask, setting his handful of plates on an all-wood dinette table, protected by two layers of durable plastic sealant.

"Depending on the outcome of our assignments, Mel grants us a healthy credit account." Jill glanced his way. She shrugged, remarking offhandedly, "And why not? It's not as if he's losing any credits."

Randolph was reminded of what Jill had said about their life expectancy and understood what she meant without explanation. After putting her plate down, Jill looked around the room as if she'd never seen it before and allowed Randolph a glimpse of her true personality.

"Being a military brat, moving every year or so, I found over time I came to find some stability in my grandmother's home, on the rare occasions we were close enough to visit." Jill smiled with memories. "I haven't the room to match the serenity I always felt in her home…" Trailing off, Jill confided in him with, "It just feels safe to me." Then sobering back into her hard as nails personality, Jill gave Randolph a hard stare, as if to silence any smart-ass remarks, before motioning him to put down his arm load.

The pair was in the midst of their meal when Jill's phone lit up. "Yes, Mel?" she called without getting up.

The Paranoid Thief

"Major, I need you and Randolph in my office." Mel's plain-sounding voice fell out of the speaker box.

"Can't it wait? I'm in the middle of dinner?" Jill said, taking another bite.

For a second or so, Randolph heard nothing then Mel asked incredulously. "You cooked dinner?"

Jill put her fork down with a sigh of annoyance. "No, Mel, Randolph did. He's here with me."

"In your apartment?" His tone caused Randolph to look at the phone speaker, then over at Jill.

"Mel," Jill snapped, "do you need us now or can it wait?"

"Oh, ah, yes, it's important. I've got an assignment for you. You'll need to leave ASAP."

Randolph looked to Jill, hearing the phone go silent, and noted she looked worried, biting her lip before wiping her mouth with a napkin. "Bad news?" he inquired.

Jill pushed her plate aside and became all business-like. "It means one of the teams has suffered capture, casualties, or both, and we're to clean up the mess while finishing their task."

Without cleaning up, Randolph followed a solemn Jill out the door to her beckoning, and found himself in Mel's office listening to events which he had no control over, and now seamed thrust into without proper research.

"Mitch and Patrick," Mr. Bennett was explaining, "haven't reported in for some days." Mr. Bennett handed Jill a folder, which she opened to inspect as the executive continued without offering Randolph a similar copy. "Their last correspondence was of normal operations, as you can see. What they'd been assigned to unravel is why one corporation is able to sell products cheaper by a third out of

China, while the mass markets are spending twice to triple the amount for the same quality."

Randolph took note Mr. Bennett refrained from mentioning China's new political strives in becoming a world leader by combining corporations in hostile takeovers and buyouts these past few years.

"So are we to locate the team and continue on—" Jill started to ask.

"No," Mr. Bennett interrupted, "you're to assume they're compromised and proceed in another avenue which would benefit our holdings. You'll find the new task outlined in basic details, redesigned for your specialties."

"What if we come across this other team?" Randolph inquired, unable to help himself as he was being purposely sidestepped in these proceedings.

"Let me put this bluntly," Mr. Bennett said with ill-patience. "If contact is uninitiated within a certain time frame, I push a button which sets off a charge embedded within the chip you all have planted in your brains. If the charge has yet to go off, it's because you're already dead or shielded. The first being because of your incompetence, while the other is but a matter of time till the signal works its way to you. Do I make myself clear?" Mr. Bennett must have seen the minute change in Randolph's facial expression; he finished with, "Good." He turned to Jill and ordered, "Get your clothes—a hover craft is waiting on the launch pad." With that he waved the pair on with a dismissive gesture, where by Jill, stiff-necked and showing tautness in her stance, walked out without comment.

As the pair reached their apartments, Randolph asked with some trepidation, "Are you all right?"

The Paranoid Thief

"Am I all right?" Jill blurted angrily. "Of course I'm all right! What makes you think I'm other than perfect, just because Mel has executed two members of our team without a thought and now is sending us out to do the corporation's bidding so they can grow in strength like an untreated cancer?"

She angrily swiped her card to open her door.

Not liking her mood, he grabbed her arm and demanded, "If that's how you feel, why have you been shoving their propaganda down my throat all this time?"

Jill slapped his hand off her arm. "So you wouldn't get me killed!"

Stepping in and slamming her door in his face, she left Randolph staring at the door a moment before mumbling obscenities of his own, wishing he'd had time to finish Mel's surprise package to give the man a taste of his own medicine should he push those buttons again. Not having any other choice, Randolph turned, pulled out his own card key, and opened his own door. Upon stepping in, Randolph took a hard long look on the scattered electronics on the table and steamed even further. Whatever he was to do could very well profit from much of what he'd gathered on the table. *But how am I to know what it is I'll be facing? And will Jill give me the time to make it?* At this, Randolph grimaced and looked skyward for help. Then on impulse he snatched up his half-built tools and supplies, tossing the lot in a brief case he'd found in the closet some time back. Next, dumping clothes and toiletries in a larger bag without organization, Randolph moved to await Jill outside his door, stewing. He waited for Jill's emergence to continue his earlier comments; some fifteen minutes later he found her in no better mood than he, carrying a similar suitcase and an aluminum case specially designed for firearms. It was then Randolph finally understood their true relationship and why'd he'd been paired off with her.

"You're an assassin!" he blurted in dismay.

"Bought and paid for by your local government," Jill admitted without evasiveness, noting with distaste, Randolph had disinclined to change his clothes. She pushed him toward the elevator, flippantly remarking, "Discarded like yesterday's trash and now recycled by Global Rift Supply and Demand, just like you." She emphasized her last words, getting Randolph into the elevator. Jill hit the top floor button then stabbed her finger into his chest angrily, saying bitterly, "And it's your job to get me past all those be-dammed-able security measures so I can take out the target, got it!"

Randolph stood next to Jill in the elevator, trembling, and knowing how useless it was, he still had to tell her, "But that's against my religious beliefs! I can't do that!"

Jill became even more enraged and slammed Randolph up against the wall, taking him totally off guard. She hissed in his face, "Get with the program, Randolph! Neither of us has any choice. We either do the job we're given or we're dead!" She let him go and stepped back to straighten out her gray suit, commenting cynically before the doors slid open to the outside noises, "Besides, whether it gives you any comfort or not, you can be damn sure the hands of our target are bloodied many times over from the countless bodies he or she buried in helping to build the corporation's foundation."

Jill walked off the elevator first, spine straight and chin held high, looking for all the world like an overpriced executive. Randolph stood in the elevator chewing on her words as Jill handed over her cases to one of two baggage handlers without even a courtesy nod then mounted the stairs and the awaiting hover craft. Absolutely hating it, but absent of any choice as yet, Randolph followed after Jill cleared

The Paranoid Thief

the stairs and gave a polite, "thank you" nod to the baggage handler before boarding the craft. The noise level out on the roof top was near on deafening. Once inside, he heard the hydraulics kick in as the door repositioned and sealed shut, cutting off ninety percent of the engine sounds and all the ambiance of a prospering metropolis.

"As soon as you're buckled in, Ms. Wander," a flight attendant was saying, "we can lift off."

Jill settled in a dark blue swivel chair, showing she understood the words without acknowledgment, then buckled herself in and crossed her legs, expressing no emotions to the situation or task.

Randolph took his own seat across the aisle from Jill and watched as the attendant made sure his buckle was secured before walking up front and settling herself behind a wall built behind the flight cabin. When the pilot announce a four-hour flight time, Randolph laid his head back and felt the powerful turbines pull in volumes of air before it sent the flow below the craft for lifting off. Once aloft, the craft shifted, angling into the atmosphere.

Regardless of the appearance he was free of Mr. Bennett and the button that would set off the charge in his head, Randolph wasted no thoughts on a vanishing act once aground. For if Mr. Bennett had not lied, that chip in Randolph's head meant he was still a prisoner no matter his location or surrounding. Besides, he was still chewing on his new realization once the craft was level and very tempted to reopen the argument he and Jill were having in the elevator when Jill got up stiffly and disappeared behind a curtain to the rear. But upon seeing the stewardess, Randolph realized he might not want to air out certain matters, lest the woman become a liability to the company. So Randolph clamped his mouth shut as she approached and inquired in a polite voice, "Mr. Arlington, would you like a drink? We have a very nice Chamblee that goes well with the Peking duck, or perhaps a glass of sherry to go with the chicken and dumpling?"

With only a modest hesitation upon hearing himself addressed by a new name, having lost the mood to send anything with flavor past his taste buds, Randolph inquired, "You don't happen to have a plain old beer, I suppose?"

"We do, sir," she smiled. "Hinkles or Donlley?"

"Just hot coffee for the both of us," Jill called out from behind the curtain.

"Hey," Randolph complained, turning in his seat to argue.

Jill pushed aside the screen and moved back to her seat, having changed her blouse and donned a gray and white vest. "We've no time for dull minds, Randolph. Now get back there and change."

Still wishing to argue but doing as told, Randolph grumbled under his breath and closed the curtain to discover a small open compartment with a complete set of business clothes. Still of a mind to split silicone chips, Randolph changed into the overpriced blue-black suit and vest, designed for snooty executives, complete with ruby cuff links, and sat to finish the ensemble with ArgonBell black shoes, guaranteed to shine without polishing for two years.

Once dressed, he pulled back the curtain and saw Jill's eyes travel about his fame before she gave him a whistle, evidently trying to lighten his mood. "You look good enough to eat."

"You may think so, but I think it's a complete waste of good credits."

Jill's brief moment of levity vanished. "A waste or not, it's necessary. Now here, put this around your neck," she ordered him, handing over a blue and gray badge on a length of cord. Randolph looked over the thing, which read "District over site committee member." This meant, in layman's terms, he had clearance to any company records and all the funding required to achieve his job, regardless of what his job was, hence the twenty-thousand credit suit.

"So what's this all about?" Randolph questioned.

"It guarantees no interference from personnel or company heads," Jill confirmed, adding, "Therefore we walk in, order what we need, including an office, and get to work."

"That maybe how you work, but it's not my way," Randolph reminded her.

"And what precisely is that?" Jill asked sounding skeptical.

"Simple," Randolph began, noting the stewardess had resettled herself behind the wall to give them some privacy. "I research an area, acquire a warehouse as a base, piggyback my equipment onto the city's grid, then get to work on the target by learning everything about them, from the building structures the target lives or works in, to daily habits. Only after acquiring all this, do I plan out what may be done to accomplish my task, whatever that may be from the contract I'd drawn out with those who hired me."

"Sounds time consuming," Jill said dryly.

"Yes, Jill, it is. First I back log the building so it appears rented out to those who rented last. Then I set up security, covering all the ways in, including the sewer system—"

"Enough already," Jill slammed her hand down. "There'll be no need for all that. All you're required to do is get me past what security measures there are for a line of sight to the target. Period."

Randolph sat back in his chair and glared at Jill.

She asked, without sounding as if she cared, "You don't like your role, I take it?"

"You got it in one," Randolph admitted, folding his arms in a statement of closure.

"Well, tough! This is how it's going to be. I've had far more experience on these missions—"

"And lost partners," Randolph threw at her, shutting Jill up with that jab. "I may be a rookie, but take a good hard look at my record. I've been pinched twice in twenty years, and those times were in my teens when I knew no better. Since then, zip-o. And I've done over sixty high-profile jobs, each one escalating my skills, and not a single fatality in any one of them!"

"Not until your last one, anyway," Jill jabbed back with a smirk.

Randolph sat up straight. "I told you I didn't kill those people. I was set up!"

"Yeah, yeah, you're just in denial," Jill said with a dismissive wave of her hand.

Randolph considered flipping her off but instead told her, "I'm not going to help you kill someone, and that's final."

"You'll do as I say, or you'll get one hell of a headache," Jill threatened.

"What, you gonna call Mel?" Randolph sneered.

"No, I'm quite capable of making you wish I did call Mel," Jill replied in such a matter-of-fact cold voice, Randolph thought he saw icicles forming in the air.

"I'll not argue"—he swallowed—"but it'll do no good. I don't believe in killing."

Jill sat back, taking a sip of her hot coffee, and tried out a scenario on Randolph. "Let's say a gunman has your family, and orders you to kill the first person you meet on the street or he'll kill them. What then?"

"I don't know."

"What do you mean you don't know?" Jill waved her hand in frustration. "What's there not to know? You take the gun he hands you and shoot the first person you meet. It's as simple as that."

Randolph shook his head. "But it's never that simple. Even if—and that's a big if—I do, what's to stop him from killing my family anyway? I'll have killed a perfect stranger for no reason, thus the reason to do so is moot."

"So you kill him instead," she countered.

"No, Jill, I can't. It's not for me to take someone's life. That's reserved for the man upstairs."

"Damn, Randolph, you really are a lifist!" Jill shook her head and put her cup down. "All right fine. I'll take out the target without your help, but you damn well better get the information Mel wants in this folder afterwards," she demanded, tossing it at him.

Randolph caught the folder and stammered, "Now hold on. Can't you at least wait till I've gotten the information? Doing him will bring down every security measure they have, making my job a thousand times harder."

"And how long would that take?"

"Cripes, I don't know. I need time to research, say a month to do the preliminary background on the company—"

"And what do I do during this fishing expedition?" Jill interrupted, taking a sip of her coffee.

"Hell, I don't know. I've told you time and again I haven't worked with a partner since the last time I got caught and convicted. Besides, I have to unravel the rat nest Mitch and Patrick left behind."

"If that's your reason, then don't worry about it. Mel wouldn't send us against the same building they screwed up in."

"But that still doesn't give me a free ride in. Security's been alerted, thus all their buildings will re-impose procedures which have been relaxed, actively looking for breeches of security."

Jill rotated her chair left and right, apparently thinking instead of arguing, then nodded. "I'll give you two weeks, after which we do it my way."

"For crying out loud, Jill, what's your hurry?"

"Cause and effect."

Bewildered at hearing such a simple statement, Randolph stared at her, whereby she sighed, explaining.

"Because you and I are supposed to be dead, thus the longer we're out on a job, the greater the possibility we're discovered, which in effect makes us useless to Mel, and thereby we get our brains fried. And being as I'm not ready to die, I'll give you only two weeks while I do some recon." Holding up a hand to Randolph's counter argument, Jill told him she would subtract a day for every minute he continued to complain.

Forced to 'shut his mouth'. Randolph rolled his eyes skyward, petitioning for patience, and stewed in his chair for the remainder of their trip.

Chapter Ten

The craft touched down as schedule on the roof of a second Global Rift Supply and Demand building somewhere in the upper state of Yanncy. Once down the steps, Randolph and Jill found themselves greeted by the chief security technician, a corporate lawyer, and two executive managers whose assistants accepted their guests bags from the baggage handlers assigned to the hover port. Escorted past sound proof doors, Jill and Randolph had their credentials verified then were asked of their needs and comfort. As Randolph's time table for even the barest essentials had been scrubbed, he begged out of the V.I.P. tour to unwind in a large conference room on the executive's level. Pulling up an over-large chair to one of two terminals, he settled in, letting his fingers fly.

First on the agenda are my four seemingly simple search programs. Randolph wrote the programs from memory, which when activated in order would combine bits of code from each to seek out hard wired lines to the outside world while looking at the security programs working on this side of the firewall. Randolph allowed these programs to run in the back ground while he wrote up a meaningless program to randomly run out on the hard lines to any nodes and open computers. Next came out of his memory a piggyback program to see what type of guard dogs ran freely here-a-bout on the hard lines; once identified, each dog was tagged and the program marked the nodes of its territory.

Randolph's next task on his cut-down list of things to do was a bit more complex, as he stripped down the second computer so he could disable any hardware allowing other eyes into the computer, including three spy-ware chips he found which had to have been installed by the security people. Next he opened up his briefcase and took an etching pen to the last quarter of the hard drive, destroying any invisible programs the operating system never sees but always installs for government agencies to have random checks for activities which could be considered criminal or detrimental to the government strangle hold on average people's lives. After this came the tedious measures of removing all bugs and optical videos attached to the video-screen that allowed a face to be attached to the program being run.

With this completed, Randolph set the computer to reformat to its original out-of-the-box settings minus spy-ware programs which send information to the builder about what the computer is being used for. Only after these start-up procedures had been accomplished did Randolph push back to the first computer and begin the next phase of capturing the strongest guard dogs and any leeches attached. This arduous task, though boring as hell, was his most important quest. For with the guard dogs, Randolph could take them apart and sic'em back on their makers, which then would give him entry codes to begin phase two.

After countless hours over the keyboards, Randolph yawned and rubbed tied eyes, pushing away from the second computer to glance over at a halo-video of an antique grandfather clock; 3:32 a.m. With a stretch of his arms, Randolph got up to walk around a bit to reacquaint his legs with movement and spied a video-phone. To Randolph's touch of the call button, a polite female voice answered without hesitation, "Yes, Mr. Arlington?"

Randolph raised an eyebrow to the prompt answer from a wide-awake secretary. "Do you have a recorder handy?"

"Yes, Mr. Arlington."

Randolph smiled and began ticking off a list of computer parts, tools and other devices he could take apart for the items inside, finishing with, "and I need them by 6 a.m., is that possible?" Once more hearing her acknowledgement of "Yes, Mr. Arlington." Randolph signed off. After a bigger yawn, Randolph used the facilities reserved for high class stuffed shirts then laid on the conference table, using the suit jacket as a blanket, and promptly fell asleep.

Insistent knocking on the conference room door made Randolph rise from his nap, grumbling, *I just laid down.* Releasing a deep yawn, he rolled his eyes to the halo clock and found it was two past 6 a.m. *That can't be right!* Grumbling yet again, Randolph rolled off the table, pulling open the locked door to find three delivery men with carts loaded. Once they waltzed out with their empty carts, a different secretary from the previous day entered unbidden, setting a tray of bagels, toast, coffee, juice and fresh water on the table. She flashed Randolph a sweet smile over an hourglass figure in a white and blue miniskirt and blouse ensemble, stitched to enhance every curve her mother and a plastic surgeon could contrive, and whispered enticingly, "My name is Gentle, Mr. Arlington. If you have any needs of something or "someone"—she winked—"all you need do is ask."

By that smile and invitation, Randolph knew her IQ was probably lower than her bust size. Still, he watched as her hips swayed side to side on her way out. With a shake of his head, Randolph headed for the door then he heard the woman give out a startled cry as Jill shoved her aside, storming in, and began his morning with an angry demanding voice, "Where the hell have you been all night? And you'd better not say it was with that piece of ass!" She glared, indicating Gentle by slamming the door.

Randolph filled his glass with water and saluted Jill mildly. "Well, good morning to you too, sunshine."

"Don't give me that!" Jill snapped, coming closer. "What is all this junk and what are you up to?"

In answer to her question, Randolph selected a slice of lemon, dropped it in the water, and leaned against the conference table. Once relaxed, he told her bluntly while pointing, "These two computers are on so many watch lists in this building, it would take me an hour to list them. Then of course there are the seventy-five watch dog programs sitting on the other side of the firewall of the outside hard line; you couldn't ask for the time of day without every one of them knowing it." He took a sip of water and tapped a key, scanning the readouts encoded for his eyes to decipher and corrected, "Make that eighty-two. Apparently my program picked up on seven more while I was sleeping." Randolph turned back to Jill and waved his glass around in a gesture of including the room, adding, "And I suggest you be careful of what spills forth from your lips, as I've found one short-range transmitter, which is lying in the corner over there."

"That's impossible." Sweeping her arm about, she told him, "These offices are swept daily."

"Okay, then explain this," Randolph demanded, taking up the coffee cup he'd used last night and dropping it on the floor then crushing it under foot. He bent over, and sifting through the remains, picked up a slightly abused bug and showed it off to her. "Now if you'll excuse me, I have a ton of work to accomplish because of an uneducated partner imposing a near impossible deadline on me."

"Hold it," Jill demanded, grabbing Randolph's arm and shoving the bug in his face. "How'd you find this?"

"My mother could have found that one," Randolph imbued his tone with an indication Jill hadn't the capability, "which tells me that's the decoy or the secretary's attempt to increase her credit account." He slapped Jill's hand off and set down his drink to go through the first of his delivered boxes. "Now, if you'll excuse me, I have to build a detector to get this room cleared of spying devices before I really get start working at my job."

"Randolph, why do you have to do all that? Why can't you simply purchase one from the supply store? Detectors are perfectly legal to buy," Jill asked with curiosity this time, now that her ego had been deflated a bit.

"Look, Jill, you may wish to put your life in other people's hands, but I don't. Working out of my own place is dangerous enough." Randolph indicated the room with a gesture. "But this, filled with people I don't know and infested with who knows how many bugs—I can't take the chance." Randolph emptied a box on the table. "And as I can't trust anyone here not to replant their bugs if I leave this room, this will be my living quarters."

After having his say, Randolph ignored Jill and scattered out the equipment.

Jill stood for a time and contemplated his words and actions. Though she held a perverse wish to continue her argument, she none-the-less left Randolph to his work with a dismissive hand-wave on her way out the door. But once on the outside of the office, she wondered how a conference room could have so many bugs without the building manager knowing? With lowered head, Jill slid her eyes over the secretary, whose only function was eye candy; Jill thought perhaps special measures might be better off on her person, rather than in her case.

Within an hour of dismantling the equipment, Randolph built from scratch a short-range bug zapper. Once activated, the device killed off seven bugs, including two implanted in the tray brought in with breakfast. After that, he spent the next seven hours constructing a sweeper with directional lights to indicate where any active video-cameras or listening devices were located. When the light on his instrument turned green, after crushing two video-cameras set to view the room at different angles, he set to work building his own computer, designed to handle the open lines of the city with its trap doors and counter spy-ware, to render the computer invisible to the public eye. Next, testing out the computer to see if he missed anything, Randolph inserted the guard dogs and leech programs he'd adjusted and sent them on basic errands to verify his competence in redesigning them for his usage.

With this accomplished, he stood and stretched his legs, ate the last of his cold pizza, downed a warm beer chaser and stretched out for four hours of shut-eye. In the morning, after shoving out the clutter of packaging and accepting breakfast from a bemused secretary, who couldn't fathom why he'd not taken her up to the executive suite for an entertaining night, Randolph finally began his real work. By the fourth day, wishing he could step out for a shower and shave, he readjusted his many guard dogs, destroyed five infested hard drives and sent out the leech programs with piggy back codes.

At this stage, Randolph wiped tired eyes, marveling he'd done two weeks of work in four days' time with only the five mistakes. He then shook his head and began sorting through the city's tax records, county building plans, state leases and a hundred other levels of bureaucracy which allowed a corporation to build and maintain a business. Next came all the support outfits which kept the place operating at peak efficiency.

As Randolph was running a basic program to pile and sort by importance, he ran into tax records and gross incomes which didn't jibe with the size of the outfit. With his curiosity tweaked, he brought up the business and tagged them for further investigation, sending out new programs and starting another file.

Another day and part of the night slipped by as he piled up more details; Randolph was in the midst of designing a special leech when the conference door opened without his permission. Glancing over and noting Jill walking in, Randolph returned to his typing.

"Well, what do you want?" Jill questioned irritably, leaning up against the wall next to the door.

"Need?" Randolph questioned; he missed a stroke and had to backup a few keys to verify the code.

"Yes, need. You left me a message to come right over," Jill told him in some anger.

Randolph looked over at her with a lead weight landing in the pit of his stomach and deigned, "Jill, I never sent—"

His alarm system went off. Four men in business suits, pointing guns and bearing badges from the Federal Building of Fair Commerce spilled into the room.

"FBFC; freeze!" the first through the door commanded while the others fanned out. "You're both under arrest under statute 2279, Corporate Espionage Act."

Randolph, however, did the opposite. He turned back to the keyboard as the words spilled from the agent's mouth and hit three keys simultaneously, causing the lights in the room to go out and a strobe light to flash. Using the disorientation distraction, he ducked under the conference table as his computer did a complete melt down from the microwave elements he'd installed. By the end of the second strobe, Jill moved and Randolph heard a yell followed by a body hitting the table. Laser beams next appeared, racing across the room to where Randolph had been as he scrambled onto the tabletop and propelled himself up into the crawl space in between floors. Without worrying about noise, as Jill was making a real nuisance of herself, Randolph scrambled across the ceiling supports till he hit the concrete wall, pulled off an opening in the air duct system he'd made, and rolled in, hearing a man scream from within the office. Without any thoughts for Jill whatsoever—she could take care of herself— Randolph hooked himself up to the descending wire harness he constructed last night, hit the on button on the payout machine and was on his way down the air shaft between the walls when he felt the concussion grenade and electric pulse scrambler go off. After a minute of disorientation, realizing his home made device had been rendered useless by the electrical pulse, leaving him hanging like a duck in cold storage awaiting to be plucked and gutted for the pot, Randolph hit the disconnect button and free-fell four stories in the air system before hitting hard, at a T intersection, wishing he'd lost consciousness.

Randolph bit down hard on the scream of pain and soon found he'd broken his leg. He wiped his blurring eyes of tears. *Where in the hell did they come from? This was supposed to be a secured building.* With great effort, Randolph ignored his leg for the moment, wiped his eyes several times, and pulled from his pocket a laser pen, which he used to make holes in the ventilation system so he could hook his belt into one after another in his quest to descend the forty floors to its end. After he gained the thirty-eighth floor, the system turned on, instantly turning the temperature to sixty degrees, which could have been a great help if it were only directed on his broken leg. Randolph ground his teeth, knowing perfectly well what was to happen next, and tried to work faster in his descent. But after gaining only a floor lower, Randolph saw below him the robotic eye of the duct cleaning robot as it ascended the shaft to the blockage he was creating in cooling off the building. With no room to disable the robot, Randolph cringed and pocketed his pen to await the clawing arm grabbing hold of his leg. Upon the machine reaching him, Randolph bit down on part of the belt and held back a scream when the grapple seized his bad leg and began twisting to dislodge the blockage before pulling him down the shaft.

Randolph closed tearing eyes to the agony as the robot moved uncaringly to its docking station, where a panel slid open to dispose of its garbage. Without hope of catching himself, he fell another ten feet into a recently emptied trash receptacle. He hit the solid surface, feeling the instant shock of temperature from dry cold to a hot rainy night and fought to regain control of his fingers before dragging himself up to the lip and scaling out of the container. With a splash onto asphalt, Randolph landed, wincing, and clawed up to a standing posture. He felt his way along the concrete wall till encountering an alcove where he could begin treating his abused body.

Randolph fought to remain conscious the whole time while he eased out of the thousand-credit shirt, using the pen knife to cut it into strips as his hands were too abused to evenly tear the material. Then locating some old paneling, he cut it in strips to use as splints. Next came the hard part in his deteriorating condition. Randolph braced himself, feeling the warm rain running down his face before he pushed and turned his right arm out of its socket. He awoke moments later after blacking out, finding his arm dangling. He pushed the button and ejected the small cylinder through his skin. Still biting back his cries of agony, using only his teeth, Randolph unscrewed the cap and swallowed the pain killers he resupplied while in the hot shower a month back. Randolph laid his head back against the building's hard surface and let the wonder drug fasten itself to his pain center, where it would block all nerve impulses to inform his brain of his injuries.

After ten long agonizing minutes, Randolph breathed a sigh of relief. Now that he could think, and understanding he couldn't show up at a med clinic, Randolph reset his arm and proceeded to do the same with his lower leg while the drug was working at full capacity. Next came the patch to his shoulder to stop the small amount of blood flow, then Randolph finished the ties to the splints and sought out a city map before morning could find him. Abstractly, while dealing with his own problems, Randolph wondered if Jill had made it out and where she might hole up. As the city was a large place, and soldiers are trained in city fighting, she should make it all right.

By the light of a liquid crystal map, Randolph identified color codes the local police used to warn travelers off the worst regions in town, and by these warnings, Randolph found where he needed to go. In those bad areas, he ticked off in his mind, *I can sell my rather torn and abused pants and shoes, buy medical supplies as well as new clothes, and hide out with the homeless till I have a couple of days under my belt of healing time.* The only flaw he saw in this was the possible bullies who frequented those places for what easy picking could be beaten out of the locals.

By morning, however, Randolph was in worse shape. The rising temperature already above eighty and the intensifying heat radiating off the building made it impossible for his system to cool itself off. Even his meds had thrown in the towel, but collapsing on the common streets meant a trip to the med clinic and a jail cell right after his ID had been established. Then again it might not matter where he collapsed, for Mr. Bennett was sure to hear the news in a short while and activate the mini bomb in his skull. Still, a portion of Randolph

The Paranoid Thief

couldn't just lie down and die, so he kept moving. Thus as 10 a.m. rolled past, Randolph stumbled into the poorer quarter wearing old clothes and a second brace to keep his leg immobile. Once settled in a small vacant spot in the "Homeless Ally," as the residents called it, Randolph chowed down on a ham sandwich then opened a bottle of whisky he'd bought with the last of his hard currency from the remains of his business suit and proceeded to drink himself into a stupor. Once in a world of fuzzy numbness, Randolph raised his bottle skyward in a salute to those he would be seeing soon, and downed the rest till blackness reigned total.

Chapter Eleven

When consciousness reintroduced itself into his still quite whole but pounding brain, Randolph puzzled over his current ability to wake, wondering if the feds had raided Mr. Bennett's building as well, thus making it impossible for the corporate sadist to flip the switch. This meant he had a short reprieve, as sooner or later the feds would learn of the device and activate it out of pure simplicity to the problem of having dead people walking around. Regardless of the short transition of ownership, if the feds really did raid the place, Randolph was in no shape to tryout his skills till he had some days of inactivity, allowing his body to mend.

This had been his plan till the noise level in the long alley told him something was wrong.

Forced to move to crane his neck like all the rest, Randolph saw the dregs of society stumbling his way, complaining, crying and making a terrible ruckus as they moved on past. Not understanding their unheard-of activity in the sweltering hours of the day, Randolph's first reaction was to scramble away and find a hole to crawl into, but then again the current activities did not fit into the feds' procedure of fugitive apprehension. Only those fitting Randolph's appearance would have been rousted from their living space, and this wouldn't include women and children. Then again, by some astronomical coincidence, Jill could have been tracked into this very alley, rendering such activity necessary. Regardless of the reasons, the group of brutish men behind the mob of undesirable dregs of polite society made sure everyone, including Randolph, was on his or her feet and stumbling to the back alley where the building's

The Paranoid Thief

support teams helped keep the flow of merchandise and garbage flowing.

Prodded into unmarked cargo trucks at the end of the alley with shock sticks, the captured residents were packed in like sardines and closed up in the sweltering tin can for ten hours before the hover truck settled to the ground. With a yell, Randolph came to life when someone used his brace to stand up. Then the back opened and the group was herded out of the sweltering cargo truck into a lighted human processing center on hard packed desert ground. Here Randolph caught a blurry vision of the surrounding buildings, but in his state of pain and dehydration, he could only remotely remember an article about such places. Besides, as Randolph was given no opportunity to realign his thought into any cohesive order, he simply deemed it simpler to limp on with the crowd and hope somewhere along the line food and water would be given.

Moved single file by rough hands and electrical sticks, like the men and women before him, Randolph was summarily stripped naked, prodded through a spray of disinfectant, scrubbed by brushes on handles, pushed through pressurized water spray and forced into a line up. As his since of self began to restore itself, a well-dressed man looked over the captive group and directed each in turn down one of two lines leading to long two-story buildings. Once in front of Randolph, the man eyed his obvious discomfort and tapped Randolph's bad leg. To Randolph's wince, the man directed two awaiting men to carry Randolph to the infirmary.

"Next," a bored and balding older man dressed in orderly clothes called.

"This one has a bad leg, Doc," the remaining guy still holding Randolph explained.

"Right, lay him down here," the doc directed.

"Where am I?" Randolph questioned, as his mind started working again.

"Shut up, you!" The brute who'd brought Randolph into the doctor's office slap Randolph's face. "Or I'll cuff you a good one," he finished, doing so anyway.

To this abuse, Randolph decided it would be less painful to do as requested for no other reason than having a doctor look at his broken leg. Lying on the cold stainless steel table, still without clothing, Randolph was strapped down without comment as the doc moved a sonic imager over the broken leg. While his leg was being tended to, Randolph looked about the facilities. The place was but a rudimentary med clinic, with low cost, basic equipment. The only pricey item he saw was the imager, and that the doc only used long enough to judge the condition of Randolph's leg. Moving the device aside, the doc walked a few steps to a wall of medical instruments and took down a leg brace with a turn knob at midpoint. For just a second, Randolph wondered about the odd thing, then he caught on to its possible use when the big brute placed a block of wood between Randolph's teeth. The doc was about to stretch out his bad leg without giving him any pain killers! With dreadful knowledge of what was to come, Randolph struggled against the straps, gaining no headway. He squeezed his eyes shut preparing for the agony to begin.

Randolph awoke to the pounding, throbbing, stabbing pain in his leg, which he alerted an orderly to by his complaints. The unsympathetic fellow advanced and told Randolph to swallow some pills he'd brought. With ill grace, Randolph took the pills, hoping they were something stronger then aspirin; in time he found they were not. This left Randolph in agony with his leg elevated in a plain splint instead of cocooned in a basic cast. Because of the cheap setup,

The Paranoid Thief

Randolph was forced to take up room in the infirmary for three months before he was able to move about on crutches.

During his time of convalescence, Randolph discovered where he was and why. Apparently, the city he'd been in had its fill of the destitute dregs of society, signing an agreement with a low-cost work force corporation. Randolph, along with all the homeless who were caught in that dragnet, were now owned by "Cheap Labor Incorporated," interred in an encampment fifty miles out in the desert from the city, and now subject to being hired out for the benefit of having a place to sleep and food to eat. As for the matter of being identified, Randolph found the encampment was run under such low funding, to better supply the corporate heads with a larger credit allowance, he held no worries of being found out. But a side effect of this low cost outfit was that the mini bomb in his head had never been removed. And because of this, Randolph had to reason the implant had only been a bluff, or somehow made useless by the electric pulse scrambler Jill had set off, as surely by now the switch would have been thrown, if not for any other reason than plain curiosity. Either way, Randolph could no longer worry about the device planted in his skull, so he could start concentrating on escaping his new surroundings once his leg was fully healed and he'd disconnected the restraining bracelets about his wrists.

"You there," a brutish guard with biceps as large as Randolph's thighs called, bringing him out of his mussing. "Do you know anything about computers?"

Randolph blink, nodded yes.

The guard's huge hand landed on Randolph's shoulder as he said, "Good. Grab a crutch and follow me."

Already having felt the heavy handedness of the guards should he use words harder to understand than a simple "yes sir" or "no sir,"

Randolph followed the fellow along the cracking concrete hallway and out into the sweltering heat of day. With the aid of his hand to shield his eyes, Randolph got his first true glimpse of the surrounding world in a few strides, only to have his observation distracted when his guard called out to another by a disabled hover truck.

"Smithy, I've an operator for you." The brute squeezed Randolph's shoulder hard, causing Randolph to wince as he threatened, "You do as Smithy tells you, or I'll break your other leg."

Randolph made the required response and limped over to Smithy.

"You know computers do yea?"

As Randolph had already established this with the first guard, he felt like saying "Duh…" but held his tongue in favor of simply nodding.

"Good, then get over here and have a look at this." Smithy gestured to the grounded hover truck.

Still doing as told, knowing the weight of the truck had likely already crushed the directional ports—making the vehicle unusable—Randolph rounded the front and froze in place, shocked to his marrow. He stared at two sets of unmoving legs sticking out from under the truck. Quickly he slapped his hand over his mouth in aid of warding off his stomach's reaction.

Smithy lent his own hands by grabbing Randolph's shirt and slapping his face a few times till he regained Randolph's attention. "Pay no never mind to them, as they're beyond any further pain; however, you, on the other hand, are not. So pull yourself together and get into the cab." With a shove at the cab door, Smithy propelled Randolph up into the cab, and instructed Randolph to get the truck up off the ground.

Weak kneed, smelling the bodily fluids from the crushed men underneath, Randolph swallowed some of the upcoming bile before

The Paranoid Thief

he looked over the dead control panel. After a simple visual inspection of the basic controls, switches, and after-market replacements, Randolph found no obvious reason for the cold panel. Adjusting himself, he lay down and popped the under covering. He fished out a flash pen and tester leads from Smithy's tool kit on the floorboard, then began an hour-long search in the over powering heat, wiping sweat from his face every couple of minutes to see. Only after Smithy's fifth interruption did Randolph find the lower-grade spliced-in wire in the harness assembly that had fried when extra power ran along the wire. This then told the circuit breaker to automatically trip, killing the panel, dropping the whole weight of the truck on the two unlucky men. Not touching the discovery, Randolph showed the evidence of a saboteur to Smithy.

"Here now, let me see that," he demanded, pushing Randolph out of the way. After eyeballing the wires Randolph exposed, Smithy sat up and slammed Randolph into the cab's door. "Here now, are you trying a fast one? How do I know you didn't just cut that wire?"

Even over his pounding head and throbbing leg, Randolph managed, "Hey, don't believe me if you wish, I'm only telling you what I found!"

Smithy glared, and his underdeveloped mind asked, "You're saying the truck was made to malfunction?" To gave Smithy the simplest answer for his abilities to understand, Randolph merely nodded yes, to which Smithy let go, rubbed his bearded chin and pulled Randolph out of the truck and told him to get lost.

Two months later, contemplating three avenues to quietly vacate the premises, Randolph endeared himself to the head foreman by lowering operating cost in repairing simple machinery and electronics. This bit of being the foreman's pet, added an advantaged of never having to pile into the trucks of human slavery, while giving him access to every building and available supplies. As for the saboteur, no one had a clue, even after discovering three more, less life-threatening acts.

After six months in captivity, Randolph was promoted to record keeping for the outfit, that is to say when he wasn't repairing something which to his mind should have been replaced two or three years ago. Now having access to a hard line computer, Randolph slowly started learning the local area outside the barbwire fence, roads, small towns and bus routes. While doing so, Randolph found an article describing two corporate executives assassinated by person or persons unknown. Bringing up the full article, it appeared to Randolph, Jill had a new partner. And thinking of Jill brought up a startling realization of what he'd been missing all these years. *In my kind of work, he mused, moving from town to town, job to job, is not conducive in discovering and maintaining a family, thus I'd settled for prostitutes, but while their only concern was getting their "John" off as fast as possible, Jill showed me what sex was really all about.* Randolph leaned back in his chair and rubbed his growing beard, as they didn't supply hair removal cream, pondering what he really knew about her, and would it be worth breaking her out of that place. *If I did,* he continued pondering, *I'd have to talk her into retiring while I continued my career. It might also be best if we vacate the continent for one where the feds have nothing on us.* Randolph nodded; he'd look into the possibilities later. He finished the daily lists before he set out for his next job.

Chapter Twelve

Three days later, as Randolph was repairing a trash evaporator, two black sedans came to rest at the front of the foreman's office. Able to eye the vehicles from within the crude shelter for the unit, Randolph felt his pulse quicken and wondered why the FBFC would be dropping in. *Surly they can't know about me?* He eyed the six men as they vacated their vehicles, dressed all in black, even on such a sweltering day as this. Randolph leaned on a support beam, wiping his hands on an old rag, and watched the men adjust their jackets as if to make certain all eyes in the compound saw the bulging holsters at hip level. As the group in dark shades acquainted their minds with the landscape, two separated themselves and headed for the office building. Unable to miss the shadows underneath the cars, Randolph pondered the possibility of escape. *Am I ready? Do I know enough of the surrounding area to chance a try at getting under one, and dropping off somewhere along the road?* Randolph knew with a glance the sun had yet to hit its peak, which meant hours of walking in the desert heat. After only a moment of weighing the hazards, Randolph wiped his brow and discarded the idea as too risky. *Others without my patience would probably have gone for it, but that's what separates me from the pack. I am very thorough in my plans.* Randolph turned his back on the possibility without regrets and began replacing the wiring which had over loaded when a safety fuse had been circumvented instead of someone spending the 10 credits for a new one.

Randolph was cussing out the engineers who designed the unit to squeeze out every credit possible when a pounding on the side panel caused him to bang his head in alarm.

"Ow!" He winced, not able to rub his head. "What do you want?"

"The boss has a job for you, so pull your head out of your—"

"But I'm not finished," Randolph interrupted the guard's favorite repartee.

"Then you'll just have it to do later. Now move it, rodent!"

Not having a choice, Randolph pulled out of the cramped evaporator, wiping his hands clean on a rag. "No one had better turn the unit on."

Marrowny, the burly rule enforcer cut him off gruffly with, "Yeah, yeah, yeah, we all know you're a genius, shrimp. Now shut it and follow me."

After Randolph obtained the ground, tall and ugly seized his neck, squeezing to notify him who was boss. "Hey, ow, come-on, Marrowny, that hurts!"

"Then mind me as you're told and keep your trap shut, you hear?" Marrowny said with a mean smile, holding tight to Randolph's neck the entire walk back to the offices, where Randolph soon found himself standing in front of the FBFC boys.

Marrowny gave Randolph one last malicious squeeze, causing Randolph to cringe as he looked on the two men in front of the foreman's desk.

"There he is Special Agent Zimmer," the foreman said evenly, "just as your wanted poster described. Though I'll admit he's not a very imposing figure, he sure knows a lot about electronics."

Randolph fought down his first instinct to take flight, reasoning. *Where would I go? There is nowhere to go but outside and even if I did manage to escape these two and the trigger-happy men still waiting out in the heat, I have miles under a frying sun to travel.* Discarding those useless thoughts, Randolph stood his ground, and upon seeing the metal collar the younger one pulled out from his jacket, he grimaced.

"It's true he doesn't look like much," that one admitted in a low voice to his senior partner while opening the neck restraint and snapping it in place around Randolph's neck without incident. The senior agent made no comment to his partner's remark but instead reached into his jacket pocket and passed over a credit card to the compound foreman. The man accepted the card and tapped the display screen, to which he smiled broadly.

It appears a bounty for my head has just been paid out, Randolph surmised, wondering with a small perverse side of himself just how much his head was worth as wrist restraints were also applied and locked into place.

The ride to the nearest Federal Building of Fair Commerce somewhere in the state of Indie, which at one time had been call Nevada, went by far too quickly. Only six hours compared to the ten hours it took going out to the pit in the desert, but then, who said the FBFC followed any rules other than their own.

The black car came to halt two levels below ground, where Randolph was prodded out, ushered through busy corridors, and settled in an interrogation room behind three ID check points, the last of which was only opened after the agents submitted to a retina scan. Seated in a small square room, looking around at the plain white walls and stainless steel table he sat behind, Randolph tried to recall all he knew about the FBFC for clues on how they would proceed. *Let's see, besides being a law unto themselves, with governmental backing, they are slaves to no district or state, which leaves me in deep kimchee.* Randolph looked down on his hands, which had been locked into wrist restraints on the table top, and amended that to *very deep kimchee*. By their locking his hands so, Randolph was forced to look subservient to them every time he bowed his head to clear away the sweat rolling down his face, not all of it merely from the overheated room.

Once an hour of the silent treatment crawled by, according to his internal clock, the room began to alternate from hot to cold in seconds of time, during which Randolph received a numbing shock-wave through the restraints, forcing every muscle to clinch two or three times before the next weather change. This went on for roughly twenty minutes before his captors picked a temperature around ninety degrees. The room remained so till Randolph sat in a puddle of sweat.

"Now then, Mr. McCann," an annoyed male voice questioned through a loud speaker behind Randolph's head, "perhaps you might like to explain how you came to be in an executive office in the Global Rift Supply and Demand building in Bakersfield, instead of remaining in the cardboard box shoved into the city of Willing's crematorium furnace?"

Randolph cleared his hearing with a shake of his head. "Before I do, could I have a glass of water?" he dared to ask.

"The atmosphere a bit over-warm for you? Here, let me see what can be done," the malicious voice replied.

The temperature dropped till Randolph's teeth were chattering from the cold. Randolph skipped useless obscenities and got right to the point of the matter. "Damn your eyes, you needn't waste your time in torturing me. I'll tell you whatever it is you wish to know! Just stop this crap and get me a glass of water or I will become difficult!"

An hour later, while he sipped at a light plastic cup of plain faucet water, ever so much wanting to throw it into their faces—*cheap bastards*—Randolph supplied the information about Mr. Bennett and his pet project.

The Paranoid Thief

My singing voice may be off key but it isn't my fault, I caught cold because the damn fools were having too much fun with the temperature gauge. Randolph sat in the now comfortable room with two agents and finished up his unrehearsed recital. The black-suited men queried Randolph on a couple of points, then pocketed their mini video recorders and left without a word about what was to become of him. *I will say I was tempted to ask my fate, but in truth, seeing their smirking faces on the obvious outcome of my life would not in the best of times be very pleasant to see.* Still chained to the table, Randolph gave a sigh of relief at their departure, coughed, and feeling beyond drained both physically and mentally, soon found himself escorted through the halls by grim-faced uniforms to a group holding cell where he was shoved inside.

Here Randolph saw for the men in black, business was good. As he'd not been offered a handkerchief by his rude captors for causing his ailment, Randolph was forced to wipe his nose on his sleeve. He walked unmolested with drooping eyes past the dregs of humanity, whether dressed in business clothes of the rich or simple attire for the everyday man. Once amidst the human garbage, Randolph spotted a lone bench against the far wall and headed for it, holding out no hope for a long prosperous future. Still wearing the restraints, Randolph coughed in both of his hands and took some pleasure in seeing the others wore the same jewelry as he, which meant no one would beat the crap out of him just to prove he was the biggest bully in the bunch. When Randolph settled on a bench, the two closest to him stood up and wandered off, whether that was because of his body odor or his apparent illness, he couldn't say. But not one to pass up an opportunity, Randolph readjusted himself so he could curl up in misery on the bench and tried to sleep, hoping his dreams would take him to a better place for a short time.

Randolph was underground, unable to witness the passing day or night. Time became irrelevant save for meal time, when the prisoners were ordered to the bars and handed a plate which couldn't be drawn in between the bars. As for bodily functions, a normal result of such activities, privacy was something he couldn't even consider. While minutes passed into hours, Randolph's misery and depression settled on his shoulders like a vulture waiting for him to pass on. *Hell*, he thought to himself, sitting with his hands between his legs one afternoon, *I almost wish someone would activate the bomb in my head. At least that way, I wouldn't have to go through being executed again.* But he had to admit the possibility of that happening was about nil. He was sure the concussion grenade Jill dropped had scrambled the electronics, because if the device was still operational, Mel would have detonated the mini bomb long ago. So Randolph wallowed in his misery as time crawled by, marked only in the occasional removal or insertion of bodies, while the FBFC agents investigated his story, one he'd told in complete detail with the one exception of any mention of Jill. Oh *they asked about her*, he reminisced, *but on that subject I am unwilling to elaborate. Why did I refused? Perhaps I'm smitten with her playful side or perhaps what she did was not of her choice and therefore I give her the benefit of the doubt. As they didn't peruse it by insisting with more torture, I figure they know all about her and set the subject aside to keep me talking on other matters they didn't know fully or knew nothing about. Oh well, however I feel about her matters not at all. She'll be captured with the rest of the group or slide away like she did when the FBFC charged in on us. Besides, either way we were both living on borrowed time, so I only hope she makes better time of it then I was able to.*

The Paranoid Thief

After battling his cold for several days, Randolph was rousted from sleep by a heavy-handed guard. "Ow! Take it easy, man!" Randolph complained to having his head tapped with a night stick as if it were a drum.

"Then get your smelly ass up," the guard growled as if Randolph had offended his family tree. Then he informed Randolph of his fate in a loud voice so everyone heard. "You can sleep all you want after your executed."

As Randolph already understood his fate, the cruel verbal acknowledgment did nothing for his enthusiasm for obeying anyone. But rather then cause himself any more grief in what time remained of his life, Randolph numbly got to his feet and plodded along like a whipped puppy. *After all, knowing all along I was headed to 'the table' yet again, I'm not very shocked to his heartless revelation.* Moved through hallways and security check points to the parking structure, Randolph was pushed up none-too-gently against the wall at the last security check point and thumped once on the head for an "attitude adjustment," before the necklace and wrist restraints were removed. Once this had been done, he was released into the custody of a surly looking local city officer; a rather fat fellow who applied new restraints on Randolph's wrists then pushed him up against the same wall and growled into his ear.

"Listen, creep, as I'd rather deliver a corpse, you best not give me a reason to pull my gun, understand?" As it was healthier for Randolph to nod, he did so, at which point the officer jerked him away from the wall and shoved him bodily into the back seat of his squad car. Once the door slammed closed, Randolph heard the doors lock, and briefly wondered how he'd already gotten on the man's bad side. *Or is he always so chipper on duty?* With a mental shrug, Randolph straightened himself on the seat without help from the rude city cop, who got in the driver's side, causing the air cushion to adjust to his heavier frame. The cop gave Randolph a glare in the review mirror before starting the car and moving up to street level and their first intersection. He then looked both ways like any good driver would but somehow missed the fast-moving woman Randolph caught sight of just before she pulled a very nasty looking gun from out of her purse! Out of reflex, Randolph ducked and caught sight of a beam of light melting through the driver window and smelt meat frying near on top of each other. Randolph turned his face so he could at least see his executioner.

Jill opened the driver's door and shoved the 275-pound dead weight with some effort over to the passenger side so she could take his place as if nothing had happened. In quick succession, the door closed and Jill moved them out into traffic. Unsure if she was there to kill him for his canary act, Randolph shrank within himself. She tilted her head back and said with humor, "Hello, partner. Miss me?"

Chapter Thirteen

"Jill! What? How?" Randolph stammered.

"Tsk, tsk, lover boy, did you really believe I wouldn't try to rescue you?" Jill said, driving one handed. She turned her head a bit more to see while she padded down the dead officer. "I told you I didn't want to train another partner." When she uncovered the keys, she touched a button on the dash console and lowered the wire prisoner screen so she could toss him the keys. "Now if you don't mind getting out of those tracking cuffs, I have a car waiting a few blocks over."

"Did you have to kill the man?" Randolph admonished, though he was relieved to see her.

Without remorse, Jill eyed him in the mirror and said, "You do things your way and I'll do them my way."

"But your way is so permanent," Randolph scolded, upset with how casual she sounded.

"Randolph, I'm sorry you feel that way about it, but in my experience, live people cause too many complications." She slowed and turned into an alleyway and settled the squad car to Earth, then motioned for him to get out. Randolph moved ahead of Jill to a blue sports model as Jill pulled out a phase grenade and tossed it in the squad car. But before Randolph opened the passenger door, Jill ran up and threw her arms around him and squeezed with a very affectionate embrace before demanding a quick passionate kiss. Then disengaging, leaving Randolph slightly dazed, she ran around the front and jumped in the driver seat. "You and I have a lot to talk about."

"I just bet we do," Randolph acknowledged, clearing his head and sliding in.

He closed his door as Jill gunned the power and shot them up and over the squad car, and into traffic.

"For starters, where are we going?"

"We're headed to a motel I've rented where you're going to get cleaned up and properly dressed for a wedding."

"A wedding? But...but Jill? Now wait just a dog gone minute. You just busted me out of jail—within an hour my face will be plastered all over the video channels. We don't have time to witness a wedding!"

"True, but don't worry, the church is on the outskirts of town."

"Don't tell me you planned our escape to incorporate this ceremony?" Randolph asked, unbelieving.

"Not at all. I planned to drop in on our way out of town." She smiled.

"Hold it. I've never heard of a wedding waiting for guests to arrive," Randolph asked puzzled.

"That's true." She patted his leg, "But we're not guests."

Thinking on that a moment, Randolph eyed her. "You're not planning to kill someone?"

Jill passed him a scathing glare. "How could you even think I'd do such a thing? That would be sacrilege."

"Well you don't seem to hold to the Ten Commandments."

Jill rolled her eyes. "I thought you were the atheist?"

"No, an atheist doesn't believe in heaven and hell. I believe in both, I simply don't believe either can influence people, places, or things."

After a bit when Jill said no more, Randolph ventured, "Uh, Jill, who's getting married?"

"I am." She smiled. "Or should I say my other side is." Jill caught Randolph's puzzled face and explained. "My other self has fallen in

The Paranoid Thief

love, and per our agreement before I entered the military, I'm going along with it. Besides, I like him too, though he can be irritating most of the time. But what man isn't?" When Jill saw Randolph's slack-jawed expression, she became more serious. "Come off it, Randolph. Can't you believe I can fall in love?"

"Truthfully, I hadn't considered the matter. Does the lucky groom know about your two sides?" Randolph tried to keep his tone neutral, lest she realize he had developed feelings for her.

"A relationship cannot last if you keep secrets from each other," Jill admitted, pulling into a hotel parking lot and allowing the car to settle in a numbered slot. "Now come on, we both need to clean up before the trip and I need to do some calls while you're in the bathroom." Jill pulled the hotel door card out as she got out of the car and said over her shoulder, "I've some snacks inside to tide you over till after the wedding, then we'll grab a bite before meeting the jet I have waiting."

Randolph acknowledged her statement on a relationship, but felt a lump in his throat as he needed to tell her what he did. Jill could only kill him once, so Randolph swallowed and warned, "But using anything connected with the company may not be advisable, you see." He spoke meekly, following her inside, thinking it might not be a good idea to have four walls surrounding him. "While in custody, I spilled my guts—I told them everything I knew about the company."

"Yes, I know," she admitted, heading for the bathroom and tossing her pocket book on the bed where two suitcases laid open, filled with clothes for both sexes.

"You know?" Randolph sputtered, flabbergasted. "Then why did you get me out?"

"Because you told them nothing about me," Jill answered with certainty, unzipping the body suit she was wearing, working her way out of it.

"But how do you know that?" Randolph pick up a waffle bar, absently watching her strip. *She and this bar have a lot in common; you have to peel off the outer layer to get to the goodies within.*

"Simply put, I was in the Global Rift Supply and Demand cafeteria in Calaway when FBFC crashed the building in force. Those of us on the first five floors held no chance of escape as the alarms didn't go off. Covering all exits to the cafeteria, they carded and ordered us all in chairs. After two hours of watching people come and go, including those who worked there, I was approached and told I could go." Jill started the shower and said as if it was an afterthought, "I guess the fake ID I always carry around saved my butt." Then looking at Randolph with a smile she said, "That's how I knew you said zippo about me, for if you had, I'd be in one of their cells as you were." Jill came back to the door and tiptoed to kiss Randolph's lips lightly before she closed the door to the bathroom. "Now relax awhile as I take my shower."

For a few moments, Randolph looked at the door in some bafflement. He chewed the last bit of the bar and sat down on the bed opposite the one with a full-blown wedding dress laid out, awaiting its engagement. *But why? She risked a lot to get me out, postponing a wedding to a man she has to care deeply about when she'd been in the clear and could have been a continent over when I got the needle, starting a new life. So why risk it?* Randolph continued to puzzle the matter over, hurt she could drop their relationship and find a whole new life in so short a time. *If she was afraid I'd give her up, she could have just as easily taken care of me in the patrol car and saved*

The Paranoid Thief

herself the added headache of my face being plastered over every video screen.

He was still puzzling over the matter when Jill opened the bathroom door, letting the steamy air out, with a towel wrapped around her midsection and using another to dry her short hair.

"Your turn, mister, and please take a little longer than I did—you reek of several days laying face-down in a sewer."

"Jill, why don't you go ahead and take off with your honey. I'm indebted to you for saving my life, but there's no reason you need risk getting caught because of me."

Jill wiped off her arms and legs before sitting down next to the dress. "Look, I can't leave you here. If the FBFC catches you this time, you'll tell them everything about me sooner or later, and don't think they can't get it out of you. I've seen some of the equipment they use and those were only the legal items. Besides, as I've already killed the snitches in our subsidiary office before getting you out, there's no place I can go where they wouldn't find me."

"That was reason forty-two why you shouldn't have sprung me," Randolph put in.

To this Jill looked pensive. "Would you quit dwelling on reasons why I should've let them give you the needle? The deed is done. Now you can kiss my feet if you feel obligated to for saving your life, but I'd rather you took a shower instead." Jill twirled her towel while he pondered, then snapped it on his leg.

"Ow! Jill, come on, that hurts."

"It'll hurt a lot more if I aim it a little higher," she threatened.

After he was washed and dressed in imitation Harmanii formal wear, Jill pushed Randolph out to the car wearing the white dress and a shawl over her hair for protection. Once on the road Randolph decided to gather more information on this event he was being dragged to. "So, is the groom's family going to be there?"

"That would be rather awkward, considering they think he's dead."

"Oh, so what is he, your new partner?" Randolph asked, a bit testy.

"Relatively new, but we've spent enough time together for me to become attached, especially my other half."

Jill turned to give Randolph a smile, and he finally saw the obvious in her eyes and yelled, "NO, you're not talking about me?"

"Oh be still, Randolph," Jill said, patting his leg. "You'll get used to me if you haven't already."

"That's not the point. I'm not the marring type! My career choice renders marriage a liability!" Randolph responded in shock and with a bit of convection.

With a sigh of unusual patience, Jill said, "Randolph, were getting married under an assumed name, so it's not as if it's permanent. The hotel I booked us into is really for lovers only, it's an exclusive place where only those with a marriage license showing them to be just married or their on their anniversary, my sign in, and with the added advantage of no children allowed." She smiled to this last. "It'll be a couples' playground. Besides, the FBFC would never think to look for you there."

"But you said...?" Randolph sputtered, somewhat confused with his own feelings.

"And I meant it. I like you Randolph, and my other half has fallen in love with you. And as we're both wanted for murder, whether you committed one or not, I've considered it and thought why not? Besides, I promised my other self if she allowed me a stint in the military, I'd settle down later and have a family like she wants."

Randolph looked skyward and sought patience of his own while he wished for more time to think things through as he tried to explain himself better. "Jill, I like you a lot too, but you don't want me—I get antsy if I'm in one place too long."

Jill gave Randolph a sideways look. "Listen, can't you at least give this a try? Being a homebody will be new for me as well. If it doesn't work out after a year we can go our separate ways."

"Okay, for the sake of argument suppose we do? Where would we live? What would we do for credits to run a normal life? And on top of the other adjustments, we'd have to sever all ties to everything we know, have our looks readjusted, and become absolutely boring people like an ordinary person, because the FBFC have long memories."

"Well, I hadn't thought out everything, of course, but I was more or less considering going native in Africa. There are still parts that use no technology, so we'd simply fall of the grid."

"Uh huh, right, and what about me? Being that totally unplugged IS a death sentence for me. My whole life revolves around the information system."

Jill shrugged. "I haven't a clue. As I said, I'm winging it. If after our stay in the honeymoon hotel we haven't decided on a direction, I have some hard credits to get us to a cheap motel where we can shack up for a month."

"I take it your partners did all the planning," Randolph remarked dryly.

"Not all of it," Jill answered. "I've always planned out the bigger aspects of a job, whether in the corps or at the company. As for the smaller details, that I left up to my lieutenant, or in your case, my partner."

"Great...okay, say I do go along with this. I'm not about to cut myself off from the world." Allowed to think on this, Randolph considered some other possibilities. "I, too, have a stash of emergency credits and with it I could set up a shop and solve our money problem. However, I'm still concerned about this marriage thing. Couldn't we post pone this till a later date?"

"Look, Randolph, we need a place to lay low for a while and I haven't had a vacation since the corps. I want to have some fun, lie on a beach, and feel the spray of the ocean and the hot sun on my skin. I want to dance the night away and not worry I could be called out to die the next morning. But most of all, I want to feel what it's like to be just a plain simple woman. Could you not argue and give me this? I promise if things don't work out I'll leave."

As Randolph listened to Jill's checked emotions, he knew it had taken her total control to have admitted all that. But a fake marriage to a murderess rankled Randolph's code of ethics and had him balking on the whole idea. Regardless of his feelings though, her notion was right about the FBFC; they would never consider searching in a private resort meant exclusively for romantic getaways.

The wedding chapel was a simple affair, white steeple roof, plain cheap wood-looking plastic doors and colored windows depicting worshipers at prayer. All this make-up was really meant for youngsters in love with few credits or any common sense, poor folks trying to get tax breaks or those like Randolph and Jill, who needed the license without scrutiny or blood tests, which in their case would light up a few video screens. They gave their I do's and two hundred and fifty credits, as was required, to the bored preacher so his volunteer staff could print up a five-credit hard chip of proof. It wasn't long till the two newlyweds were flying over the Island of

The Paranoid Thief

Jewlopo, a small span of land out in the ocean that used to be one of the many islands of Jamaica till it was bought out right by a resort hotel conglomerate moving out of the over-populated and rundown gambling cities in Indies, a state now owned by the remaining full-blooded Indian nations.

The craft settled down in the middle of the island so every space of beach property could be exploited. The fugitives were greeted with fake smiles and insincere welcomes all the way to their overpriced room, which looked out over the island and not the ocean, as that was another three hundred credits extra a night. *However,* Randolph thought, *looking about with a calculating eye, if you ignore the obvious insincerity's and over priced drinks, meals and gift shops, the place is as advertised. Warm to hot weather, clean beaches with miles of sand, sun, and ocean. As for activities to lose yourself in, everything is designed around their theme of couples getting acquainted or reacquainted. Including the lax dress code I witnessed when checking in. Seeing couples walking around, even indoors, without clothes, some of whom really shouldn't, while others fit into my wish some people should be forbidden to wear tight-fitting clothing.* Randolph shrugged off the image with a shiver. He unpacked as Jill sat down in a round chair big enough for two and flipped the video channels to see what other amenities the place had to offer.

Their first day on the island, Randolph had to admit, was very enjoyable. Jill had let her softer side out and after only a few hours, and Randolph felt as if she were just another average woman. She giggled, laughed, played coy and all the while held onto his arm with true affection, something he'd never experienced with a woman. By mid-afternoon, Randolph could truthfully say he was pleasantly surprised. Although he'd already had a taste of her softer side back at Global Rift Supply and Demand in Calaway, this was the first time she was out the whole day long. The following day turned out quite differently, as it was Jill's tougher side's turn to enjoy the local festivities. However, because she was constantly looking for danger or an alternate meaning in anything said or done by the staff or couples they came across, she acted and sounded like a nervous virgin, finding it hard to appear normal because of her training.

"I'm sorry if I'm such a burden, Tom," she confessed, using his marriage license name as they stood in line for the parasol ride. "I normally withdraw for activities like this, as my other side is so much better in dealing with the normality of civilian living."

"In other words, you never let your hair down and tried to enjoy the small pleasures in life?"

"Not true," Jill defended herself. "I can drink any man under the table and bluff with the best of them at poker."

"I see; so any activities usually associated with the males need to challenge and over come, besides making a fool of themselves," Randolph remarked. Considering this after her acknowledgment, he inquired, "Perhaps this part of you is better suited as a man. Have you considered dating another woman?" Randolph looked down into her eyes.

Jill looked up into his eyes with such disgust, Randolph thought for a moment she might hit him, but all she did was say in total conviction, "No Tom, I LIKE men. I'd rather be around men then women, and as for sex, there's no substitute for wrapping myself around the hardness of a man's body…even your body," she added with a smile.

The Paranoid Thief

Still looking for a way out of her marriage proposal, even though it would be very hard to say goodbye, Randolph asked, "Have you ever even tried sleeping with another woman?"

"Tom, drop it!" Jill snapped, becoming more like the military Jill he knew. Then subsiding after a bit, possible trying to apologize for her gruffness, she asked, "Tell you what, why don't we try the tables after this, then later I'll show you what I mean."

"As much as I'd enjoy the tables, it's the one place we need to avoid." Leaning closer to her ear so as no one could over hear him, Randolph whispered, "We'd be photographed the instant we walked in, run through the works and before we even made it to a table, they'd know who I am."

Jill pulled away skeptically, receiving a shrug and look of regret from Randolph as he answered her unasked question.

"Before I knew any better, I used what I knew about their random number computer systems, knowing full well computers are nothing but precise, as long as they've been programmed sufficiently."

To this Jill looked forward, frowning, and said with a sigh, "And they won't let me in on my own."

"A good thing too," Randolph hinted. Jill gave him a grimace, understanding what might happen if she were video graphed.

Afterward, the two chose other activities which ended with them both in their hotel room enjoying the extras which enhanced that night's intimacy, something they both had already done last night, save Jill was more submissive with her softer side out.

Chapter Fourteen

At the end of their two weeks within the paradise of adult pleasurable sins, Randolph used some of their dwindling credits to find and rent out a cheap office and hotel on the main island of Jamaica, to work up new credentials and unshakable identities. But to make them survive a total investigation even by the FBFC, he knew both of them needed facial changes in order to fool the matching programs into discarding their videos without notifying their operators.

This then was the tricky part as Randolph also knew these programs considered any facial video down to a low sixty percent match good enough to present to its human controller. But even knowing plastic surgery to be a necessary evil, this time Randolph truly felt a face change was a real shame, as he'd gotten to like how he looked with the long face, short stubby nose and cropped blond hair. *Oh well,* he sighed, *it comes with the territory. I just hope Jill will be as understanding.* After hooking up a hard line to the local net, Randolph typed in a simple ID program any small corporation would have to investigate the seventeen passports he'd lifted during their first three days on the pleasure island and set aside any thoughts of surgery till he'd paid back Mr. Hilden. This little mission he'd already discussed with Jill in some length, assuring her they'd have the credits to disappear afterward, but for the moment they only needed passable IDs to get them off the island and back on the mainland without setting off any alarms. "Simple enough to do, as long as I do it by the numbers," he'd assured Jill.

Randolph typed out the last of the code to set the program its task but before he hit enter, he heard Jill shift in her chair next to the white office wall and file cabinet. Today she chose to wear an outfit that best showed off her all-over body tan she'd received, with her legs crossed like any lady so no one could look up between her purple mini skirt covered thighs to the dark green bikini underneath.

With a glance her way, seeing the soft and affectionate look in her eyes, Randolph knew the softer side of Jill was out, watching him with interest. Seeing he'd taken notice of her, Jill smiled lightly and said with feeling, "You look quite handsome in that pin-striped suit, John. You've good fashion sense when you wish to use it."

Randolph spared Jill another glance, now quite sure her softer side was out, because only that personality called him John. Mildly annoyed with her presence, as he needed no distractions, Randolph let his fingers work over the two keyboards to the two computer systems he was using to verify and correct any mistakes he might make.

"Are you too busy to tell me what you're doing, love?"

Still confused with Jill's use of that particular endearment, Randolph kept his voice natural. "At present, I'm checking my programs. Debugging as I see errors in my test runs. As these are simple programs, I'm peeling off tracer programs which attach themselves to mine, looking for government watchdogs, search and destroy viruses, advertiser spiders and security programs that gather up information on computer users. And while I'm doing that, I'm learning the current sophistication of possible threats, like the one I'm mutating to worm through the firewalls to the information I'll need to get us set up with new passports and ID cards." After a couple more key strokes, Randolph picked up his coffee and noticed the look on Jill's face. "I take it you're not following me?"

"Sorry, love, but I lost you at tracer programs," Jill admitted, taking a sip of her diet soda.

Randolph scratched his ear to the usage of the L word and suggested, "This will take awhile. Why don't you go out to the beach and finish up your tan?"

"I'd rather sit here and watch you." Jill kicked off her native beach sandals and folded up her legs beside her in the chair, as it was larger than most he'd gotten from a used furniture store.

"All right, but what say you go out and get us a bite to eat?" Randolph ventured, to get her out from underfoot while he concentrated on an especially tricky problem.

Apparently Jill caught his hint. She unfolded her tan legs in getting up and stretched out her hand. "All right, I'll leave for a bit, but I'll need some hard credits for food and something to gain my attention."

Randolph opened the top drawer and handed over a hundred-credit chip, which she slipped it into her bikini cup underneath her purple, tie-dyed half shirt. She threw Randolph a kiss before walking out the office door.

As Jill walked away, Randolph watched her slender feminine form and the easy way she moved, still not believing within that innocent-looking average-minded woman lurked a cold-blooded military-trained killer with an IQ at least 20 points higher. With a shake of his head and a rub to his neck, Randolph banished thought of the packaging encompassing the two entities and took a deep breath before he put himself back to work.

By the end of the second day, Randolph had peeled away all he needed from the captured leech and watchdogs his simple programs brought into the trap. Using their information, he tapped into the city's registry and reviewed passport records, IDs, and devastated counties from natural disasters. When he discovered a natural volcano and following earth quakes had wiped out a Scandinavian county's records, Randolph began an in-depth task of working up solid identities. Thus spending the next couple of weeks on all possible angles any agent could uncover, he pieced together two unshakable identity cards with an eleven-year background that could be traced back to that county's disaster, eleven years ago. Standard procedures for ID checks rolled back ten years. Randolph had to smile briefly, knowing if further investigation were applied, they would hit that dead-end. To further guaranty untraceable backgrounds, Randolph made Jill and himself both orphans, having their parents killed in the border wars some fifteen years prior to the volcano's eruption, rendering a check on their parents impossible, since neither of them were ever claimed by any relatives. In fact, the only flaw in his deception was their DNA. Neither held Scandinavian DNA, but who was to say their parents weren't there on business or vacation?

Randolph was doing touch ups on their background history to render polish and color to their new identities when the door to his office opened and two poor-quality-suited native muscle men walked in. As Randolph hadn't flipped the sign over to let the public know his accounting firm was open, their entrance caused him some concerned. *On second thought, make that very concerned,* he corrected, as an average native wearing beach attire walked in behind the two as if he owned the world, smoking a large cigar, totally ignoring the very plain 'No Smoking' sign in the window. At once Randolph applied a business man's smile on his lips to possible clients, even though he knew quite well these men had other agendas. He calmly tapped up his accounting programs and sent his work to a back file, and waited for the spider to tell the fly how much of his blood he would have to provide to stay alive.

At first Randolph fell into natural habits of playing unaware of what was to come, then he remembered Jill, and the fact she would be back shortly. Even though he felt certain Jill's harder side could handle the situation, her softer side could endanger them both, and of late Jill softer side had been the controlling personality. This by necessity changed his tactics to get the men on their way before she arrived.

The native boss man arrived at Randolph's desk, and rudely turned Randolph's cheep video screen around for his viewing pleasure before beginning his shake down spiel. "Tell me, Mr. uh…"

"Tabor, Luke Tabor," Randolph supplied, even though his fake name was clearly painted on the door window in broad letters and printed in sliver on the white name plate facing the local crime boss.

"Tabor, right. So tell me," the relaxed native asked in a heavy Jamaican accent, "why is it you have chosen to open an accounting office here in my lovely island."

Since any answer given would be the wrong answer, Randolph declined any response and watched the man sit in Jill's favorite chair next to the wall. With a careful look to the two heavies, Randolph folded his hands slowly on the desktop to keep the over-watchful goon squad from becoming anything more then they presently were. After a moment of silence from Randolph, the native boss blew smoke Randolph's way, tapping the ashes off the end of his cigar onto the clean floor without any thoughts for even looking for an ashtray. Crossing a leg, he asked, still in a calm but menacing voice, "You haven't answered my question. Now, why is that?"

"Because any answer I give is truly irrelevant to you as I know you don't care, so I'm waiting to learn how much I owe you for the protection you'll grant me from the abuse of your two friends,"

Randolph said in the nicest manner he could, so the native boss wouldn't take offence to his reaction to this shakedown.

The native took another drag of his cigar and eyed Randolph, judging, saying at last, "You appear to be relatively calm about the facts of life." He faked a look of thinking and said, motioning with his lit cigar, "I like you. You understand the price of conducting business." Adjusting his sitting posture so he could lean back a bit more, the extortionist opened his mouth to spell out their new-found relationship when Jill chose this inconvenient moment of time to walk in.

The native turned his head in annoyance to the interruption, and saw what everyone else does, a brown-haired, white and yellow bikini-clad, shawl-covered good looking woman, missing entirely what Randolph saw—a soft and easy going personality fading out into the background while a hard, cold-blooded killer took her place once she noticed the two suited goons and the cigar-smoking native in her chair.

"I'm sorry, Mr. Tabor," Jill improvised, clearly taking in the situation. "I had not known you'd be entertaining clients this early in the morning." Jill made a motion to the bag she was holding from "Savory Delicacies Emporium" and said mildly, allowing no hint of alarm to enter her voice, "If you wish, I could return with a nice selection to include your clients?"

"That won't be necessary." The boss man smiled, signaling the over-steroided goon nearest to Jill to move in behind her and close the door as Jill continued to look the mild, low-IQ assistant who was beginning to realize something was amiss.

"Mr. Tabor?" she questioned with a tremor in her voice.

"Have no fear, Jill. These men are here to collect on a debt I owe, so if you'll remain calm, we'll finish this quickly so they can be on their way."

"Now, now, there's no need to rush things," the over-confident boss expressed with a smile, now adding Jill's presence as a bonus into his extortion plan. The native stood, taking the few steps over to Jill's side, looking her up and down in a calculated fashion to add more intimidation into his proposal before he slid a finger along her jaw line, enjoying Jill's fake fear.

Or is that her softer side she's allowed out to give off a truer response? Randolph wondered.

"First we must consider all the tangibles of your business," the native boss said with superiority coloring his voice, "before we may negotiate a proper account of its worth." He gave a signal, to which Jill's arms were seized, and the goon behind Randolph landed a blow to the back of his neck. Jill give a squeal of fright—whether true or faked Randolph couldn't tell—and look wild-eyed on the goon who sat Randolph back up in his chair. But since she let out the high-pitched tone in the boss man's ear, he viciously backhanded her, growling, "Enough! I'm becoming bored with the two of you."

The native extortionist fingered Jill's bikini top strap, while Randolph stepped up and played his part in this game of cat and mouse. "Please, mister, don't hurt her, I'll pay anything you want!"

"Oh, I know you will," the native said smugly, letting go of Jill's strap to pat her face, "because if you don't, she and I are going to get well acquainted with each other while my men give you a few pointers in being a good client." He took another puff of his cigar as he turned to Randolph and smashed it out on the desk. "Now then, as you are not of my native island and have neglected to hire local help, my fees by necessity have to be doubled." He explained with a wave

The Paranoid Thief

of his hand, indicating that was Randolph's first and second mistake. "You see, you're taking away the livelihood of some of my other clients, and that's not good for our rather poor economy." He pulled another offensive cigar out and with the help of the hormone-infested goon behind Randolph, lit it and continued the shake down by approaching Jill's face with the newly lit cigar. "And as I can see the local custom of my lovely Island women will suffer due to this rather scrawny secretary of yours, I must therefore charge a bit more to make up for that loss of income." He tapped out the ash on her new white shawl and took another long pull as if thinking up a number. "Adding this all up, your weekly fee well be, umm...say 1,000 credits, half of which is due right now!" His menacing voice presented no room for arguments. The arrogant native slid a glance Randolph's way, knowing full well a business like this held no such hard credits like that on hand. With a cruel smile the native boss fingered Jill's strap once more in anticipation to Randolph's up and coming statement of that fact.

Randolph grimaced inwardly, wishing Jill hadn't waltzed in an hour early, as it seemed Randolph now had to figure out how to make 182 hard credits, which was all they had left, look like 500. *Something I hadn't worried about as we were already booked on a flight off the islands. But now it's very relevant, as these men are not leaving till I hand over the required amount or*—Randolph never finished that thought as Jill came to the same conclusion as he and acted.

With expert military training in hand to hand combat, Jill used the muscle man's tight grip on her forearms like supporting straps and gave the native boss a rude kick to his pride and joy between his legs. Then she use her other leg to connect solidly with his lowing face, sending him backward, crashing into the wall and side table before making the floor. To this treatment of his boss, the muscleman's IQ registered surprise to actions he'd never had to consider while holding a frightened female, but Randolph held no time in witnessing her next moves as he was a bit busy reacting to her distraction. Jumping up, he shoved the muscle man behind him into the wall with all his strength and grabbed the cheap suit's jacket in both hands to sent him stumbling into Jill's favorite chair, over balancing him into his struggling boss. *We're dead meat now if either one makes it to their guns!* Randolph grabbed a potted plant to bounce off the muscleman's skull when he saw a light beam burn a hole into the man's temple, frying the brains inside. This action caused the newly dead man's body to slump over the boss with his massive body, pinning the boss in place for a brief second. To this Randolph risked a look over in Jill's direction, and he saw her put the pistol up under the jaw of the other muscleman and pull the trigger, then she deftly stepped away from the mindless body that slowly crumpled to the floor and looked at Randolph, taking note of his frown.

"Hey, don't blame me," Jill defended herself, raising her hands, allowing the pistol to dangle on her finger tip. "Numb nuts here had the thing set on max."

Randolph rolled his eyes skywards to her declaration, and shook his head in some pain as he knew they both were in deep kimchee once the boss got out from under his man. Never mind it was the boss man's fault this all happened, his kind never considered the consequences of their actions could ever result in retaliation, kind of like the woman crying her eyes out, declaring her son to be a good boy at his execution for murdering the school teacher who flunked him for not learning his lessons.

Jill eyed the boss, who was taking stock of his current situation, and asked Randolph, "So what do we do with him?"

The Paranoid Thief

The fact she actually asked surprised Randolph, causing his thinking to short-circuit a moment before he said calmly, "Well, I've a few more hours of work here, which pretty much renders letting him go out of the question, as he'll become a problem later if we do." Still considering, Randolph glanced down on their unwanted guess, whose eyes looked over Randolph trying to figure out how he'd killed his men so efficiently—that is till he saw Jill standing not far off with his bodyguard's gun dangling from her small index finger.

Randolph turned to look out the fourth story window so he could think in terms of *Now what?*

But when his back was turned, Jill proclaimed calmly, "Okay, problem solved." To which he smelled the odor of ozone and meat burning.

Randolph Jerked his head her way, seeing the gun she acquired being tucked down the back of her bikini bottom. With dread, Randolph turned to look on the native boss, finding his lifeless eyes staring up at Jill with a clean little hole in his forehead. Randolph turned hardening eyes onto Jill. "Will you please stop that!"

"Calm down, Randolph, we both knew he had to be killed if we were to leave the island alive," Jill told him in a level voice, walking over and relieving the other bodyguard of his gun before she sat in her favorite chair. "I was just hoping you would come to the same conclusion and allow me to do what was necessary."

With a sigh, Randolph looked about the remains of humanity's burden on a growing society and rubbed his face and cheek, going over the other possibilities they might have had. *Rather redundant now,* he considered, but instead of facing the truth, Randolph stood there, thinking. *There just has to be another way this could have been solved without killing them.* But no matter how he approached the matter, Randolph came to the same conclusion she'd already reasoned out. The fact that she was right, knowing she was right, was what stuck in his throat, because taking someone's life was always against his principles. *Thusly not saying aloud she was right makes me, oh I don't know, "a hypocrite" comes to mind.*

"You're not going to give me the satisfaction in admitting I'm right, are you?" Jill asked, annoyed, watching how Randolph was now starting to pace with his growing agitation. "You're just going to pace about and blame me for introducing you to the real world."

"Give me a break Jill," Randolph snapped, "you've killed four people since breaking me out of jail, and now I have to justify in my own mind the growing body count of my freedom."

"Well, while you're at it, why don't you flex those wonderful muscles you have hidden under that suit and help me stuff these three in the closet for now?"

"Yeah sure," Randolph mumbled with a shrug, knowing if anyone happened to come in, the sight of three dead men might make leaving the island a bit tricky.

By four in the morning, Randolph had all they would need. The laser printer he'd modified did a right fine job to the scroll work on the front and back of the passports, set in place to make such forgeries impossible to copy, but how they reasoned that out with all the forgers in business was beyond him. As for customs stamps, they were not as critical to match, for the bored customs agents tended to smear the activation of the archaic hand-held stamp. Next came video pictures, IDs, credit accounts originating in Scandinavia which he filled with 10 percent transfers from his few clients' credit accounts, which provided them a modest 230 credits from three clients. Their uninvited guests supplied them with a meager 468 hard credits between the lot, but later when Randolph held more time to do some

The Paranoid Thief

poking around, he'd check into their personal accounts and see what could be withdrawn. For now, it was a small matter of popping by a bank on their way to the skimmer port and depositing half of their hard credits before boarding their flight.

Once finished, Randolph stretched tired arms and rubbed his eyes before he nudged Jill, who'd fallen asleep in her favorite chair. When Jill's eyes slowly opened and she began the process of orienting herself, Randolph saw a sight he'd never seen before. Perhaps he'd never really looked in them before, but he swore he saw both personalities, one looking out of each eye, before the softer Jill retreated and the colder Jill completely surfaced.

This Jill took stock of her surrounding, stretched and yawned, asking, "What's up?"

"I've got all we need. Now what do I do with the bodies?"

"Oh them." Jill yawned again, standing, bending over backward and forward to wake up her resting muscles. "That's easy. The boss man goes in the chair behind the desk. The cronies are placed thusly, one in a chair across from the boss and the other draped over the desk."

"And this is supposed to do what?" Randolph inquired.

"Silly boy, it's for body placement after the fire crews put out the blaze."

"Jill, they'll never believe they simply allowed themselves to be burned up."

"Well of course not. The autopsy will show the laser holes, but that won't happen till sometime tomorrow. By then we'll be well on the way to where, uh, hmm…where are we going?"

"Telangrade County. It's a hundred miles from the city of Willing, where Mr. Hilden resides."

With time delay incinerators set and the office sprayed with DNA residuals—gathered over the course of their stay—to render their own DNA impossible to discern out of the mix, and the specialty equipment Randolph acquired or procured from other offices neatly restored back in their original offices, Randolph disconnected the fire retardant for the office they'd rented only and started walking out. Jill, however, gave Randolph an annoyed look, as she'd seen he'd made sure only their office would go up in flames, but he guessed she decided it wasn't worth arguing over. After pressing the two guns in the goons' hands, she followed him out to a rental car.

After boarding the skimmer, Randolph figured Jill's softer side most have emerged. She snuggled up to him once they were in the air, placing both her arms around him possessively before falling back asleep. Even though he was becoming attached to her warmth, Randolph wondered what in hell he was going to do with her. She was rendering his justification in clearing his name a bit moronic, for what did it matter who the records showed he'd murdered? Because of her, he was now just as guilty of murder as if he really had killed the Henderson family and servants.

Chapter Fifteen

Once back on firm ground, the pair disembarked the atmosphere skimmer for a regular hovercraft which took the couple to an old outdated hotel where Randolph kept his emergency funds stashed. Closing the door to their room on the 23rd floor, Jill looked about its simple appearance and plopped herself on the bed, testing its firmness, while Randolph took off the ventilation cover and crawled into its dusty interior with a pen light in his mouth. Over his many years of research, Randolph discovered corporations came and went depending on their accountability to their owners. But hotels tended to stay hotels no matter who owned them, so unless the owners were willing to drop the building, it was a relatively small gamble to stash hard credits and IDs in the ventilation shaft. Updating the HVAC system was always the last resort in a refurbish job.

After emerging, Randolph dusted himself off and dumped the contents of the dusty box out on the bed Jill was lounging on, reading a home fashion magazine she'd picked up on the way to the elevator. Jill looked on the pile with little interest and laid her magazine down to point at a picture. "Honey, what do you think of this?"

"Of what?" Randolph picked up an account card, tapping in the twenty six digit code to allow him access to its total funds.

"The color of this wall design. Don't you think it would look nice in our den?"

To the word 'our', Randolph lost his sequence then looked skyward for patience. "Jill, aren't you being a little premature? It'll take months before I'll be ready to move on Mr. Hilden, after which we'll decide if we'll stay together." He tried the pin code again, but Jill shifted her position, dropping her magazine and sitting up so her back was to him. To the distinct sound of sniffling, Randolph lost his cool and his place a second time. *Of all the—* "What's the matter?"

"I want a family, John," Jill's softer side said with sorrow in her voice as her shoulders shook. "Jill promised I could have my family once she'd established her carrier and to that end I've given up ten years of my life." Jill raised her chin and used her arm to wipe her face, saying with some heat, "Now because of her cold-hearted ways we're condemned to death should the court system catch up to us, which is really only a matter of time." She turned some so he could see her profile. "I don't want to die, John! I want my time in the sun. I want a home, children and—and a husband! And that husband has to be you!" Jill stood and cleared her eyes once again before she turned fully to him. "You know exactly who and what we are. With you there'll never be inquiries into our past. John, please, I'm begging you. I do love you and I want your children, our children. Please don't push me aside, I'll be good to you, I'll—I'll—"

To his blank stare, she began balling in earnest and ran for the bathroom, slamming the door behind her.

Still confused, Randolph held no idea what to say or do. He even felt like a heel, though he'd done nothing wrong. Then the bathroom door jerked open and Jill came out, striding his way with murder in her eyes! Randolph knew full well who was in control, and remembering the last time she looked at him in that way, Randolph panicked and held his hands up in submission, trying to get his throat working while backing up.

But he received a right cross before he could, sending him into the bedside table, to which Jill growled just below a yell, "What did you do to her?"

"Ow! Jill, I did nothing!" Randolph declared in innocence.

The Paranoid Thief

Back handing him next to keep him in the corner, Jill snarled, "What did you do? I can't even feel her in the back of my mind!"

"Honestly, I didn't even touch her!" Randolph looked into cold and deadly eyes which he desperately wanted to calm before he became her punching bag. "In fact, you should know that; I thought you told me you two talk to each other."

She folded her arms instead of abusing his face more then turned around, taking a couple of steps away. "It doesn't work that way. I get glimpses like pictures now and again while she's in control if she allows it, then a video of all that's happened when we change places, but this time I fell in control without a single thought!"

Randolph ran the back of his hand against his stinging mouth, tasting iron saltiness in his mouth, and come away with blood, grimacing to the pain. Jill looked back on him, sighing with annoyance; she walked over as Randolph tried to meld back into the wall holding his hands up in capitulation.

"Oh, quite acting like a baby," she accused, picking up a tissue box on the way and handing it to him. "I didn't hit you that hard. Now take this and sit down, I want to know what you two talked about."

"Sure, if you'll move to the other side of the bed," Randolph said, still trying to protect himself.

"For crying out loud, Randolph, I'm not going to hit you again. I'm now in complete control of myself."

"Well, I'm not saying anything till you do," Randolph argued, dabbing lightly on his split lip.

"All right! Fine!" Jill snapped in exasperation, throwing her hands in the air.

Once Jill settled on the far corner of the bed, Randolph began his recital of her softer side's words and feeling, being a bit cruel in tone, holding nothing of that conversation back.

Jill turned her back to him and faced the room's entrance, making no sound or comment. Standing after a bit, she straightened her shoulders, thanked him for being truthful, and headed for the door.

"Where are you going?"

As the door closed behind her, she said with just a hint of emotion, "I'm going for a walk."

Once he heard her footsteps recede along the outside hallway, Randolph was able to sigh and relax, though now for some reason he felt like a total heel. He grumbled, and reminded himself Jill was a big girl now and if she had half the report with her other side, his news was no revelation. So as he had tons of work to start, Randolph called room service for medical supplies, hot tea, a turkey sandwich and picked up the old standby stationary tools the hotels always supplied to make a list of common items he'd need to begin his newest and possibly last adventure into the world of documentation, security measures, and credit accounts.

After verifying he held ten thousand credits in his own account, Randolph authorized payment for the room with an extra 300 credits to draw on from the hotel for incidental living expenses. Then it was off to the local electronic building for a mobile computer and the few things he'd written down to occupy his time while he thought out minor details during the intervals between his search programs and finding a suitable place to set up shop. When he returned to their shared hotel room with the required equipment, Randolph's mind had already categorized possible avenues of basic surveillance he considered Jill to be perfect for, and only remotely noticed she hadn't returned from her walk. With a glance about the room, Randolph shrugged her out of his thoughts, and set up his equipment on the provided table, hard wired the computer to the net, then cracked his fingers out of habit before he let fly his fingers, as his mind settled in on this grand adventure.

When Randolph sat back in the cheap upholstered chair to rest his eyes and roll his neck about, he took notice of the time. *1:00 a.m. and Jill isn't back yet?* He stood to stretch his legs and open a window to take in somewhat fresher air and had a moment of guilt roll around in his mind. *Surely she wouldn't have taken off for such a minor argument? A bit painful yes, but—*

Letting his thoughts drift, parking his butt on the windowsill, Randolph absently activated the video screen and flipped to the local news. He looked out over the neon-lit city as the broadcast rambled about the day's news. *Having only a few credits on her, she couldn't have gone far, but then again she did survive for years without me.* As his stomach complained of malnutrition, Randolph decided to try room service and finding it still open even at this time of night, ordered up a snack platter of cold cuts and cheese along with a light beer before sitting back down to reason further; he could do nothing till she showed up. With his conscience settled, Randolph tapped on the keys to read up on any latest advances in computer technology, thus his attention was diverted when his ears picked up part of a news story of a woman trashing a local bar.

Quickly turning his head to the video screen, he saw the smartly-dressed woman behind the news desk saying, "As details become known, we'll update this story at the top of the hour. Next up, why is city hall so desperate to—"

Tuning out the video, Randolph raced his fingers across the keyboard to search out any reference to the news broadcast. While his search program popped up with the most likely articles he sought, Randolph hoped his concerns were wrong. But when the video came up, and there on the top of the list was Jill's picture, Randolph's heart took a flying leap into the well of guilt. With a sense of dread, Randolph punched up the article and listened to the news broadcast.

"It was a chaotic scene today as violence broke out in a midtown bar. After interviewing police officials, had this to say."

The camera trained on a uniformed police officer. "This unidentified woman," he said to Jill's face posted to the left side of the screen, "having had far too much to drink, began a brawl, leaving customers to run for cover. At present we're still gathering evidence at the scene which can be used in a court of law."

The scene changed and a smartly-dressed fellow filled out the remainder of the story as Randolph sat back heavily in his chair, his mouth dropping wide open.

"As this had been reported some hours ago, we now have fuller details on this incredible story through our public relations liaison, Lieutenant Morison. Lieutenant Morison," asked the anchorman of a hard-nosed man in his fifties, "can you now elaborate more on this unidentified woman?"

"Yes I can, Mr. Taller. As your viewers learned earlier, an unidentified woman in her early thirties, with obvious combat training, set about wreaking havoc in a local bar. She is currently incarcerated in the downtown public enforcement building on charges ranging from inciting to riot, property damage, assault and resisting arrest. Presently, as she has yet to give a name, we are running a DNA test to gain her identity for official documentation and booking. In the mean time, we are asking your viewers if anyone happens to know this woman, please come forward to help us sort out her reasons for such a destructive display."

Randolph mechanically turned off the video report and rubbed his face, over whelmed with anger and hopelessness. *A DNA report will take 24 hours as long as no deaths were reported, and depending on*

The Paranoid Thief

the work load at the facility, that could push the results back a few hours but no more, and I can't count on that. With a glance Randolph saw it was now 2 a.m., and she'd been picked up around 5 p.m.; this left him with less than a day to figure out what he should or could do. *Once they get the results, it will be a simple thing to put her in the computer and discover exactly who they have on hand. If only she'd carried her ID or gave them her new name, that would have given me more time to investigate what options are available. Now by afternoon, regardless of what she or I tell the police, the DNA report will be in, and in a matter of hours Jill will be picked up by the military for completion of her execution.* Not liking the time crunch, Randolph drummed his fingers on the table, trying to reboot his brain for what by necessity would be a fast and dirty job.

He hit the escape key and dumped all current programs to type out possible scenarios. Not holding at bay his imagination, Randolph created even the most ridiculous ploys, and developed ten choices in minutes. Next came common devices he'd need, programs, tools, IDs, vehicles and clothing. Strapped for time, Randolph accessed the nearby electronic store by net and placed an order for the required equipment, adding in a large tip in order to guaranty prompt delivery. Then came the accessibility of vehicles, clothes and incidentals which made any job look just that bit more legitimate. Next came forging prescriptions for the pain killers he'd need for resupplying his arms with tools and down loaded this to an all night pharmacy with credentials of a the medical doctor he'd done a job for. After which, sitting back in the chair with over-tired eyes, Randolph ignored how many hours he'd been working. He ordered up additional sandwich supplies to add to his plate of cold cuts and cheese, which he knew would help energize his lagging energizes and took a long hot shower.

After finishing his meal, Randolph looked over the last of his inbound packages, and set to work unpacking, arranging, familiarizing, setting up, plugging in and all the other necessary acts before he truly could buckle down and weed out by availability his options for carrying out the possible campaigns open to him. By 6 a.m. Randolph chose his path, set appropriate tools in his arms, and dummied up fake IDs in the name of a military colonel who fit his body description; that should withstand normal inquiries, as long as they failed to require a retina scan for Jill's release. With all this accomplished, Randolph yawned deeply, stretched, and reasoned he could catch two hours' sleep before places he needed to visit opened for another business day.

Dressed and checked out of the hotel, Randolph dropped off all the unusable equipment at a handicap facility, making a bee-line to his first acquisition. Three hours later, with a rented vehicle loaded with military police clothes and acquired equipment, Randolph was waiting in the law offices of a local documentation attorney for the weasel behind the desk to down load his credits for a private viewing of documents he'd need to pull the job off. After paying the exorbitant fees, Randolph was escorted with a fake smile to a private booth, where he proceeded to hack into the system to over write its security measures and bring up Colonel Anderson's files for printing out with only slight detail changes, like his video picture and hair color. Next came legal wording which would get Jill released into his custody and orders to transport her over state lines. Next came introduction orders to the local military base with added orders for the colonel in charge of the military police to aid in his assignment. Carefully comparing his drafts to real orders on file in public records, Randolph polished them up and printed them out. After he received the required stamps, for a fee, Randolph slipped them into his briefcase and proceeded to

The Paranoid Thief

his next goal. By 1:15 p.m. Randolph held a valid ID and driving credentials; by 2:30 he'd lifted a bag and seating tickets form an incoming flight to add to his ensemble and rented a vehicle suited to his new position.

A little past 5 p.m., coming to a rest in the visitors parking space in the underground structure, the no-nonsense corporal in the passenger front seat got out and opened Randolph's door. Once on the concrete floor, Randolph straightened out his hip equipment, and started moving with his two man escort, for the double door entrance into the police building. *Thus far all is working as planned; now if I can keep up this facade of a hard-nosed colonel,* he reminded himself as he walked into the lion's den to extract Jill from the jaws of justice. *With luck, we'll both be lost in the city after disembarking the atmosphere skimmer I've already booked, dressed like any other low-level corporate manager and secretary.* Head held at an arrogant level, Randolph passed uniformed officers on all sides as he and his men entered the building, while he mentally hoped his deodorant held up its promise. He was jumpy as hell on the inside, like a bright fledgling chef offering up his best dish to the city's most acclaimed food critic. And in a way, that's exactly what he was doing, save he hadn't the time to properly prepare his dish for this display. With a wish he could adjust the itchy military collar, Randolph folded his hands behind his back to keep them from showing his anxiety and allowed the two corporals to escort him deeper into the lion's maw, hoping no one would look past the uniform to place his wanted photo over his face. Still rigid, though trying as hell to look relaxed, Randolph rode the elevator to the twentieth floor, then walked past cubicles not un-similar to any corporate operation until he arrived at his destination. He allowed his subordinate to knock before opening the door and then entered the master lion's den.

Regardless of knowing everything could go wrong, Randolph knew now was not a time of worrying, and reestablished his airs of superiority to walk up to the man in charge, extending his hand to the captain as the man stood. "Captain Russell," Randolph began, projecting his voice to sound hard as plastic-steel, "My name is Colonel Don Van Hasting of the military police."

"Colonel," the captain acknowledged, clasping Randolph's hand with strength, "what can I do for you?"

"I'm here on a matter of some embarrassment. Apparently a woman by the name of Major Jill Wander somehow survived her execution and vanished from our mortuary." After receiving his hand back, Randolph extracted the documentation he'd made from his briefcase and handed it over. "I'm here to correct that mistake by escorting the major back for completion of her sentence."

"I see," Captain Russell said, receiving all the legal papers and motioning Randolph to the chair in front of his desk while he read through the ten sheets of legal wording which could have been reduced to half a sheet if it weren't for all the "whereas, first party, second party," and countless other double talk words used to make the legal system near impossible for normal people to understand.

With his fat in the oven now, Randolph sat down stiffly before Captain Russell, and crossed his legs, trying to look comfortable, though every neuron in his brain was screaming for him to take the first emergency exit out. Although he'd done stunts like this before in commerce buildings, Randolph never imagined such a stunt where he sat in a building filled with hundreds of law officers while using two military trained police grunts as an escort. *I hope if there's such a thing as gods of audacity, they were paying attention to my exploits this very day. Damn, my antiperspirant had better live up to its guaranty. And if it does, I'm buying stock in the company.*

The Paranoid Thief

"Mmm..." Captain Russell responded in his chair, apparently reading every word on every page Randolph had handed over; what he'd created in hours, what should have taken days. "Colonel, could you clarify something for me?" Captain Russell asked, eying Randolph over the papers. "According to our files, we only identified Miss Wander two hours ago, so how is it you've had time to cut these legal documents and arrive here from Fort Chasing in that short of time?"

Not having his entire story intact, Randolph began slowly. "As with any good organization, we keep tabs on all local and foreign news videos. When the major's picture hit the news cast, our facial recognition program tagged her face with military records. Once done, my office was notified and the appropriate orders cut."

"But what if she turns out to be just someone who has a striking resemblance to this woman?"

So far so good, he's asking only reasonable inquires, Randolph thought. "A plausible outcome, Captain, and if that were true you'd be showing me the results in which I'd apologize for taking up your time and be on my way. However, as you haven't, after I returned her to our base, she'll undergo some intense identifying procedures and interrogation before her sentence is carried out."

Randolph watched the captain's face as he tapped on his terminal, noting his expression changed not at all in reaction to whatever he was reading.

"You're in luck, Colonel; all work-up on Miss Wander has been completed and conforms to your documentation. As she is then a military prisoner under a harsher sentence then our prosecution can call for, your claim supersedes civilian laws and saves our tax payers the expense of a trial." Captain Russell hit a couple of buttons and assured Randolph, "She's all yours. Presently she's resting comfortably in her assigned cell, so I'll clear you for entry. It'll take me a few moments to go over her file and print out a hard copy of her disposition. So why don't you and your men head on down and I'll have it delivered to you there?"

Randolph acknowledged the request by standing as the captain's door opened and an officer stepped in.

Without looking up, Captain Russell instructed the lieutenant, "Please see Colonel Van Hasting and his men to holding block 27J."

"Yes, Captain," the lieutenant answered. He looked to Randolph and asked, "If you'll please follow me?"

Randolph acknowledged the captain one last time, clasped his hands behind his back and followed the lieutenant out as warning bells rang out in his mind, screaming. *This is far too easy! He knows! Quick, get out while you can!* However, instead of taking such credible suggestions from his experienced brain, Randolph dutifully traveled along the corridor to the elevator where their guide pressed underground level 14. While descending, Randolph pondered what might he have done wrong besides stepping into a building filled with people who'd toss his sorry butt out the highest window were they allowed. On the 14th floor below ground level, the hallway encircled the elevator shaft with plastic-steel doors set mid wall to each designated holding block. 'J' block sat directly in front of the elevator doors with a key pad, slot card identifying plate and call box. The lieutenant escorting Randolph and company waited till all were off and the doors closed before using proper security measures, by blocking the panel to his company's view as he tapped in his identifying pass number and slipped his card in the slot.

Without obvious interest, Randolph watched a red bar of light over the door turn yellow, signifying thus far procedures had been followed correctly. Next the sound box squawked with a tin voice.

The Paranoid Thief

"Who is it, and what business have you here?" The lieutenant answered the required questions and was instructed to bring his party into the next hallway while his claim was authenticated. The bar over the door turned green and a pressure release valve sounded a warning. This allowed the hydraulically sealed door to rotate open by remote.

"As this is a secured area, Colonel. All weapons must be relinquished and placed in this holding bin," the lieutenant instructed once in the hallway. Already being prepared for such normal measures, Randolph nodded approval for his escort as the pressure door behind them closed and he sensed a slight tingling as body scanners gave the group a once over. Never having tried a stunt like this, every understandable security procedure implemented had Randolph that much more certain they knew exactly who he was and were allowing him to crawl deeper into the web before springing the trap. Covertly watching the lieutenant for any signs of recognition, Randolph felt a sigh pass over him as the lieutenant pressed the button which locked all batons and fire arms from the party members, including the lieutenant's. With all weapons securely out of hands' reach, a second scan was made, followed by a yellow light above the far door they were facing changing to green. Once more Randolph heard the hiss of pressure valves releasing as the door rotated open. The lieutenant motioned for them to follow while compounding the unnecessary gesture with the spoken words, "If you will follow me, Colonel?"

Randolph nodded for him to lead, and followed him into a twenty-by-twenty white-gray room furnished with uncomfortable hard plastic chairs and harsh lighting to illuminate everyone in the room from all angles. Given no time to adjust to the room, Randolph was led up to the guards station with the guardian sitting easily behind a protective plastic-steel glass panel set in the steel wall some feet from a reinforced door.

"Colonel, if you'll inform Lieutenant Bran who you're here for, he'll help you from here." So saying, Randolph's escort walked back into the hallway, allowing the pressure door to close behind him.

Randolph eyed the lieutenant as he left, hearing more warning bells go off in his head as he now had no escort out of the building. *Which very well could mean I'm not leaving!* He tried to swallow. With all options but one left to him, Randolph squared his shoulders, still clasping his hands in back lest they start shaking in response to his nervousness, and walked up to the duty officer.

"I'm Colonel Don Van Hasting. I'm here to claim Major Jill Wander."

"Right, Colonel," the wide-awake lieutenant answered, ringing more warning bells in Randolph's head. "Captain Russell has informed me of your coming arrival. If you and your men will have a seat, I have a couple of notations to make before I can release her into your custody."

As sitting down was the last thing he wished to do, Randolph had to reason with himself. *If I've blown this, there's nothing I can do.* And admitting this, all he could do was play out the scene till whatever happened, happened. Trying to radiate confidence, Randolph sat as suggested, crossing his legs in a casual manner to help with his deception, whether blown or not. His two muscle men remained standing in the middle of the room, quietly conversing to one another about some sporting event and why the outcome had happened, as if they owned the team. *A rather useless activity.* Randolph rolled his eyes, in an effort to help steady himself. *Some psychiatrist insist it's a good way to stimulate the brain in problem solving. If that were even remotely true, our society would already be colonizing other worlds instead of still stumbling on problems with the twenty-year-old moon base.*

Randolph decided to put his own mind to better use, like nonchalantly looking the room over for vulnerabilities, but as he started, he heard the pressure door open and glanced that way, somewhat knowing already what was going to happen. His escort mildly turned to look, and watched in surprise as ten hard-nosed officers sporting hypo dart guns hurriedly came in and spread themselves about, ready to fire. The military-trained muscle men, perceiving danger, though a bit late, reacted in self-defense instead of rationalizing they were nowhere near the jungles and this was not a fight to the death. Even so, Randolph had to give them credit as they dropped two men and were engaging two others as he sat, apparently calmly, eyeing a pistol leveled at his chest and very unwilling to give the holder a reason to use it. Regardless of his guards' valiant attempt in a situation which had gone afoul by their simply stepping into the building, the two MP's sagged to the polished floor from the tranquilizer darts as the officers picked themselves up off the floor, or straightened out there clothes, while the two covering Randolph spread out a bit more in-case he should be so foolish. The next sound Randolph heard was higher-quality shoes treading on the hard floor. To this Randolph turned only his head and watched Captain Russell walk in.

Chapter Sixteen

"Colonel Don Van Hasting," Captain Russell started, "or should I say Randolph McCann?"

"Randolph will do," Randolph sighed, still wishing he knew where he'd gone wrong.

"By your reputation, I'd have thought you'd have known better than to try a stunt like this after killing that city sheriff."

"I didn't kill him."

"Accessory after the fact then, which will be added to your other crimes of murder."

"I didn't kill them, either!" Randolph snapped, still offended by that frame-up.

"Whether you did or not might have been taken into account had you surrendered yourself and turned in Miss Wander." The severity in his voice indicated the captain didn't believe him, a reaction Randolph was well aware would be upper most in every-one's thoughts till he made Mr. Hilden confess to the crime. Even so, it made little difference now as Jill had indeed made him an accomplice to murder, no matter if he had asked Jill's help or no. Understanding the routine, Randolph carefully stood and turned to the wall so they could start processing him.

Once more running the gantlet of security measures to extract any objects considered not skin and bones, Randolph was finally clothed in a bright yellow short-sleeved jumpsuit, given a number, videographed and incarcerated in the same cell block as Jill.

Evidently one of their more maximum security blocks, Randolph mused, *which in truth is rather lucky for us as they should have kept us well separated, given my track record, which Captain Russell*

The Paranoid Thief

made plain he'd read in some detail. Randolph shrugged off this fortunate mistake, now that he was in a more familiar role, and sat down listening to the magnetic lock being activated which brought to mind plan B. For obvious reasons, Randolph couldn't indulge himself in planning out plan B as he also had time restraints on this activity, due to Jill's lack of the same. *In other words,* Randolph reminded himself, *it's put up or shut up, as this is our very last chance at escape. If this fails, I have no magic hat to save our butts from the sterile stainless table top and that cold, cold needle.*

Randolph shook off that morbid thought as he sought out the video camera and microphone then flipped a mental coin on whether or not to leave Jill to her fate and save his own butt. Letting that imaginary coin fall unnoticed to the floor, he went to the corner under the video camera, and twisted and pulled his arm out of its socket while the building celebrated their illustrious capture. With his head pressed into the corner, Randolph bit back his scream of pain, as he gathered out the precious tube which had saved his life several times over the years, and extracted with teeth and suction the miracle pill, which made morphine seem like a mild can of beer.

Unable to use the dislocated arm till resetting it back into its socket, Randolph bit down on the cylinder like a cigar, plastered against the wall blinking watery eyes as he waited out the few moments for the pill to take effect. When Randolph felt its wonderful molecules attaching themselves to the pain centers along his brain stem, stopping the news from his arm of the misuse, he kept the first cylinder between his teeth and reconnected his arm then disengaged the other arm for its cylinder. After making certain his arms and hands worked as normal, Randolph palmed both cylinders and put a depressed look on his face, playing the part of a whipped puppy, before he walked back into view of the video camera and settled under a light wool blanket with his back to the room to begin his work in earnest. Once the tools were assembled, Randolph took several deep breaths before sitting up. With a look skyward in a plea for any help from the man upstairs, or any help from the imaginary gods of stupidity, Randolph activated the video jammer and shot to the door frame, activating a laser pen. Within seconds he was in the wall and jumping the circuit board without consideration for extra security measures as he had no time to dawdle. When he heard the power shut off, Randolph pushed out the door and ran down the hall to the guard's station as fast as he could run. With the aid of his non-slick shoes, Randolph halted at the guard's station and lasered the key hole and bolt assembly till it fell to pieces when he yanked the door open and charged into the surprised face of Lieutenant Bran. Yanking a clipboard off the wall he'd seen before being captured, Randolph applied this to the lieutenant's cranium more than once to introduce his displeasure of being locked up. With adrenalin racing and his breathing elevated, Randolph stripped the lieutenant bare, swapping out their clothes, even to the lieutenant's slightly larger, imitation leather work shoes, and then searched out Jill's holding cell. When he gained her cell number, Randolph grabbed up the keys, and downing the lieutenant's coffee to wet his dry throat, hurried back the way he'd come, dragging the unconscious, naked lieutenant along so he could wake up knowing how it felt to be incarcerated unjustly.

 Still adjusting the bothersome tie the uniformed officers were forced by ignorant managers to suffer, Randolph dropped his cargo off on the floor next to Jill's cell, and slid the lieutenant's card key into the slot, hitting the green button which informed the electronics he wished the door open. Once the powerful magnets released, Randolph yanked open the door and barely caught a glimpse of something inside moving. With but that fraction of movement,

The Paranoid Thief

Randolph managed barely to deflect Jill's dinner tray from full contact with his skull.

"Ow!" Randolph stumbled back and saw a brief blur of movement as Jill landed on him, forcing him back to the hall where he lost his balance and sat down hard on the floor with her on top. "Jill, it's me!" Randolph tried, his face coming alight from her fist. "Geez, is that anyway to thank me?"

"Oh shit, Randolph, are you okay? Can you get up?" Jill intoned worried-like, scrambling off him.

With Jill's help, Randolph stood, and saw her face take on so many expressions of joy, fear, relief and uncertainty at once, he said tasting blood, "If you'll give me a moment, I'll find out."

"You could have told me that was you, for crying out loud!" Jill told him in considerable anger.

Still feeling wobbly, Randolph leaned against the wall. "Sorry, I was rather busy concentrating on getting us out of here instead of worrying on miner details."

"What do you mean—don't you already have a plan?" she asked, recovering faster than him.

"Hey! I had a perfectly good plan, a wonderful plan, save I had less than 24 hours to get every detail figured out, with the added disadvantage of having to use public facilities never designed for my type of work to gather the documentation needed with no sleep in the last 48 hours. So after that disastrous try, I've spent the last three hours being prodded and poked then shoved into a cell two doors over from yours." After running his mouth out of nervousness, Randolph took note of a change in Jill's eyes that vaguely reminded him of cat eyes becoming filled with mischief, then he ended up on the receiving end of two engulfing strong arms. "Jill?" he began, hearing her sniffle, "now is not the time for your softer side. We still have to get out of here before the guard wakes up and discover I'm wearing his clothes."

Jill pulled away from him, wiping her eyes with a hand, and said with a catch in her throat, "Your right of course. It's just over whelming to know you'd risk your life to try and get me out of here."

For a second, Randolph thought to point out she'd done the same for him, save that could wait till another time as they really needed to get moving. Jill stood a foot from him, her arms trembling as if she were fighting them from grabbing him again. Randolph looked into her eyes to see her looking at him expectantly, as if he already knew how to get the pair of them out of here. *Trusting, isn't she?* He then looked down on Lieutenant Bran, without his clothes; Randolph once more verified to himself. Women *are far more pleasing to the eyes,* then snapped his fingers, coming up with an idea. But before he began, Randolph pointed an accusing finger at Jill, remembering her past words. "You will promise me you will NOT kill anyone on the way out."

"Randolph—"

"Promise me—"

Jill chewed on his words and stern face made a face of disgust before she improvised on his words. "I promise to kill no one as long as they're not a threat."

"Jill," Randolph warned, "everyone in this building's a threat."

She shrugged. "That's the best you'll get out of me, sweetie."

"Sweetie? Since when do you use endearments?"

"Oh come off it, Randolph, can't I try to sound appreciative of what you're doing?"

"Not in our current situation. I need to know who I'm talking to."

"All right, fine. So what am I supposed to be doing?"

Randolph looked skyward in thanks just as a moan and thud sounded from Jill giving Bran a swift kick to keep him quiet.

"First things first, you lock our bundle of joy in the cell and I'll see what can be done at his console."

Jill gave him an exaggerated "righto" salute, to which Randolph rolled his eyes before jogging back to the lieutenant's work station. After seating himself in the chair in front of the console, Randolph began typing up programs, document, copies, and information on all resident criminals. Then he looked over the make and model of the printer, and found what he had in mind was feasible, as long as no one really looked hard on his forgeries.

In a matter of minutes, Randolph cut and pasted their papers and geared up to start printing the documentation when he realized he was making a seriously stupid blunder. As he was still thinking in linear terms, Randolph had naturally made the documentation up to transfer Jill to another facility. A momentary review of a clip board on the wall holding a large video picture of his face, he understood instantly the paperwork would get them nowhere but back in a cell before they could step ten feet beyond the elevator.

"Shit!" Randolph exclaimed as he rolled over other possibilities.

"What? Is something wrong?" Jill asked from her place at the door.

"Yes," he grumbled trying to rethink, "as long as I have shit for brains."

"Come again?"

"Be quiet will you!" Randolph snapped unnecessarily, regretting the words but needing to think. He drummed his fingers on the table, looking for inspiration, as Jill sat her butt on the same surface, crossing her arms. *Waiting for the master mind to remember he isn't alone in all this!* With a blinding flash of inspiration, one he should've had precious minutes ago, Randolph started the cut and pasting all over. After ten minutes of rework he started the printer and told Jill to strip.

"Randolph, this is hardly the time." Jill smirked but did as asked.

"Actually, I should have asked you to do so ten minutes ago," he remarked, irritated with himself, shucking off his stolen clothes as well. "As a cop killer, my video would be all over the place, regardless of the fact I'm now safely behind a cell door. You, however, having just been identified and currently sealed inside a cell, will not have had one issued. Therefore it should be you escorting me out. Besides," he admitted, "you have a mentality near on similar to the police."

"How's that?" she asked, trading clothes.

"You have a way of carrying yourself I could never emulate. Besides you're far better trained in combat then I am."

"Oh, so you've noticed, uh?" Jill smirked.

"Shut up and get dressed."

"As you say, sweetie," Jill said with a smile, receiving a glare in response.

Jill was zipping up the fly on the pants as Randolph contemplated this might not be a good idea, for Lieutenant Bran's clothes were far larger than her body type could support. This little piece of news he should have considered when he was wearing the lieutenant's clothes, but in a time where he was improvising like crazy, he was bound to make a few mistakes. The problem was they couldn't afford them.

"Uh, I may have been wrong about this."

"No, no, it's all right. I'll tuck them in here and there and if anybody asks, I'll tell them I'm new and these were the only clothes they had on hand."

"Will that work?" Randolph asked skeptically.

The Paranoid Thief

"Sure. You don't really think the military has on hand all sizes of clothing for women, do you?" When he shrugged, Jill continued. "No. Besides every woman's hips are different, if you hadn't noticed, and the brass insists on crispness in the ranks." So tucking the shirt in, she sized the belt by using the laser pen and cinched up the pants.

As she bent over to roll up the excess length in the pant legs, the couple were interrupted by a buzzer and a yellow light flashing on the board. Randolph turned to look over the console, worried-like, and found the screen above a readout as it dawned on him they had guests.

"Cripes, not now!"

"What do we do?" Jill asked, becoming very professional.

"We do nothing. You sit here and answer those two." He pointed to the screen. "With these words," he hastened to add. Jill did as asked, working her tie in place, and fumbled her way through the routine as best as Randolph's memory remembered, till the group of men were about to come through the last door. After Randolph sat down at Jill's feet so he wouldn't be seen and yet could still direct her if she hit a snag, he heard the buzzer for the last door activate and saw Jill's face set with a light but bored attitude. Randolph marveled on her control, somewhat envious, when he heard the room speaker pronounce, "Where's Lieutenant Bran?"

"Went home sick. I'm covering while he's out. So who's this joker?" Jill said mildly, with no real interest implied.

"Tom Jenkers, ID 271712DC. You say you're taking over for Bran, how come I've never seen you before?"

"I transferred in from Stockwell two days ago. Supposed to have a five-day leave to settle in when I was called in to cover." She made up the lie without batting an eye, sounding irritated. "Disposition of prisoner?"

"Held over for trial. Here's the plastic workup on him."

Jill reached and collected the plastic card through the rotating container, dropping it next to Randolph as if by accident. "Sorry," she said, looking annoyed at her own clumsiness, "hold on a moment." She bent over to retrieve the card and asked in a whisper, "What do I do now?"

"You got me. I think I remember Bran using that slot by your elbow when I came in the second time," Randolph suggested.

With a nod, Jill sat back up, examined the slot then flipped the card twice before sliding it in. "So," the speaker began, "are you going to be permanent here?"

"I don't know yet," Jill answered, looking up at the screen, eying the information. "Damn, you're my first customer and your system's entry information is different then I'm use too." Jill looked frustrated and apologized, "This may take a few minutes."

"Don't sweat it, uh…?" The speaker wanted her name. Jill gave him a fake one and he continued. "Linda. Bran keeps an instructional clipboard there on the wall."

Jill swiveled her head, then pulled down the clipboard with step-by-step instructions. "Damn, I'd forgotten about that. How'd you know it was there?" she asked, easily following the instructions.

"Bran likes his baseball games. If there's a good match up, he'll play sick to stay home and watch it."

"So you've helped out others I take it?" Jill asked, typing in the appropriate words in the empty boxes.

"Yeah, I wouldn't be surprised if they cancelled his card at this easy gig and put him back on a beat."

Randolph heard the buzzer go off that allowed the new officers access to the hallway and frantically signaled Jill "NO," pointing at the door lock which was no longer there. Jill gave it a quick glance before she pulled the card from its slot and met the men at the door to

The Paranoid Thief

keep their attention off the obvious entry point into the control room. "I'll just walk you back and forth to make certain I know the whole procedure, and if you ask me out after only being here a few hours," she said, blocking the door with her body, "I'm going to be rather upset with you."

"Um...all right, fine." The officer agreed, then took note of Jill's clothes and shoeless feet, gesturing. "Uh..."

At which Jill folded her arms in a huff and complained, "You try and get a set of fitting clothes when all yours are being altered for this district's dress code."

Randolph wished he could see how the situation was unfolding behind the door, but he dared not take a peek, even when he heard them start to move off with Jill leading the way. But then he felt a chill of apprehension, hearing one ask Jill who'd hired her on; for no one asked such questions unless they perceived something amiss.

As Jill knew no names they would recognize, Randolph stood and walked out. "Actually, no one hired us yet."

Their reaction was every bit what Randolph was hoping for, turning as one to his voice. Jill shoved the prisoner into one officer and kicked the knee joint out of the second before either one knew what was happening. In the next seconds, Jill silenced the pain-riddled man while Randolph stormed down the hall, shoulder-blocking the prisoner and officer as one, felling both as he stumbled and hit the floor rolling on past. Back on his feet, Randolph found the other officer was far quicker then he and tried to block his oncoming fist. This failed, as the officer's fist connected with his face, sending him back a step while Jill, a second or so late, swept the officer's feet out from under him. Randolph and Jill separated themselves to either side of the downed officer while the prisoner, still having his hands cuffed behind him, stepped into the second recovering officer, resulting in distracting the man so Randolph and Jill could move.

Once the unconscious man hit the floor, Randolph ignored the griping of the prisoner, who objected severely to Jill's insistence he get into his cell.

"Well, that went rather well," Jill commented, closing the door, "and I didn't kill either of them," she finished, making sure Randolph knew she could have.

"And no one appreciates it more then I, save these two when they think about it." Randolph remarked, stripping the one closest to his size. Jill checked out the size of the other man while Randolph went back to the console and assigned a room for their uninvited guests. As he was punching in the last codes, the buzzer on the console went off, indicating company coming. This time it was two men in black suits.

"Damn it all, when it rains it pours!"

Chapter Seventeen

"What is it now?" Jill asked, looking on the screen as Randolph tilted his head up with a silent plea of *Stop already with the surprises*. He rubbed his face in frustration, his mind ragged with all this improvising.

"Who are they after, me or you?" Jill asked.

"No way to tell until I ask," Randolph shrugged. He pressed the intercom button and asked the men to explain their business.

"Special Agent Grant and Agent Dunn to take custody of Major Jill Wander," the FBFC agent declared in a no-nonsense monotone.

"All right Special Agent Grant, please step into the hallway as I verify your request." Randolph directed, watching the pair move in as he rubbed his neck, thinking furiously.

"Have you any ideas?" Jill asked. When he shook his head, signaling her to hush, Jill laid a hand on Randolph's arm, saying with a quirky smile, "Well I do. Give me a few minutes then send them to my cell." Randolph turned to eye Jill as she instructed, "Just make certain you're behind them after you open the door."

"What are you up to?"

Jill laid a gentle hand to his face. "You've been beautiful up to this point, but it's time I started carrying my own weight. Now do as I say, as we have little time to pull this off."

Jill left him there questioning, pulling off the tie. Somewhat perplexed by her touch and his own reaction to it, Randolph shook himself and pushed the button which would open her door and release Lieutenant Bran then opened the cell next to hers so she could stuff the officers into it before turning to adjust his mind for the new party crashers in the hallway.

After removing his video picture from the board and pinning on Bran's name tag, Randolph opened the hallway door and waited as calmly as he could while the two men walked up to the window. With confident movements, the older of the two handed over the documentation giving them full custody of Jill, while the younger partner took in the room. Randolph took up the paperwork and read over the pages, noting a word placed here or there would make these documents invaluable in obtaining equipment he'd always wanted—that was if he and Jill got out of this alive.

After some minutes to give Jill time, Randolph nodded his acceptance, buzzed the door to allow them in the hallway, and stepped out to block the damaged door. He motioned with his hand. "This way, gentlemen."

Once in front of her door, Randolph fumbled out the card-key trying to prepare himself for anything Jill might do while hoping his nervousness did not show. Tensing so he'd be prepared to aid in her scheme, he pulled open the door, but what he and they all saw inside the cell was nothing comparable to what he'd imagined in the short walk along the hallway.

Instead of being set to deck one of the two men upon the door opening, Jill sat astride Officer Bran's hips facing them, wearing absolutely nothing, sounding as if she were coming near to a climax as she moaned and moved herself up and down on his uncovered lap. As with any male whose mind is never very far from thoughts of sexual pleasures, Randolph and the two agents stood a moment gaping on the scene till she lowered her head. Opening her eyes, noting the trio watching her, she commented, "Come on, guys, one at time, please!"

The Paranoid Thief

"All right, Lieutenant, what the hell's going on here?" Special Agent Grant turned. His partner did likewise as Randolph stammered, trying to find an answer.

Jill leaped off of Bran's lap, landing on her coveralls between the two men on bent legs, and rammed her right palm upward into Special Agent Grant's family pride. The resulting blow even had Randolph wincing as she repeated the action to the other agent with her left hand. Not above capitalizing on any opportunity even as stunned as he was, Randolph lifted Agent Grant's wallet and shoved him into the cell as Jill used the other agent as leverage in standing. She pulled him in further as she bolted out and grabbed the door, swinging it shut.

When metal hit the magnetic lock, sealing the door closed, Randolph couldn't help himself. He grabbed Jill in a bone-crushing hug of relief and gratitude. Jill's first reaction to his sudden affection was to tense up, but she soon melted in his arms after the first couple of seconds and returned the embrace.

After only a short time, Jill pushed herself away, but caressed his face with her hand and sought his eyes. "As much as I'm learning to enjoy being in your arms, I'd suggest you let go so I can get dressed before I pull your pants down and jump your bones."

Jill gave Randolph a quirky smile as he backed off, coughed into his fist and nodded. "Yeah, I guess that would be wise."

"Now if you'll be so kind as to open your cell, I'll get dressed." Jill smiled up at him, patting his face.

Randolph nodded and returned to the control room, which was not doing its job, and explored the agent's wallet. While he was engrossed in the many possibilities an FBFC's credentials could contribute, Jill entered and donned a second pair of socks before trying on the smallest pair of shoes present.

"So what's the plan now, sweetie?" Jill asked, tying the laces for a snugger fit.

"We get the hell out of here is the plan, and we'll be doing it by walking out the front doors, as I'm tired of changing clothes."

Jill eyed him speculatively, shrugged, and gave him a big kiss for good luck.

Thirty minutes later, Jill and Randolph were in deep discussion as they walked right out the front doors and continued their lively talk along the block, right into the first clothing store crossing their path. The pair picked out new clothes to replace the uniforms, and used Bran's credit account to pay for their new wardrobe while Randolph refrained from waving at the video camera, sighing. It would be unprofessional of him to do so; however, he couldn't resist giving a wink to the video camera as they left, just to let them know he knew they would find this video shortly after he left.

Each had purchased two sets of clothing, wearing one set upon leaving. Jill and Randolph sought out public bathrooms to change into the second set to make it harder for the computer technicians to use the clothing store's video on the streets to locate them.

Using public conveyances till dusk, Randolph and Jill traveled all over town till he hot-wired a conveniently located car and sold it to a junk dealer for hard credits to rent out a hotel room, where the couple lay arm in arm for some hours, expressing their joy in being alive and free.

But once settled in with some rest under his belt, Randolph's mind returned to reality and began wondering if they shouldn't split up. "After all," he explained, "By now my face will be—Ow! What's that for?" he complained to her stinging slap.

"Now you just shut it!" Jill ordered, stabbing a finger into his chest, causing him to sit on the bed. "It's my fault this happened, and

The Paranoid Thief

you damn well knew what would happen when you bailed my worthless butt out of the slammer. So don't you dare sit there and say you care nothing for me! That hug you gave me back in the station was not just out of gratitude for my actions—you feel something for me as I know my other self is in love with you. So you can trash those thoughts and tell me what are we going to do next?"

Randolph looked up on Jill's stern stance of immovability, rubbed his cheek and admitted, "I've no idea what course to take now. I've been running on adrenalin for so long, I need a day of rest and time to clear my head."

Jill closed her eyes and rubbed her temple. "This is all my fault, but I have to ask, are we safe here for a day or two?"

"Yeah, we're safe. The staff never saw my face and we're paid up till next week," Randolph assured her, breaking out into a yawn, his body no longer active.

"All right lover boy," Jill said, taking up his robe and hauling him physically off the bed. "We both need a shower, after which you can sleep as long as you like." With her body and voice giving out orders, Randolph knew it to be futile to argue with her, so he did as bidden and never felt his head hitting the pillow.

The body can only take so much, after which it needs a respite, and Randolph's body had decided a full day was a good beginning before any nourishment was requested to continue replenishing itself. As for Jill, her body felt just as badly as Randolph's, for when he finally stirred, she was deeply asleep, curled up as close to his body as she could get. Trying not to disturb her, Randolph slid out from under the warmth of the covers and sought out the bathroom. He then took a good hard look in the mirror on the face he'd chosen during his last facial change and ran his hand over the stubble, wondering if any crooked doctor would have anything to do with him, now that he had the city police and the FBFC after him. Randolph leaned his exposed butt up on the cold porcelain sink, folded his arms and wondered. *For that matter, would one even see Jill even if she allowed it?* Still pondering after some minutes, Randolph heard movement in the next room moments before Jill walked in wearing a robe.

"Good morning, love," Jill's softer side greeted him, enveloping him in a tight embrace and a kiss before shifting her robe to sit on the toilet. The way she casually took care of private business while he stood inches away reminded Randolph so much of his parents, that is until his father ran off with his mother's entire savings. Childhood feelings reemerged which left him uncomfortable. Guilt and blame followed on the heels of his mother's tears. *What if I'm like my father? Is this why I never settled down?* Randolph tightened his arms about himself, for a fierce chill ran through him.

The sound of water thankfully ended his destructive feelings. This brought about awareness of his surroundings, and with it, why they had enveloped him so.

When Jill finished up, she stood and wrapped her robe around him. "The bed's warm and much nicer with you in it. How about ordering breakfast in bed, then afterwards we could use up the newly-acquired energy?"

"Jill, we still have things to discuss," Randolph said trying to be serious, but in answer she buried her face in his neck, nuzzling, pressing herself up against him so he could feel the warmth and pleasure she was very willing to give. When his arousal grew near her hips, she squeezed him even tighter, knowing he was capitulating, and affectionately kissed his neck before drawing away, pulling his hand to draw him back to bed.

The Paranoid Thief

Sometime later, after they'd caught their breath, Randolph sat up against the headboard while Jill lay besides him with a possessive arm and leg intertwined with his own. "As nice as this is, we really need to discuss events and how we wish to have them play out."

Jill nuzzled his arm and kissed his elbow, murmuring, "Such are things that can wait till tomorrow. Today I wish to show you my appreciation for saving my life."

"Did you not just do that?"

"That was more or less a bribe to get you back in bed, and now that you are in bed, I plan on keeping you here all day and throughout the night, of which I promise little will be used for sleeping." And in keeping to that promise, she shifted to sit astride his hips, though he was far from being ready again, and holding the headboard to either side of his head, Jill leaned into his face and demanded Randolph kiss her as she passionately kissed his lips.

"Jill," he tried when she pulled back a little to catch her breath, "we really need to discuss the future."

"The future can attend to its ugly self today, as tomorrow will come soon enough. So let's leave it outside the door while we explore paradise here inside this room." She sat back further to help invigorate a response from Randolph's lower half, and took both of his hands to place them on her breasts. Then shaking out her lengthening hair, Jill moved her hips over his two boys, trying to draw out the strength of the man between them. After only a short time of encouragement, Jill smiled at his response from her combined talents, and shifted, lowering a hand in aid of taking him in with such a look of passion in her eyes, Randolph felt his heart flutter in anticipation. He was going to give her multiple pleasures before he succumbed to his own.

By nine that evening, Randolph's lips were beyond tired as he held Jill, slowly drifting off to sleep. Jill kept astonishing him with how often she managed to get him up for more activity beyond what he felt a man was capable of. And now as their hearts slowly began settling in for a well-deserved rest, his mind took over, briefly comparing the two sides of Jill which he'd seen today as they both shared equally their joining bodies.

The next morning as Jill finished off breakfast, sitting Indian style with the bedclothes covering her bare legs, she asked, "Well, what of the plan involving this Hilden character, can we still go ahead with that?"

"Oh sure, if you want to start World War Three," Randolph remarked, wearing a brown robe, relaxing in a chair angled for best viewing pleasure, and nursing a decent cup of coffee. He looked up into the growing irritation in her eyes, and explained further. "After getting you out of jail, there's no way Mr. Hilden couldn't know I'm a live and free, practically on his front door step, and knowing this, he has to surmise I'm rather pissed at him." As she finished off her orange juice, Randolph elaborated further, partly for his own good. *As I'd really like to do some serious damage to that SOB.* "To have tied the noose so securely about my neck in order to make certain of my participation in his murderous scheme, he'd had to have gotten detailed records furnished to him by the police and possibly some of my victims."

"But they can't know everything about you, or you would've been caught long ago."

"True, but he knows enough. I may be able to circumvent all kinds of electrical components and dig my way into software programs, but there's one factor I can't work around, and that's old fashioned bodyguards and roaming patrols."

"But I thought you didn't have to get into his home or office to do your thing?" Jill put her plate on a pillow and adjusted the covers, to the disappointment of his eyes.

Briefly he considered upping the temperature to encourage the removal of such obstacles to his viewing pleasure; even if he couldn't physically enjoy her body right now, he could at least enjoy looking while they talked. Shrugging that thought aside, Randolph stretched his legs to work out some kinks. "In most cases that's true, but Mr. Hilden is a professional, the proverbial silent partner, who can pull the strings so no attachments can leave physical traces to his handiwork. Such a man would only have damaging evidence in his personal computer which I can guaranty is unplugged to the world at large. And as a home is much easier to guard against intrusions then a public building, everything I'd need would be safely hidden deep in the hornets' nest."

Jill propped her elbows on her knees to rest her chin on her hands and asked, "If this is so, considering you're an unwelcome security risk, how safe would it be for us to simply get lost?"

Randolph sighed with regret, and put his hands behind his head considering Jill's perfectly logical suggestion, putting himself into Mr. Hilden's shoes. "Not very. Being a personality needing power, his insecurities would conclude rightly I'd show up sooner or later and become an inconvenience. Thusly I know he'd have a large reward already posted for my death to insure I kept on the run."

"That won't do," Jill said with such finality in her voice Randolph turned his head to look at her closely. "If we're to have a life and family we can't be looking over our shoulders fearing a laser shot to the back of the head. I'll have to take him out first."

"Jill, you know my feeling about such an act. Besides, even if you did, the credits for my disposal will still be enforced."

"How do you know that?" Jill asked, waving a hand in the air.

Randolph turned on the computer and typed in a simple question, "Who are the walking dead?" In seconds, a list of names and videos appeared in alphabetical order. Scrolling down to one with his likeness, he hit enter and allowed Jill to see what he meant. "As you can see, in case of his untimely death, funds will be allocated from the dispensation of his holding to insure I and the one who killed him will not live to enjoy his retirement." Randolph scrolled down a bit more to a detailed description of himself and pointed out, "And it appears he's already gained some information on you as a second target. Thus, he's covering all the bases."

"Well, what can we do?" Jill asked, slouching to this news.

"That I haven't figured out yet." Musing aloud, he concluded, "To remove our problem, Mr. Hilden has to become credit-less. To do so thoroughly, I have to walk into the hornet nest and spend some quality time with his files."

Now that Jill had reawakened his thinking process, Randolph spent the next two days working over plausible paths to Mr. Hilden's computer, ignoring Jill in his adventure, stressing to Jill's softer side he needed the time alone to muddle out their problem.

On the third day, when a plausible plan took shape, Jill took his idea with extra enthusiasm, throwing him down on the bed and taking him like a man would a woman, not understanding Randolph was still in the developmental stage of his plan and therefore prone to tune out surrounding activity till he hashed it out—

"Ow! What was that for?" Randolph exclaimed, rubbing his cheek as she glared down on him with her hand readied to land another hard slap.

"If I'm going to make love to you, you damn well better be paying attention!" Jill angrily said, dismounting and donning her robe before sitting at the table.

"How'd you know I wasn't?" Randolph asked, sitting up, closing up his own robe least she decided to take out her wrath on his two boys too.

"Because I could feel you softening up at the very point I needed you to be otherwise," Jill growled, reaching into the cooler and extracting a beer. "Just because I'm not the one in love with you, doesn't mean I wouldn't like you showing me a little affection too."

"Look, Jill, I'm sorry," Randolph tried as she downed half the bottle.

"Yeah, sure, don't mind me, I'm tough as nails, so why should you waste any affection on me?"

"Jill, please, it's not like that. I've details to work out and an inspiration hit me in the midst of what we were doing, that's all. Once I had it securely implanted in my mind I would have been back with all the lust any man has in the midst of sexual pleasure."

Jill downed another quarter and ignored him with a huff of disbelief. Sighing, Randolph got up and pulled one out for himself. "Whether it was you or your softer side out wouldn't have made any difference at that moment, but if you need reassuring, I'll, uh...um...make it up to you somehow." He snapped off the top, and took a swig, deciding to drop the subject. "As it appears I can't convince you just now, do you mind moving so I can follow up with my idea—owww—!" Randolph moaned, dropping the bottle and grabbing her hand, which had moved with speed under his gaping robe.

Jill squeezed his nuts, using her finger nails to dig even deeper. "This is how I feel right now, and instead of being reassuring, you push me aside. Well I've news for you, Jack-O, I'm just as much a woman as she is, with all the emotions and sensitivity she has. So I'd suggest you think of them the next time we're involved or I guaranty you'll be missing these useless things." Jill gave his nuts one more crushing squeeze before she got up and shoved him out of her way.

Chapter Eighteen

Randolph folded up around himself on the floor. Curled up for a time, Randolph wondered if Jill was really worth the trouble, but while he was running over those thoughts, gentle hands touched his shoulders, causing him to flinch out of reflex.

"Oh, John, I'm so, so sorry. Here let me help you up."

"If you don't mind, I'd rather you get away from me for a while."

"But, John, I didn't do this—I could never hurt you so callously."

"I don't care which one you are, just get the hell back!" Randolph snapped.

She scooted away. "John, please…" Jill sniffed, making him feel like a heel, knowing which Jill he was snapping at.

Using the bed as support in sitting up, Randolph saw Jill standing some feet away, tears rolling down her cheeks, looking for all the world as if he'd slapped her hard. *And in a way I guess I had.* Not liking the way he felt, Randolph relented and waved her over to aid him up into the chair.

"Can I get you anything? A cold pack, perhaps?"

"No thanks, just give me some room to work, okay?"

"Yes, love, anything you want, just ask."

While Randolph reset his security codes to begin his search for the perfect candidate to get the ball rolling, Jill cleaned up the mess on the floor and opened another bottle for him before settling on the bed, picking up a magazine pretending to keep herself occupied as he worked.

To find the right person involved a lot of research, for Randolph knew they couldn't just go to anyone with greed standing on his or her shoulders. No, the perfect candidate had to have clout and be willing to strike lasting bargains, so when he came across Mr. Sterling's profile, Randolph knew he had their man. So he dug out their Scandinavian passports, typed up an irresistible letter, and sent it to Mr. Sterling's office. With that out of the way, he started in on the Jamaican boss's bank account, though he knew by now it should be emptied by the state or his partners. *But then again, one never knows.* As he began the process, the table moved under his fingers. Looking for the cause, Randolph saw Jill had planted her robe-covered butt on the table. As she hadn't slapped him to gain his attention, Randolph looked up past crossed arms and a set chin below watching eyes, looking as if she had a bad taste in her mouth.

"Randolph, I'm sorry. I should not have done that to you."

"No, you shouldn't have," he remarked, turning back to the screen, typing to let loose the dogs of inquiry and leeches of passwords.

She sighed. "You're not about to make this easy for me, are you?"

"Why should I? Anytime you get mad, I get hurt."

Jill stayed quiet for a bit; he imagined she was searching her thoughts, trying to come up with some rational reason for her disposition, then must have concluded there was none. "Come on, it's three in the morning. How about coming to bed?"

Randolph glanced at the time, having lost track of it, then shrugged. "Maybe later. I'm busy right now."

"In other words, you're still mad and you'd rather sleep with her than me."

Randolph leaned back in his chair and sighed before he tried to explain. "Look, Jill, this has nothing to do with you or her. Whenever I'm on a job, I'm like this. I lose track of time, I don't eat, I don't sleep, I don't do much of anything till I've accomplished what I set out to do, or barring that, I work to a point I'm comfortable in leaving it for a time." After that admission, Randolph guessed Jill chewed on that for a minute or so before concluding he wasn't lying, for she nodded and left for the bathroom. Regardless of what she did next, Randolph stayed at the computer till the yawns became too frustrating. At which point, rubbing his face and feeling the stubble, he stretched tired arms and legs, noting it was eight in the morning. Shutting down his work, he stretched his stiff legs in a walk to the bathroom for a hot shower and shave before heading to bed.

Their flight out to the frozen lakes was miraculously uneventful, even with the price on their heads by Mr. Hilden and nearly all law agencies, proving good makeup and body-adjusting clothes made a world of difference while one was surrounded by rush hour crowds. As for getting in the building to see the senator, that took far more elaborate measures; retina-changing eye-wear, finger-print altering skin grafts, and other basic changes, all compliments of the Jamaica's bank account, which Randolph was delighted to find still intact. A rather blessed windfall, considering the amount of the bribe he had to render to the physician for the specialty items to secure the changes for the pair of them without having to worry about being handed over to Mr. Hilden or the authorities.

Seated in Mr. Sterling's outer office under the eyes of his competent secretary after an hour of security clearance, Jill looked lovely next to Randolph in her long-sleeved, ankle-length blue and green dress, high heel wrap-around shoes of black, and a thousand-credit finely-crafted sterling silver chain necklace and jewel-encrusted green hand bag.

Randolph leaned close to her stylish hair, which still held a whiff of pleasurable perfume and whispered into her ear, knowing full well the directional microphone on the secretary's desk would pick him up,

"Now, dear sister, let me do all the talking—the senator is a very busy man, and we mustn't confuse the issue with the pair of us talking." Jill nodded her acceptance as they'd discussed before entering the building, whereby Randolph sat back comfortably in his chair wearing a middle-priced suit of black, the standard suit for up-and-coming managers and business secretaries of low rank, chosen specifically to give off the impression they held no threat to Mr. Sterling's growing empire.

"Mr. and Mrs. Jurlkus, the senator will see you know." The secretary messed up their relationship, likely to gain any new reactions to add to their growing file on her computer.

To her bait, Jill corrected the secretary in the high-and-mighty-style voice she'd been practicing all morning. "That's Miss Jurlkus, and I'll ask you to correct that in your records now," Jill indicated, with a strong emphases on the now part.

"Beg pardon, Miss Jurlkus, I'll see to it immediately," the woman said as Jill straightened out her dress and stood by Randolph. The secretary pretended to do the changes but was more likely typing up Jill's mannerisms before the door to Mr. Sterling office swung open for their convenience.

The senator's outer office, like that of most politicians, was smartly decorated; white walls and pleasing scenic painting, comfortable couches and end tables doubling as drink centers to invite leisure talk, which might come in handy when dealing with his guests or other matters he might wish to invest his time in. His office had been decorated to his own tastes of mostly modern furniture, easy on the eyes natural lighting provided by strategically placed amplifier/reflectors, and very expensive cedar paneling about the walls.

The Paranoid Thief

Mr. Sterling stood behind his finely-polished desk of enriched etched glass and offered up his hand in a friendly gesture most politicos advocate in a first meeting. "Mr. and Miss Jurlkus, what a pleasure it is to meet you. Please, make yourselves comfortable. Would you like a drink or muffin?"

"You're very kind, Senator, and thank you. I believe my sister and I would like a chilled bottle of water by Cornelus Lake, if you have any?"

"A very good choice." Mr. Sterling smiled; his guest had done some homework on his holding, meaning they weren't merely part of the crowd but an integral ingredient that helped inaugurate change in the system. The senator had his secretary deliver the water personally to help placate Jill's act of irritation, then shooed her out to close the door for better privacy.

"Now then, I must say I'm very intrigued by your letter, Mr. Jurklus. Although you remained purposely vague on details, I'm in hopes we can come to a mutual agreement so I may possess the full knowledge of this incident you say was not in truth an accident, but an orchestrated murder of our gallant men and women in the service."

"That is our firm wish too, Senator. As journalists, we sometimes come across illicit matters such as this deplorable act which are swept under the rug or ignored entirely. Although never of this magnitude, still, our work can be damaging to reputations of companies and/or business men."

"I see. So to gain this particular tale, with documented proof, you both wish protection in my great county?"

"With certain concessions, so we may keep providing the public with the truth, while not forgetting exceptional materials we feel you would be interested in, to better serve the man who would be in truth our benefactor." Randolph meant they could be of mutual help to one another.

The senator sat with his arms resting on the glass and his fingers interlaced, pondering the obvious implication of Randolph's offer, whereby Randolph saw the instant he had the senator hooked. Once Mr. Sterling's word of support and hand written agreement on the terms of his help were attained, Randolph presented public documents on the events leading up to and after the murder of Jill's squadron, including documentation on her sworn testimony at her court-martial, which until Randolph found them, had been hidden in the bureaucracy of double talk and misfiled information. Randolph handed over everything relevant, including names, ranks, dates and places, and saw the senator's eyes alight with possibilities as his fingers shuffled the papers with glee. The last two sheets Randolph pulled out of his case were the names of the entire unit, their next of kin, and exactly where he'd found all the lost files of the incident to better illustrate the cover up.

When at last the pair exited the building, Jill emitted an audible sigh. "So that's all there was to it? All I had to do was hand over those sheets of paper and all those involved would have been prosecuted?"

"In truth, no," Randolph eyed her, deciding they deserved an expensive meal. "Had you done what I just did, it would have been swept into a drawer of I.O.U's, then held till a day he needed them to save his butt or put someone higher-up under his thumb."

"So you're telling me we just used my men to gain us a reprieve on a miner infraction of the law?" Jill puffed herself up, preparing to make a scene in the middle of a public walkway—not a good thing considering they were still wanted.

The Paranoid Thief

But before Jill went ballistic, Randolph grabbed her arm, got into her face and hissed, "You know me better than that. Now drop the attitude and I'll explain." When it looked as if she had settled, Randolph enlightened Jill's naiveté. "As you know, this is the information age—whoever holds the most information wins. Any and all transactions revolve around this one goal. Had you gone in with this information alone, nothing would have happened save when it benefited Mr. Sterling. However, I informed Mr. Sterling if he followed through on this matter I'd supply him with dirt on people he would like to have under his thumb."

"But I didn't hear you say that."

"That's because you've been trained to react to a situation without really listening, while I've learned the hard way information is the true gold of our age."

Jill thought this over before asking, "So when will he act on my case?"

"Just as soon as I, uh, we make good on my promise."

"And just how do we go about that?"

Randolph turned her into the Ah La Palette restaurant, and watched the entrance through reflected glass and mirrors, or any surface offering a reflection till they were seated where he could keep his eyes on it directly. "I'm in hopes Mr. Hilden's files will have some tempting offerings. If not, all I need do is see who's infringing on Senator Sterling's holdings and acquire some leverage he can use."

"I thought you only went after the guilty?" Jill whispered across the table.

"At his level no one's an innocent, as you so eloquently pointed out, but so you understand, I have my own levels of innocent and those who surpass those levels will be targeted." Randolph took note of their waiter approaching, and waved Jill silent to concentrate on the meal and the two men who walked in a minute after they'd arrived. He then took note of all other dinners, and made certain he and Jill enjoyed a full-rounded meal, taking two hours to see the change in faces, noting dinner selections and what drinks were served. This then identified the two men he was watching were not here for the ambiance of the establishment, and to his pleasant surprise, Jill informed him so.

"We're being followed," she announced softly as she dabbed a napkin to her lips.

"So you've noticed?"

"How could I not? They were so obvious when we walked out of the elevator in the Senator's building. I was just wondering if you'd seen them and therefore chose this place for verifying they were indeed on our trail."

"In point of fact, no. I choose this place because we deserved it."

Jill took some surprise in this and giving Randolph a smile, her eyes softened and she said, "Thank you, the luncheon was quite spectacular. I've never been so treated in my life."

"You're quite welcome. Now, have you any ideas how to lose those two without going through the kitchen?"

"What, you're trusting me?"

"Why not? You keep saying we're partners. So, partner, how do we go about it, as I couldn't have any of my surprises stashed on me to visit the senator."

Jill smiled. "As I had an understanding why you made certain these clothes were reversible, why don't you give me a few minutes in the ladies room before heading for the men's?"

Randolph eyed Jill across the table, and crocked a finger, mouthing, "No one is to get hurt," whereby she smiled, wiped her mouth, and announced she'd be just a moment. While Jill was in the

The Paranoid Thief

ladies room, Randolph paid the bill in his brother's establishment, regretting what the next few minutes was going to cost Mick. But as Randolph really had no choice if he and Jill were to lose their unwanted escorts, his brother would simply have to absorb the cost till Randolph could apologize properly later, after he cleared his name in those murders Mr. Hilden slandered his name with.

After leaving a considerable tip, Randolph left for the men's room and entered a stall. After inverting pants, jacket, removing goatee and working in place a different-colored rug on his head, he waited for Jill's distraction. When a loud explosion sounded in the ventilation vents, followed by alarms, Randolph walked out, took a hold of Jill's arm, and hurried out like all the other panicked diners.

An hour later, while they changed clothes in a department store, Randolph had to ask, "And how did you manage that?"

"I'm sure you haven't forgotten I'm trained in demolition. How hard do you think it is to make a bomb out of house hold items?"

"Okay, I'll grant you that, but I know we hadn't ordered anything which would cause that explosion."

Jill smiled and leaned into his ear to whisper, "A man's playground is not exclusively for men's toys." She kissed his cheek and pushed away to find Randolph a bit startled with that admission. She patted his face in affection and added, "Not everything fits nicely in a woman's purse." Jill became serious after this, and while Randolph looked over the latest video-cams for sale, she asked, "So who were those men?"

"Probably Senator Sterling's. It would've served him well to have kept tabs on us, in-case turning us over was more advantageous then running us in the field."

"And we trust him why?"

"I never said I trusted him. I said we can work with each other," Randolph corrected, checking out a video-cam, and considered what it would take to adjust the resolution and zoom for the first step in taking down Mr. Hilden.

Chapter Nineteen

Two months later, after careful research into an apartment's security system and available hard lines, Randolph set up four work stations, one counter measures station and two remotes, unplugged for diagnostic program checking, plus inexpensive amenities for the two of them while living in the apartment. Although this was not very comfortable for Randolph, Jill made a good point for not following his normal route of setting up shop, and it galled him to know she was right. Mr. Hilden knew Randolph's MO, thus he was sure to have Mr. Stanton and company checking out warehouses throughout the city. Randolph also had to admit lying low, allowing Jill to do his errands, was also advisable so as not to come into contact with Mr. Hilden's roaming people, who Randolph couldn't possibly know were working for him. Besides, Randolph told himself, Jill's face is still not associated with the killing of that sheriff; it will be my face paramount in all law officers' posters and not hers.

When it came time to consider his specialty equipment, Randolph held a short, heated argument with himself. The smells of constructing, and the oddity of having such equipment arrive at an apartment building in the west side area of Harcuss—a college district in the city of Barbella, twenty miles from Willing—just screamed something wasn't kosher. Randolph had to leave this up to Jill to construct, from the plans he gave her as soon as he had her enrolled, at a small workshop the local college rented.

Dressed in tight-fitting, Tom boy-styled clothes of yellow and green, sporting no less than twelve bracelets on each arm and hoop ear rings, Jill's softer side gave Randolph a playful embrace and a farewell kiss before bouncing out the door. She was absolutely bubbling over with pride that Randolph entrusted her to carry out this part of his plan; not that it mattered, he had no other choice. The equipment he needed would have to be custom made for the job, and Randolph never knew what was required till he'd done his homework. So while she built some basic tools he used in any job, Randolph surfed the hard line net, matching businesses to the county grid to understand who was where and what possible run-ins he might have on the electronic highway. Even though he had circumvented countless counter measures before, new programs were designed and implemented every day, and unless he attended to them, one could infiltrate Randolph's own system. *Which does happen, as I'm not infallible,* he reminded himself. In fact, Jill returned later that day to find Randolph in a very black mood, staring down on a box full of hard drives with a worm on each he couldn't trace down.

"Love, what's the matter?" Jill asked, concerned, laying her burden down and wrapping her arms around his neck.

"We've a smart-alack kid in that college who I may have to deal with," Randolph said in irritation. Jill glanced at the box of hard drives as Randolph elaborated. "As soon as I hit the node near the college, a program hit my inquiry and traced me back to my fire wall, where it's sitting, and no matter what program I've designed to counter it, it leeches on to the new drive and embeds itself, and I've yet to discover how."

Jill let go and picked up one of the drives. "Is it on this one?"

"It's on all of them!" Randolph exclaimed in disgust.

"What does it do?"

"At present, I don't know. Like normal when I hit an unknown, I pull it out and run programs to dissect it. After that, I can learn its purpose, but as soon as I hook it up to a clean drive, it invades the programming so I've no way of activating it."

The Paranoid Thief

"Well, how's about I make an inquiry or two at school? Perhaps I can find out what it does. You know they have an excellent computer theory class," she reminded him.

If he'd been located in a warehouse, Randolph would have simply ordered boxes of drives and worked the problem out, but being forced to down size in all avenues by his choice in work environment, eyebrows would be lifted if he tried that here. So mulling over the advantages and disadvantages, Randolph reluctantly agreed, only he couldn't have her take any of his drives; they had information on them he'd not like anybody to discover. So instead Randolph sent Jill out for a new laptop from the local store then took two days setting it up like any college kid's drive before introducing it to the worm.

Jill gave Randolph a peck on the cheek after breakfast, then took her arm load of books and new laptop with her as Randolph worked on another possible theory on the worm's programming. Hypothesizing the very flow of electricity as its catalyst, he took a palm computer with a lower voltage, reduced its usage even further so the CPU acted like a vacuum tube compared to today's technology, then he hooked up the leads to his screen and connected it to an infested drive. What he saw rolling across the screen floored him. It wasn't a program at all, but rather an algorithm which hadn't been used in a hundred years! For a time, Randolph watched the peaks and valleys roll along, hitting every circuit, resister, and diode, anyplace the current flowed. To this revelation, Randolph stood and walked away to stare off into space, so he could puzzle over how to purge something embedded in the very thing that gives society life. *This is far beyond me,* he thought to himself as he put his hands a top his head. *It's the ultimate in security measures, and not built by some smart-alack kid, either. This is far too sophisticated for some college kid. No this is a corporate-financed worm, one designed to do...what?*

Randolph took out a beer and settled on the couch, and nursed the drink, thinking.

That's where Jill found him some hours later, when she triumphantly walked in declaring, "John, love, I've got it!" She displayed a chip before his up-turned face with the biggest smile on her lips. "I was told all I need do is insert this chip into my computer and the worm will be neutralized."

Not liking the note in that, Randolph still gave Jill a smile when she handed him the chip.

After a quick examination, Randolph plugged the chip in a new clean drive and checked the programming out, and had to sit back in wonder at its genius. Jill's arms encircled his neck, before she kissed his cheek. "Did I do good?"

Still looking at the registration code, asking for identification of the user, Randolph asked her, "Uh, when you asked about the problem, did they happen to look at you oddly?"

"Now that you mention it, I did get some raised eyebrows. Whys that important?"

Randolph disengaged her arms. "Jill, please don't take this personal, but I need to speak to your other half. Now." Her eyes turned sad, then they dilated and her posture changed slightly, letting Randolph know when she changed places.

"What's up, sweetie?" Jill asked, her eyes sweeping the room.

"Jill, I need you to search your memories—did anyone follow you?" Randolph asked urgently.

Upon hearing his tone, Jill stood straighter, folded her arms, and looked inward. After a bit she looked squarely at him. "I can't be sure, but they may have."

"That's it then. We've been nailed!" He jumped up, gathered the drives and shoved them into the oven, setting the dial to high. Jill asked no questions but headed briskly into the bedroom, gathering up clothes for the pair of them as Randolph activated a special chip in each computer that would melt them down into useless sludge. He then snatched up the few tools he'd been able to make, and wondered how long the pair of them had till the local police arrived. Not having had the time to acquire a proper DNA scrambler, Randolph pulled out a box of insect fumigator canisters and headed for the bathroom, tossing a mask to Jill in passing before he pulled the tabs. After dropping one in the bathroom, he open all drawers and cabinets and moved to the next room. In this manner, business like, the pair of them moved with practiced efficiency. After Randolph set off the last canister, he crawled into the kitchen cabinets after Jill, and down the escape hole he'd cut out into the lower apartment he'd rented under another name. Closing up the hole, Randolph followed Jill out the door and moved swiftly down the hall to the elevators. As Jill pushed for the elevator, Randolph gathered their masks and ditched them in a carry bag she held, before he combed his hair back, trying to look publicly presentable as they watched the elevator pass them by going up.

While they awaited the elevator to come down, the unmistakable sound of multiple feet moved swiftly down the hall overhead. Randolph grimaced, hating his paranoia when it was right. But for the moment he gave thanks and followed Jill on the elevator when it opened on their floor.

Randolph pushed the ground button. "They'll have the lobby covered, as well as the stairs and service door."

"Don't forget the garage," Jill added.

"That's why you're driving." Randolph sighed as she fished out the keys and he took up the luggage. Even though Randolph knew Jill's car had been tagged, it made little difference in their choice, for both of their DNA could be retrieved from the car's interior. By necessity that made the car their next priority to scramble.

Randolph hit the passenger door as Jill piled in.

"Any preference on our heading?"

"Some place underground with lots of exits so I can trash the car," Randolph replied, buckling up.

"Hmm, monorail station should do." She activated the lifters before setting them in motion.

"And, Jill," Randolph warned as she pick up speed, "try not to kill anybody, they're just doing their jobs."

"Okay, sweetie…" Jill smiled over at him before her face hardened.

Randolph knew that look. He grabbed the door handle when they neared the exit. Jill gunned the motor and crashed through the blockade, rammed a car on the street jarringly before she changed gears and hit the boosters. Pushed back into the seat, Randolph felt a momentary tingle in his feet from the fast-acting officer who got off an electrical pulse shot, meant to fry the motor. Fortunately it was a glancing blow.

Jill called out, "Hold on!" before turning sharply, slamming into another car to keep them from rolling over because of their momentum.

Shaken by the suddenness, she hit one more car before righting theirs and punched up the map of the city. Belatedly knowing what she sought, Randolph took over so she could keep hands and eyes on the street. With blaring sirens notifying them of oncoming police cars, Randolph cussed under his breath and dug out a police scanner from under the seat.

"You really aren't used to this kind of business," she observed, as he worked the controls to pick up the signals of the tracking cars.

The Paranoid Thief

Not sparing Jill a glare, Randolph answered, "Being around you, I'm taking a crash course."

"Speaking of crashes, sweetie, hold on!" Jill made another hard turn, and purposely slammed into some parked cars to aid in making another tight corner going the wrong way down a one-way street. With a glance of Jill's face as she dodged the oncoming traffic, Randolph could swear she was really enjoying this. As coded calls came over the scanner, Jill picked up, as he did, the interception street the police were shooting for to shut them down.

"Randolph," Jill said seriously, "as they only have my face on video, why don't you jump out and I'll lead them a merry chase?"

"No dice. If you're caught, they'll have your picture match up in minutes. Then knowing who you are they'll bury you so far under in maximum security, I wouldn't be able to get a remote controlled ant in the building to see you."

"They have things like that?" Jill asked, shifting into a higher gear.

"I'm being facetious," Randolph told her. Jill let a smile touch her lips as they heard the next junction was being blockaded. "If you avoid this one, they'll know we have a scanner," Randolph warned.

"I'm quite aware of that, sweetie, but you told me not to kill anyone."

"And that still holds."

"Then I've no choice," she said. "You know, the high school I attended had a very nice coffee shop across the street. I'll see you there."

She turned a corner so fast Randolph had no time to prepare. Once the car straightened out, Jill stomped down on the brakes and surprised Randolph with a right cross, hard enough to cause stars to dance about his eyes. While his world remained in a daze, Jill disengaged his buckle and opened the passenger door without completely stopping. Shoved out, Randolph hit the pavement with enough sense to roll and heard Jill call out as she drove away, "I love you!"

Shaken after his tumble, Randolph gained his feet and stepped off the street moments before two squad cars, sirens blaring, sped by. To clear his mind, Randolph leaned on the building towering over him and shook out the remaining stars. Once able to think, he cussed under his breath at Jill's idiocy, adjusted his clothes, and set off at a causal walk in the opposite direction.

The fact he never saw that coming had him mumbling; the fact she did it so deftly made him truly consider their differences. Jill was trained for uncontrolled action in combat situations of life and death where he was but a liability. By tossing him out on his ear, she knew she'd lead the chase after her so he could escape in his own way while she could do the same in hers. Even so, her last words didn't make his knowledge any easier, nor did it help to know she was sacrificing herself for him.

Randolph took a deep breath and sighed with guilt, knowing how he'd been trying to handle their relationship when Jill had been straight up with him all along. And of course this doubled his regret as he stuffed his hands into pockets and joined the street crowd, heading for the nearest monorail station, trying to hold back his deteriorating emotions.

A day after Jill left him on the street, Randolph located The School House Coffee Cup, across the street from her old high school, with but a simple search program any six-year-old could use. For the first few weeks after traveling to Fresno, located in what was the middle of old California before it had been gutted by large corporations, Randolph had shown up in the teenager-riddled coffee shop, dressed in a low-level business suit for the area, and quietly sat in a street-side table reading a hard copy of the local news while he sipped on a medium-sized decaf cappuccino.

Thus far the local paper, which Randolph deftly used as a shield against video cameras and direct eye contact with the high-spirited kids, had revealed no outcome to Jill's mad dash down a one-way street in Harcuss. And although the news videos were of the same useless information regarding her flight, Randolph wondered how much longer he could give Jill before moving on. Although no videos of her capture had appeared as yet, lack of news in no way proved she'd escaped. It was quite possible the FBFC was withholding such information in the hopes she could be broken and learn of his whereabouts. Though Randolph hated such thoughts, he had to face the hard truth; given time, drugs will break the hardest of men, which meant he'd been coming to the coffee shop for far too long. With a heavy heart, Randolph finished off his cooling drink and set the cup down with a sigh. *It's best I moved on,* he firmly told himself. *For Jill's sake, I'll forget about Mr. Hilden for the time being and contact the senator for a target he'd like information on so he'll proceed on Jill's military case.*

Randolph folded the paper as he stood, kept his face turned down and away from the video cameras as he paid for lunch in hard credits and strolled out of the quaint little place for the last time. Breathing in the cold air, Randolph shrugged his jacket tighter about his shoulders to ward off the chill and hopefully stave off his emotions, which were threatening to override his good judgment. Unable to stop himself, Randolph paused at the entrance of the shop, whispered a gentle, "Farewell Jill," then stepped out into the moving crowd and headed for his apartment.

With a feeling of remorse, as if he left apart of himself in the coffee shop, Randolph walked the block and a half battling an inner argument when he was startled by an arm sliding around his own and Jill's lovely voice playing patty cake with his heart.

"Hello, sweetie, I nearly missed you with that beard and shades."

Randolph seized his startled emotions, and settled instead for an un-noteworthy turn of his head to plant a kiss to her forehead, before he whispered, with a tremor in his voice, "And I've really missed you too."

"Is that for a fact?" Jill smiled up at him as her eye shifted.

"Yes, Jill, I'm afraid you have me hooked," he assured her with moisture blurring his eyes.

Jill hugged his arm even tighter as they walked like any other couple in love and confessed after they stepped into an elevator, "I've waited a very long time to hear someone say that to me. Even so, can you truly say the words instead of hinting around them?"

"As I've never said the L-word to anyone other than my mother, it might take me some time." Randolph smiled, leading her off the elevator and down the hall in his apartment building. Jill lowered her face and became quiet as he opened the door. With a motion for her to precede him, Randolph made sure the door was closed and locked before he spun her around and pulled her into his arms, allowing her to see the passion blazing within his eyes before he confessed to her and to himself, "I love you, Jill, both of you!" Then took her lips hungrily.

Chapter Twenty

What they did to each other for the next two hours would never make any record books, but Randolph did believe their love making was somehow that much more enriching, now that he'd admitted openly how he felt about her. *The both of them,* he amended.

Reluctantly Randolph surfaced for air and caught his breath when he heard her stomach complain of emptiness. With a smile at Jill's girlish giggle, Randolph ordered a simple pizza for delivery and entangled himself in her arms a few more minutes before he pulled out to install himself in a cumbersome robe in forced readiness for the door bell to ring.

Once settled at the kitchen table in separate chairs, enjoying the cheese pizza while they sipped elegant wine meant for special occasions, Jill's harder self filled Randolph in on her adventures between bites and sips, finishing with, "And as far as I know, I was able to clear the city without killing anybody."

"I'm very proud of you, Jill." Randolph smiled happily.

"Please, Randolph, could you use the word love in place of my name now and again? It means so much to hear someone finally say it and mean it. That is, if you're feelings apply to me as well."

Randolph gave her a light smile. "I'll do my best, and yes, love, I've fallen for you both."

Randolph motioned Jill to follow him to the couch with glass in hand and settled her on his lap. Without the need of any prodding, Jill did as motioned but once settled on his lap, she asked, "I'm far to keyed up in emotions to settle down as yet, so why don't you clue me in on what I did wrong?"

Embracing Jill, knowing she was wondering in how she gave the two of them away, Randolph shifted her weight a bit more comfortably on his lap and explained. "You did nothing wrong at all—that trap was set for me, but not me personally." When Jill looked in his eyes with puzzlement, Randolph continued, "What they were doing is probably a prelude to a new system designed to catch system hackers. I imagine they were testing it at the school, using the kids in the computer course to ferret out bugs in the programming. You see, there really wasn't anything wrong with the drives, the worm I ran across only showed up because I was hacking, and as all hackers do when confronted with a worm, I tried to work around it, and in doing so, I found the built-in signature leading me to believe someone at the college designed it. Thus when your other self showed up asking about it, they couldn't believe they caught someone."

"You mean someone like her," she said with a snort.

"Well, yeah, but regardless, they fed you the pre-discussed story, I'm assuming, and followed you back to the apartment, whereby they called the police."

"Okay, I'll buy that, but how did you know it was a trap?"

"I didn't. I was just being paranoid," Randolph confessed.

Jill leaned away from Randolph and looked him in the eyes for a moment before taking a sip of wine and nuzzling his neck and whispering softly, "My lover, the paranoid thief." Jill remained close for a few seconds before she pulled away and told him in a demanding voice, "You are going to shave that thing off before coming to bed tonight."

Randolph rubbed the weeks' worth of growth and wondered how long it took to get used to the itching before he reasonably agreed he would follow her request.

The Paranoid Thief

The next morning while enjoying a spicy omelet with onions, bell peppers, tomatoes and bits of sausage, Jill smacked her lips in delight and asked, "So what's our next move on this Hilden character?"

With a motion of his hand to ask Jill if she wished any more grapefruit juice in her glass, Randolph admitted, "None. We scrub the task and check in on the senator's list of targets."

"Now, sweetie, I seem to recall you saying he was our retirement fund," Jill reminded Randolph mildly, pointing her fork at him before dipping into the hash browns. "Besides, he owes you."

"True, but the area is far too hot right now."

"Now, now, a hot LZ only quickens the blood flow, making one's eye sight sharp and the mind focused, so I'll ask again, what's our next move?"

Randolph looked at his lover over his own partially-eaten breakfast and shook his head before he added fresh ground pepper to his hash browns. When he didn't agree in any physical signs, Jill added, "What's the first rule in any undertaking?"

"Jill, the subject is closed. They have a description of you and a hot sheet for me. Mr. Hilden's not stupid; you don't get to where he's at being so. He knows I risked a lot to get you out and seeing your description on the watch sheets, he'll dig further and see my MO in the way I destroyed all the DNA with a bolt hole waiting in case of emergencies."

"Oh come off it, Randolph, you're not the only hacker who takes precautions."

"Maybe not, but I'll lay you odds I'm the only one who has a very competent and beautiful ex-military partner backing him up."

Jill cocked her head at Randolph with a light smile touching her lips to his endearment before she told him, "I thank you for that praise, but my mind is made up. As you have done so much for me, how can I not help you take down the one man who's screwed you royally?"

"I didn't say I wouldn't take him down," Randolph backtracked in his statement after he swallowed the last of his omelet, "I just said the area's too hot to attempt at this time."

"And trying to live a half-normal life together will be pretty impossible with that contract out on our heads, so no, Randolph, we either go in your way, or I'll take him out my way, because I'm not about to let him live while we worry when we'll be assassinated."

Randolph put his fork down and rubbed his clean shaven face in irritation while staring at her. In answer to Randolph's look, Jill put her own fork down, leaned away from the table and folded her arms.

"I mean it, Randolph, I'll kill him, his lawyer, his staff and begin working down the list in the city corporation till someone takes us off that hit list."

Randolph wiped his face, having lost his appetite for the last of the meal.

Jill, on the other hand, swallowed the last of her juice before she pushed away from the table and in getting up, declared, "I'll give you today to decide. In the meantime, I've someplace I wish to visit before we leave town."

"Where are you off to?"

"At present, that's none of your business," Jill threw over her shoulder.

"You'll put your family at risk if you contact them."

Jill turned and glared at Randolph before heading for the bedroom to get dressed.

"I mean it, Jill," he called after her, "you'll only bring them grief." But then Randolph got to thinking about family and realized Jill was ultimately right. Whoever picked up their contract would only look so

The Paranoid Thief

long before targeting both their families in order to draw them out into the open. Randolph sighed with disgust and put his face in his hands and his elbow on the table, feeling trapped between two vicious killers who held no values on life as he did save for one difference—Jill's value of right and wrong was far preferable over Mr. Hilden's. So hearing the door close some moments later, Randolph remained at the table considering the concept of what needed to be done. Mr. Hilden now knew he'd work out of an apartment building as well as warehouses, so what other avenues did that leave him in gaining the intelligence to Hilden's vast holdings?

For no small amount of time, Randolph drummed his fingers on the table top and stared at Jill's vacant seat before an idea began forming. Abandoning the cold meal without cleaning up, Randolph sat on the couch, pulled out his palm computer, and began noninvasive inquiries into city maintenance, layouts and underground maps and piping. It wasn't until the smell of chicken chow mein drew Randolph's appetite out later that evening when he noticed Jill quietly watching him on the couch next to him. With a smile to her offer of Chinese takeout, Randolph realized Jill had started to learn his way of tuning out the world when he was deep at work in his world of electronic information. Gratefully accepting a carton, Randolph also took up the chopsticks she wasn't using and opened a package of soy sauce.

"First off, I don't like being pushed into anything, understand?" Randolph said plainly before taking a bite.

"Yes, love," Jill answered over her sweet and sour pork.

"And second, don't let this go to your head, but you're right. Mr. Hilden has to go down and not because of your threat but rather for the welfare of our families."

"I wondered when you'd see that," Jill said over a sip of cold beer, tilting the bottle his way in offering.

"All right," Randolph said, waving the offer off. Then softening his voice he asked, "So tell me, how is your family doing?"

"As far as I could see with my binoculars, they're doing well, I just—I just wish I could have talked with them, let them know why I did what I did."

Randolph looked on her sad face and reached out and took her hand. "They will. I'll make certain the senator shames the military by condoning your actions for doing what should have been done."

Jill gave Randolph a half smile before she finished off her meal and started in on cleaning up the kitchen.

A couple of weeks later, Randolph wiped sweat off his brow from the overpowering heat of the city's tunnels, even in the dead of winter, and rubbed his hands clean on a rag before he activated his program. With luck, by noon tomorrow he'd have the blue prints of Mr. Hilden's home and he'd be able to match them up with the videos Jill had taken for him yesterday. Today, however, as Randolph gathered intel on the electric highway, Jill was out doing the same on the people surrounding Mr. Hilden, as it would help to know who was guarding him and how efficient they were at their jobs.

Randolph shifted his weight trying to find a more comfortable position on the five gallon oil can he was using as a seat, still musing over Jill's cavalier manner of having to live in the sewers, as they were out of credits. *Completely taped city,* he'd explained, hell—they couldn't even afford a tooth brush unless he did some pick-pocking. And that bit of exposure was annexed, being Mr. Hilden had upped the ante by plastering posters of Randolph's mug all over the city with a sizable amount to entice even the mildest of citizens to cash him in

The Paranoid Thief

if he were spotted. When his bottom agreed to his new position, Randolph reflected over Jill's light comment, "War is hell," before he settled back into the piping and conduits. After lacing his fingers behind his head, he eyed the antiquated computer and monitor screen Jill had acquired out of a dumpster and waited patiently for its CPU to churn out his program. This single-tasking was irritating but necessary, as he would over-tax the memory banks with Jill's videos that should render the normal devices installed in walls and roofs to discourage the average everyday thief. Once Randolph identified these, he could examine the videos frame by frame for the security systems in place for the real professionals. Once he labeled these, he'd look even harder for the new ones now installed simply just for him. *Paranoid, me? You betcha!*

While Randolph was relaxing in the oppressing heat, Jill tromped into view and plopped down on her can, flipping a chip his way. "Sorry, boss, we hit a snag."

"Oh?" Randolph chimed in as requested.

"I had this rather rude but well-dressed guy and his cronies come up to me on the street and tell me in no uncertain terms was I never to approach Hilden's property's again." Jill looked rather put off by the incident, but was trying to hide it by calmly examining her finger nails.

"Let's see, gray-eyed and built like a wall?"

"A bit sexy looking, but yeah, that's him," Jill admitted.

"That'll be Mr. Stanton, Mr. Hilden's right-hand muscle and dirty job enforcer."

Jill took out a plastic nail file and retorted, "A bit of a coward isn't he?"

"How so?"

"Needing all those guys to get up the gumption to tell little old me off," she replied, adjusting the single light fixture in the cubby hole to better see her fingers.

"It may appear that way to you, but remember, Mr. Hilden's no fool, he'd have given Mr. Stanton your jacket file and knowing who he's up against, I'd imagine he'd take all precautions in addressing any woman of your build."

Jill eyed Randolph over the working file. "If I'd wanted him dead, no amount of back up would have saved him."

"And that flows two ways—by not killing you, he's telling me to give it my best shot."

"I thought you said he didn't recognize me?"

"That wouldn't stop him from killing a perfectly innocent stranger if it would achieve a goal. After all, he did kill an innocent woman in the park simply to get me framed for her murder while they framed me for blowing up the Henderson's home."

This caught Jill's attention and she glared off into the dark tunnel. "I should have killed him, and the next time I see him I'll correct that error."

"Love," Randolph said, trying to bring her back, a bit shaken from the venom in her voice, "I'd rather you didn't just yet. Mr. Stanton may be a cold-blooded killer, but he's a known commodity in my equation in taking down Mr. Hilden. Taking him out would replace him with someone I don't know, which would make us stay in these luxury conditions far longer then I wish to."

Jill turned her cold eyes on him, causing a shiver to run down his back even in this heat, before she softened and made a face to his comment, settling back to do her nails.

"By the way," he asked in an afterthought, "did he touch you in anyway?"

The Paranoid Thief

"You don't see my hair messed up, do you?" Jill answered, annoyed.

"No, but I had to ask in case he put a homing beacon on you."

Jill gave him such a glare, Randolph held up his hands in apology. Jill snorted her acceptance, and pulled out a soda from the portable cooler he'd purloined from the public works truck in a supply yard and tapped the screen on the computer, bringing his attention back to his side of the job. Randolph gave Jill a half smile, then plugged in the new chip and set about studying the new information she'd gathered.

For another week, Randolph sorted out details and designed tools they'd need to infiltrate Mr. Hilden's fortress when Randolph came across a certain restaurant owner and company being indicted for tax evasion and other lesser charges. Quickly recognizing this as a simple countermeasure instigated by Mr. Hilden to color Randolph's thoughts, Randolph had to admit it still made him mad as hell. Even so, hating the trouble this would cause and the risks involved, Randolph felt he owed his brother his help.

He was unhooking the computer when Jill stirred from her sleeping pallet and inquired, "Honey, what's up?"

"I think it's time we had a decently-cooked meal. So why don't you pack up and we'll head for the public showers to clean up for a flight out to the frozen lakes."

"Frozen lakes? Why do we need to see the senator?"

"We don't, but I've business there I must see to before we begin the raid on Mr. Hilden's residence."

"John, love, I thought we were flat broke?"

"We are, but my brother's not, at least not yet."

Jill sat up straighter and her voice lowered into a commanding tone. "Randolph, what the hell's going on?"

"I've business in the frozen lakes, that's all you need to know," he snapped, putting the computer in a protective carry bag.

Jill stood and without provocation slammed Randolph against the wall, holding him in place by his shirt and throat while she placed a knee very close to his groin. "Answer my question. We're far too close to simply drop things and go running off, so what's happened?"

"Jill, I can't talk this way," Randolph forced through his teeth, dropping the bag to take up her arm, trying to push it away.

"You can, however, breathe, a condition I can alter if you don't answer me. It's your brother isn't it? Someone's done something to hurt him and like a good big brother, you're running to the rescue."

Randolph eyed her, wondering how she connected those dots even as a smirk touched her lips and she let go, stepping back, folding her arms so he had room to move while he rubbed his neck. "Randolph, it wasn't that hard to figure out. You seemed to already know your way around that town, including the layout of that fancy restaurant. So tell me, what's happened?"

"I could just happen to have had a job there," he grumbled.

"That statement would've held water if you hadn't mentioned your brother paying our fare. In all the time I've known you, you haven't trusted anyone but yourself and that still holds, even now after admitting your love for me," she finished, sounding hurt with that last part.

Randolph straightened out his shirt. "Okay, fine, you're right. It is my brother. The bastard's done some manipulation and probably some payoffs to get my brother in trouble. As he's an innocent in all this, I'm going to see him and straighten out the people who think Mr. Hilden is far more of a threat then I am."

The Paranoid Thief

"Uh-huh, just as I thought. Well, go ahead then"—she waved a hand at him—"play right into his hands, and while you're at it, I'll take out Hilden and company."

"Jill, no!"

"Jill, yes..." she snarled back. "This Hilden character will have the place crawling with paid assassins knowing you couldn't help but show up. So go ahead, make it that much easier for him to kill you, leaving me alone, a widow and husband-less mother."

"But don't you un-der...uh, what did you say?"

"Nothing of any consequence to you. Now be off with you, I've got plans of my own to make." She turned her back on him.

"Jill? Honey?" Randolph asked, swallowing, stepping up and placing his hands on her shoulders, gently turning her around. "Are you...are you pregnant?" Randolph looked down into her eyes.

"And what of it?" Jill demanded. "What do you care? You've got your brother to bail out, so go on and leave me in peace."

Floored by the unexpected news, Randolph stammered, "But how...uh I mean, when? Uh, how far along?"

"For that answer you'll have to ask my other self. Now why don't you quite pretending you care and—"

Randolph didn't let her get any further as he pulled her in for a tight embrace, totally at odds with himself. The fact Jill was pregnant with his child had a part of him jumping up and down with joy, while another screamed great obscenities at the timing as a third part crawled into a corner, balling up into a tight ball of scared uncertainty. *Gad, how does one handle so many emotions at once?* She resisted for a moment before melting into his arms, holding on so tightly her strength was causing him trouble in breathing.

"Oh, Randolph, I was so scared you'd resent me for this, I—I had no idea how to tell you."

Randolph swallowed, nuzzling her hair then tried to fish out his emotions so he wouldn't say the wrong thing. "When did you know? How far along are you?"

Her tears wet his shirt and her body shook; Jill was quietly sobbing in his embrace before she admitted, "I don't know how far along I am, she won't tell me? Hell, in all the time we've known each other, she's never withheld such important news from me." Still shaking in his arms, Jill pleaded, "Please don't leave me. I never meant this to happen. I've been taking all the precautions necessary to prevent this. But my body is not solely mine, how am I to prevent something she desperately wants?"

"Shhh, it's all right love, neither of you have done anything wrong. Shh now, there's no need for this, I'll not leave you. Now please assure her she's done nothing wrong and find out how far along you are."

Randolph felt the change in Jill's grip, as her softer side surfaced, and he was glad of it as he had been about to ask her to loosen up her hold shortly—something in her state he didn't think she would take very well.

"You're—you're truly not mad at me?" Jill questioned, slacking her arms so she could look up into his eyes.

"Now, I didn't say that," Randolph said gently, so she wouldn't withdraw. "I am mad, but only on the timing. Now tell me, how far along are you?"

"I'm not getting an abortion," she stated with strength, "and I'll not let her get one either," she assured Randolph, jutting out her chin.

"Now who said anything about an abortion? You know perfectly well my stance on a human life."

"You—you mean it? I can have my baby?"

Randolph nodded.

The Paranoid Thief

She bit her lip, not quite trusting him. "Three, maybe four weeks."

Randolph nodded with a smile, and kissed her forehead before he asked, "Thank you, love, now, may I talk to Jill?" Her eyes filled with tears before she turned away and leaned into him, crying anew. "Honestly, love, I have no intentions of hurting our child, although your timing alters my time table, I also look forward to holding our child." He felt her nod, knowing she still didn't trust him at his word yet, then the harder Jill surfaced and she pulled away to hug herself.

"If we're to get the abortion, we better do it now while she's in a state of sorrow," Jill said, trying to calm her voice.

"Love, I meant what I said, I couldn't conceive of hurting our child. But what I need you to know is that you're out of the assault. I'll not risk you getting hurt, jeopardizing the life of our child."

Jill turned around, a fierceness hardening her face as she told him, "If you think for one damn minute I'm going to let you do this alone because of my stupidity, you've another thing coming. I'll do the abortion myself if I have to, for there's no-way no-how are you taking on this asshole by yourself."

"Jill—"

"Don't you 'no, Jill dear' me! We're a team, and as such we'll take this chance for a wonderful life together, or I'll follow you in when you leave and there's no way you can stop me." When she saw him taken aback by the venom in her voice, she waved at the computer. "Now set up that thing and I'll see about obtaining the parts on your list you made last night."

Jill slipped on her shoes, but before he could argue further, she held up a finger, pointed at the computer and promised, "If we want another child later, I'd suggest you get back to work."

To this direct implication of harm to his two boys, Randolph swallowed, knowing Jill didn't threaten to hear herself talking. So backing away from her, he pulled out the computer as Jill set off down the tunnel.

Chapter Twenty-One

Once Jill was out of sight, Randolph had to admit she was right; he was acting the fool in thinking to run off in aid of his brother. If he truly wished to help him out of his jam, he needed to finish this feud with Mr. Hilden once and for all. *After that,* he promised himself, *I intend to make it perfectly clear to everybody messing with my brother is going to cost them everything they have!* His only drawback was Jill's condition, regardless of Mr. Hilden's attempt to push him into acting sooner then he'd wished; Jill being pregnant accomplished this goal in a way Mr. Hilden could never know. So setting up the computer, Randolph set to the task with a will far greater then he held before, for he wasn't only fighting for his life, he was fighting for his wife and child, and that fact he felt, made him that much more dangerous.

Only a few days later, they sat on a park bench under a street light Jill had disabled yesterday, holding each other like a couple taking advantage of the semi-privacy the darkness granted. Randolph looked though spectrum sensitive goggles he'd also purloined from the city truck, and checked wall and front structure to Mr. Hilden's manor. He adjusted the dials, changing the sensitivity of the filaments, and noted the placement of security devices he already knew about.

"How's it look so far, love?" Jill whispered into his ear, her cheek nuzzling his in affection.

"Like I own the place," Randolph answered, flipping the channels slowly, taking note of the electrical currents and the direction they flowed.

"So are we still a go?"

"Hang on, I'm still looking." Lowering the goggles to reset for audio, Randolph took another look at the wine-o sitting next to the city dumpster and the couple still talking at the corner, ignoring the fact the dog on the leash had already done its business some time ago. "He's got two men and a woman patrolling the street outside the walls," Randolph mumbled into her hair, enjoying the fresh scent of the light perfume she was wearing.

"So tell me something I don't know," she commented, shifting to kiss his ear.

"Besides the fact you're distracting me?" Randolph admitted with a smile, looking back through the goggles and finding what he'd hoped Mr. Hilden would have disregarded as a "pain in the butt system." Sighing, Randolph grumbled, "He has a sound array up."

"Never heard of it," Jill whispered, shifting to hide the fact Randolph was putting the goggles away.

"No reason you should have. It's a sloppy system. I ran into one a few years back. The salesman I talked to claimed it was a military development, annexed from active service because it was too sensitive, which made it that much more marketable to the public. But in truth, the active ears overload the CPU with so many incoming sounds to identify it pretty much classifies anything as a threat and activates the alarm."

"So why would anyone buy it?" Jill asked, kissing his lips.

"Because with the sound array he can legally kill a stranger and blame the manufacturer for the wrongful death, at which time the manufacturer blames the military for releasing a known dysfunctional product, whereby the city has no choice but to drop the case because the government won't allow lawsuits on the R and D department that reduce its funding for more developments of weaponry."

"Boy, that's a mouthful. And you know this how?"

The Paranoid Thief

Kissing her lips, rubbing a hand up and down her back for show and pleasure, Randolph took note she was wearing an athletic bra and answered her question, "Because I do my homework—and out of curiosity, why aren't you wearing a more supportive bra under your shirt?"

Jill smiled, kissed Randolph passionately then said, "Old habits; the military teaches women to wear easy-moving bras so as not to restrict any movements, and as I haven't as yet regained any real size, I felt it best." Jill slid his hand up under her shirt to caress her breast. "Besides, I like the freedom it affords me, even if they're a bit sensitive."

"Jill, love, if you keep this up, we'll have to postpone our attempt till tomorrow night."

She met his lips again, and whispered, "Spoil sport."

Randolph reluctantly let go of her breast so they both could straighten out shirts and jackets as a patrol car, like clockwork, started down the street. After the city cop rolled past, Randolph collected their bag of goodies, which had far more goodies in it then he'd have liked.

But Jill's argument from earlier had a certain ring of truth. *Most people would call the police. Somehow I doubt Hilden to trust the police in holding you a fourth time, so it's either these, or be carried out in body bags.*

Remembering these to be four hand grenades, a bag of mini mines, two laser pistols, two extra power packs and six strips of plastic explosives, Randolph wondered over her devilish smile, *Where in hell did you get all this equipment?*

After some thought, Randolph resigned to the fact she was right; however, he had to inject his objections. *You're not going to use those unless it's absolutely necessary, right?*

Whereby Jill granted him one of her ambiguous statements, *Define necessary.*

Randolph looked skyward, mentally asking for forgiveness for what might happen.

Jill asked, "Okay, so how do we bypass this sound array?"

"Pay no attention to it. Just keep watch for the relief group. We've about ten minutes before they show," he instructed as they both hurried over to the gate.

Randolph knelt, and pulled out his laser pen to cut a circle in the plastic-steel door. After removing the piece, he activated the light to see the inner workings. Next went on clips and wire to circumvent the alarm before he glued the cut-out piece back in place, taking all told three minutes. *Not a great record for by passing a gate alarm.* But he was in no hurry as yet. Once he turned on the infrared goggles, Randolph eased the door open enough to see the three lines of red lights, knowing only the top and bottom ones were important. With precise angled mirrors, he inched them in place and signaled Jill to step through to take them up so he could slip in. After closing the gate, Randolph pocketed the mirrors for later use as Jill joined him in his crouch to view Mr. Hilden's front yard, which would've been rather hard without the night vision goggles she slipped on.

"Well, we're in the front gate, now what?" Jill whispered in his ear.

"Hold still while I check." Randolph reapplied the spectrum goggles. Although they had good intel on the outside alarms and some of the inside ones from surveillance and recent contractor blueprints, it was still good to run the dials and see what they might have missed. And sure enough there they were—electrical wires running under foot in a zigzag pattern. "Pressure plates," Randolph whispered, motioning

The Paranoid Thief

her to follow as he moved along the inside fence to the side of the house.

"Why aren't there any next to the wall?" Jill inquired.

"Good question," Randolph remarked with no clue, knowing he hadn't missed anything along the wall.

"And why hasn't the sound array gone off?"

"It has, the moment they turned it on this evening, so now they have a bored technician manually logging in every sound it's picking up, and as it can hear even an ant's fart, it'll be awhile before the tech comes to the sounds we're making."

"Any guess how long?"

"As we're surrounded by the sounds of the city, perhaps an hour, may-hap's longer, depending on the tech. Of course it could've been upgraded since I last read up on it, which means they could be listening in on our conversation right now," Randolph added, his polite way of telling her to shut up. He caught her *Oh, sorry* look.

After making the side wall of Mr. Hilden's home, Randolph marked the wall where he would cut, then took off the bulky goggles. With a glance at his watch, he noted the time of 10:41 p.m. *Two minutes ahead of schedule.* He half smiled, wanting to pat his own head, but refrained from such frivolity.

"Hand me one of your pistols."

"I thought you hated guns?" Jill remarked dryly, still wearing her goggles to better watch their backs.

"I do, but this wall's been doubled and my pen knife hasn't the strength to cut through."

"So I'm useful after all," she said with a bit of sarcasm.

"Jill," Randolph said, annoyed, "the gun please."

"Yes Daddy," she replied, sounding just like her softer side, a personality they truly didn't need out guarding their backs at this time or point.

"I really wish you'd be more serious from here on out," he grumbled, setting the power level to half, "I really need to know you're with me on this."

"All right, sweetie, if it keeps your boxers from bunching up."

Randolph shot her a glare which she reacted by giving him a toothy grin before pulling out the bag of mini mines.

"Excuse me, but what do you think you're doing?"

"You're about to cut a hole in the wall, right? Well, these will give us a few seconds extra if someone spots the different shades of darkness and investigates."

"By blowing off his leg?"

"They're not that deadly—more likely a foot, but it'll give the guard something other to worry about than your hole."

Randolph rolled his eyes skyward, then took note of his watch. Two minutes had passed in their exchange. And here he wanted to be inside the house by midnight before the security systems did a back up of the last four hours, before applying the extra security measures which had yet to be activated. As he held no time for arguing, Randolph stuck to the time table, ignoring her antics as he applied gun to wall. After a check of the hole depth the gun made, Randolph adjusted its strength till the beam burned through. After making a large enough hole to work comfortably, he returned Jill's gun and activated the pen light using the laser to cut into the electrical tube. With the light held between his teeth, Randolph spread out the wires and checked them against the schematics on his palm unit.

"Can you cut the security line from here?" Jill asked.

The Paranoid Thief

"Yes, but that's not what I'm doing," Randolph explained around the laser light between his teeth.

"Then why are we wasting time here?"

Randolph spared her a glance. *Now that's the Jill I understand.* "The security lines are hooked to a volt meter which would register the current change and set off the alarm. What I'm attempting to do is locate Mr. Hilden's security computer and deactivate the system net on the inside by hacking into it. With luck, the crew watching the system will assume he's gotten up and switched off the alarms so he could do some late night work."

"I thought you said his computer isn't hard wired into the net?"

"It's not; however, eighty-five percent of the professional population use a second computer as a backup system, with all the commands installed. In this way they have complete control while at their desk."

"Uh-huh, and if it's not?"

"We're screwed." He located the wire he needed, and hooked up his random code generator. Able now to relax against the wall, as his palm computer might take a while, Randolph hoped Mr. Hilden hadn't a secondary unit as redundancy.

Jill stood and flattened herself against the wall, looking right and left.

"Jill?" He'd heard nothing to be alarmed about.

"Hush, love," she hissed, easing out the two pistols in her waist band, flipping off the safeties and stretching out her arms to either side, "You keep doing your job and I'll protect your sexy buns."

Sexy buns? Randolph wondered how any man's butt could be thought of as sexy. Regardless of the repulsive image of a male's butt, Randolph shook his head and returned his eyesight to the screen. The first green dot was on, indicating Mr. Hilden's computer was up and running. *Good.* Next came the second and third LEDs, letting him know he was in. Now with something to do, Randolph rubbed his hands together to warm them up a might before connecting the keyboard to the code breaker and eyed the screen as he let his fingers fly.

Ten minutes into his work, Jill slid down the wall. "How much longer will this take?"

"Depending on where he has the codes and files I need, upwards of an hour, perhaps more."

"An hour?" Jill hissed, "Are you crazy? We're sitting ducks out here!"

"It'll take longer if you keep distracting me, now hush!" Randolph spared only a glace her way as she pushed back up to a standing passion.

Forty-seven minutes later, twenty-eight before the program reset for late night settings, Randolph unhooked the wires with a sigh of satisfaction.

"So can we go now?"

"I assume you're talking about getting inside the house," Randolph remarked, pocketing his equipment.

"I had hoped the way you were smiling he had left his bank account on the computer so we could leave the grounds."

"That's wishful thinking, and something I did explore, but alas no. All I've done is shut off his security net in the house and gained the entry codes to the door's key pad so I don't set off any silent alarms I hadn't known about."

"What alarm?"

"Exactly." Randolph moved along the wall to the side door. He pulled out the lock picks and set them in place before punching in the entry code. Once entered, Randolph moved the instruments deftly with his fingers, unlocking the door easily. After a look in the darkened kitchen, he moved in and held the door for Jill while his eyes adjusted to the night light. He closed the door silently and resetting the inside pad, paused to look over the kaleidoscope of pots, skillets and utensils hung over a preparation table in the middle of the room. To his left, the cleaning station took up part of a wall, including a hydro steaming unit. *The latest model, even.* Over to their right, a walk-in cooler with variable locality temperature controls, very expensive and absolutely indispensable to connoisseurs of specialty dishes whose ingredients need a certain degree of temperature.

"Do we have time for a light meal?" Jill jokingly asked, trying to soothe away some of her tension.

"Oh sure, just give me an hour and I'll whip up a meal to discuss his bank account over while we sip on his favorite wine," Randolph remarked dryly, secretly wishing he could.

Jill stuck out her tongue then snapped her head to the entranceway further in, instantly on guard and waving Randolph quiet.

Randolph waved off Jill's deadly intentions, signaling her to hide as the lights in the other room turned on.

Jill shot a glare at Randolph as he squeezed behind the dishwasher. Obviously not wishing to lose the element of surprise, and only for his sake, she stepped into the cooler.

Randolph took note of Jill's decision with thanks, and settled comfortably a moment before he heard talking in the other room, drawing closer to the kitchen.

"I'm telling you, there's something wrong," Randolph heard an angry voice complain as the kitchen lights came on and the door swung open. "Mr. Hilden's bedroom lights are not on, yet I saw movement flicker on my screen in this room."

Randolph ducked low as he could get, and only then noticed the washer was polished stainless steel. Upon seeing the reflected images of the two men approaching, Randolph knew to a certainty if he could see them, they sure as hell could see him if they were even remotely careful in looking around. Sending a glance upward for help, Randolph watched the men separate around the preparation station as the other man commented.

"Well, I don't see anyone. The outside alarms are not going off, nor are the ones in here. Mr. Hilden must be up if he was even down here or we'd have our ears blasted off with alarms."

"But what if it's that guy Mr. Hilden's been so upset about? He's supposed to be the very best at circumventing even state-of-the-art equipment."

"Jeff, you're giving the guy way too much credit. Mr. Hilden has four systems alone covering the grounds, and if that doesn't get him, the explosive pressure plates in the yard will."

"But what of his new companion, isn't she supposed to be a top notch assassin?"

"She's an ex-military sniper, you dolt, which makes her absolutely useless in close combat. Besides, if she does make it to the house, Mr. Hilden has a special surprise for her. Now will you get your look see over with, so I can get back to my video show?"

"I still want to report this," Jeff grumbled.

"Oh, for the love of...there's no one in here damn it!" The other pulled open the cooler, motioning his partner to have a peek. "If there was, this is the only place a person could hide."

Randolph closed his eyes briefly in anticipation of the coming seconds, but surprisingly nothing happened. No shouts. No bodies falling. Nothing! To his surprise, Randolph opened an eye and saw Jill within the cooler, spayed-legged, both guns raised, but as neither man looked in the cooler before the door slammed closed, she never fired a shot.

"Satisfied?" the one nearest to the cooler griped. "Now cut the crap and let's get back to our office, perhaps your equipment needs a diagnostic test."

Jeff grumbled, but seemed to concede the point to his partner as they left Randolph alone with his heart attack.

When the door closed and the lights went off, it took Randolph some moments before he could get his rubbery legs to support him in squeezing out of his hiding hole and over to open the cooler door for Jill to step out.

Chapter Twenty-Two

"Thanks for not shooting," Randolph said with sincere gratitude.

"Don't thank me yet," she said, closing the door and rubbing her arms. "Because I didn't take them out when the opportunity presented itself, we may have to deal with them at a later point, more likely at a time most inconvenient for us."

Randolph regretted the fact Jill could very well be right if he made a mistake; still, he feverishly hoped he lived up to Mr. Hilden's expectations.

Reapplying the night vision goggles, Randolph motioned Jill to follow, and moved up to the door. He opened it enough to look both ways down the wooden hallway.

"Which way?" Jill whispered.

"I don't know—this hallway's not supposed to be here," Randolph said over his shoulder. The front of the home would be their best bet. He slipped out, and made himself like a piece of wallpaper, moving with practiced ease along the wall.

Randolph stopped at a door on their side as the wall in front of them ended in an entertaining room. With a look-see in the door, he breathed, "Bathroom."

Jill nodded as he flattened himself up on the other wall so he could peek around the entertaining room with relative concealment. From where he stood, the wooden flooring below his feet vanished, and a white polished marble floor began. Next he took note of the sheep-skinned furniture, oak trunk tables and the absolutely beautiful redwood coffee table with an oblong glass top. With a stray thought of his mother, and how she would like that table, Randolph looked past the sound system and found the stairs by a low-level glow.

The Paranoid Thief

Having learned from the guards' inspection there was a secondary alarm running to register movement, most likely installed to keep track of any guests, Randolph signaled Jill to the floor and they crawled along like two water spiders till making the stairs.

Once seated on the first rug-covered step, Jill whispered, "Did you catch a look at his video pictures? They're quite lovely."

Randolph glanced sideways at Jill, removed his goggles and looked about. Four video pictures, each depicted the Virgin Islands before the last storm some twenty years back wiped them clean.

"Yes, they're quite lovely," he admitted, as he watched one move between night and day in only a few seconds. "Now keep low and your weight evenly distributed as we ascend."

"As you say, love," Jill whispered with a bit more affection in her voice then the present situation dictated.

Randolph looked more closely at Jill, wondering if she'd allowed her softer side out; she was only one of the two to use terms of endearment with such feeling. But then Randolph discarded the notion, knowing full well Jill wouldn't be that stupid. As the pair moved between duel saltwater tanks to either side of the stairs, with an abundance of sea clams, colorful coral, clown fish and the very poisonous but beautiful lion fish, Jill took that moment to tap him on the shoulder.

"Darling, this gives me a grand idea."

"Oh, what about?" Randolph asked, stopping mid way up the stairs to turn and look her in the eyes, trying to see if he was wrong about his assessment.

"Our home-to-be of course, wouldn't a tank like this be absolutely adorable in the wall between the living room and kitchen?"

What in the hell was Jill up to? "Jill," he began kindly so as not to upset her, "as much as I love you, this is not the time for you to be out. Could you please trade places?"

"Oh, sorry, love, it's just that I've never seen how the rich live. And by the looks of this place so far, those entertainment videos don't truly do the rich any justice if their homes look even half as good as this place is, even in the dark."

"Tell you what—if this pans out, I'll build a place for the three of us. Now, if you don't mind, please let your other half out."

"Hmm, of course, love," Jill's softer side intoned with some regret, then stood on tiptoes to lean into Randolph so she could passionately kiss and hug him.

"Jill, please, this is neither the place nor the time," he scolded quietly.

"As you say, love," she answered, then her eyes changed and the other Jill was out. "You're lucky that's all she did. I got an image she was trying to come up with a way to pull you back into the bathroom we passed."

"What for?" Randolph asked mildly, much relieved.

"I'm afraid both of us are feeling horny right now," Jill explained without embarrassment.

Randolph turned with raised eyebrows to her admission.

She shrugged. "I can't help how we feel. My only thoughts on the matter is it's this tropical setting. Perhaps he has the air scented with some stimulants."

"I don't smell anything," Randolph remarked, irritated. *How could anyone get turned on while deep in enemy territory? But then there are those who like the thrill of doing it in public places where the risk of getting caught heightens the sexual experience.*

The Paranoid Thief

When Jill gave no other comment, Randolph took her words at face value, as they were far too deep in Mr. Hilden's home, to argue the matter out. With a quick check into Jill's eyes one last time, Randolph signaled her to proceed up the remainder of the stairs.

Silently he replaced his desire to throttle Jill for allowing her softer side out. *If the truth were to be told, I'd rather rob a business any day over the simplest home break-ins. For two reasons really; one, there really ought to be a place a man can relax without having to worry about fighting off the wolf after working a full day at his job; and two, businesses don't have little surprises like yappy dogs or animals—like the cat that just shot by us heading down stairs!*

"John, are you all right?" Jill whispered, touching his shoulder with concern as he looked skyward holding a hand to his pounding heart.

Randolph patted her hand, nodding, then caught the name she'd called him by and hissed, "What are you doing out? I need your stronger self out right now."

"It's all right love, she's having a hard time with something and told me she needs time to think about it, but don't worry, if she's needed I'll tell her."

"Uh-huh. Jill, this is not a time to keep switching about. I need to know who I'm with and if truth be told, I really need your stronger personality out right now," Randolph explained, starting to lose his patients.

"That's what I thought as well. But she assures me this is the best for the three of us."

"No offense, but how is having an inexperience person guarding my back an advantage?" He argued softly, trying not to let his agitation spill out to upset her.

"She didn't say." She shrugged.

Her response held no signs indicating she knew how really dangerous this was.

Catching another look in her eyes that made him wish he could risk backing them out of the home, Randolph decided to try once more. "Jill, please, would you ignore her wish and change places?"

"Anything for you, love," Jill whispered, putting her arms around him, squeezing.

Randolph awaited the transition; she hugged him tighter as if not wishing to let go. Then she pulled away, allowing her hands to slide down his arms before looking up into his eyes with adoring passion.

"Well?"

"I'm sorry, love, she won't do it." Jill smiled up on him, allowing her fingers to linger on his palms before she put her hands behind her as if trying to control them. "She said, and I quote, 'Stuff it, sweetie, this is best for all concerned.'" Longing filled her eyes as she shrugged and smiled.

Grinding his teeth, not believing they were having this hushed conversation deep in the lion's den, Randolph rubbed his face and hissed. "All right. Fine, just please keep alert."

Jill nodded she would. So Randolph reluctantly moved them deeper into the ants' nest, because in truth, if they left now, he would never get in this deep again.

By now the systems outside had backed up and reset, meaning it would be too risky to leave anyway, especially dragging along an inexperienced child, which is how Jill's softer side would react to the alarms and armed guards. With a gesture she was to stay put at the top of the stairs, Randolph slipped quietly along the wall, checking out three doors in succession along the right end of the hallway. Once near the first door, he pulled out an ordinary stethoscope and placed it on the door; hearing nothing, he silently opened it to reveal a spare bedroom. Next came a bathroom at the end of the hall, then loud snoring from the next door. With Mr. Hilden located, Randolph moved to the other side of the stairway, finding the study.

Randolph reapplied the spectrum goggles, dialed through the selections and found nothing. *Good.* Randolph smiled. *That's how it should be.* Signaling Jill to come over quietly, he checked the door once more out of anxiety and felt her arms go around his middle before she snuggled up to his back.

"Jill, what are you doing?"

"Hmm? Oh, sorry, darling," she said giving another squeeze before letting go. "It's just that I love you so very much."

"Well, I'd appreciate it if you didn't love me quite that much right now, okay?"

"I'll try," she smiled, using a finger to brush a stray lock of hair out of his eyes.

Not understanding what was with her, Randolph got them inside and the door closed. "Jill, what's going on with you? You're acting crazy—you're all touchy feely at a time I don't need to be distracted!"

Jill looked on him with eyes uncomprehending to their situation, and laid a hand on his face tenderly.

Randolph grabbed her wrist. "Stop it! This is neither the time nor place. Now sit here"—he indicated a chair next to the door—"and be still!"

Jill nodded she would, and took off her jacket, laying it across her lap and interlacing her fingers, resting her hands on the jacket just as if she were waiting for him to try on clothing in an apparel department.

To her apparent submission to his will, Randolph nodded approval, and turned to view the room with the night vision goggles. Wood paneling made the room seem cozy, with the added lingering scent of cigar smoke. This told him Mr. Hilden had a habit of spending hours relaxing in the leather chair behind the desk, most likely eyeing the activity scrolling across the two screens, each angled to face the chair from the opposite corners of the desk. Behind this and in the corner was a coat and hat rack with a smoking jacket hanging off one prong. *Possibly waiting to be worn for another day of destroying someone's life,* Randolph remarked dryly, envisioning the evil smirk Mr. Hilden had given him in the execution chamber. Shaking off that bit of memory, Randolph noted no windows but eight video screens, each exactly placed, so it was child's play to pick out the one with the wall safe behind it. With a smile, Randolph walked the few steps to the wall and set out his tools carefully on the rug floor. After eyeing the video frame a moment, he pulled out and turned on the pen-light, laying his head close to the wall to look over the edges without touching its surface, as some had movement sensors. Checking that security measure off the list, Randolph slid two exposed wires up underneath the frame and watched his palm meter screen. For a moment, Randolph puzzled over the lack of protection a blackmail artist used to keep his files locked away. But not one to argue that matter, Randolph looked over at Jill to make certain she was still seated, and found her bouncing her legs and gripping the jacket as if trying to stave off something.

"Bathroom?" he mouthed.

Jill bit her lip, and denied the need, though to Randolph she looked as if she needed something and whatever it was she needed it now. With a hope she was simply reacting to the stressful situation, he turned back to the frame and calmly moved it out of the way.

Seeing the Craymore 6000 nestled in the wall, Randolph smirked, remembering the sales commercial, advertising it as the ultimate in home security, with a forty-number keypad and switchable dial for

The Paranoid Thief

changing the numbers to symbols, making the Craymore 6000 home security safe virtually un-crackable. *Virtually.*

Digging into his pack of goodies, Randolph removed two alligator clips and a length of electrical cord, but before he put them to use, he heard a whimper from behind and shot a glance Jill's way. To his dismay, he discovered Jill sitting on the edge of her chair, in some agitation, watching every move he made. Not liking the situation, as he held no idea what to do with her, he proceeded to clamp the clips on the handle and dial of the safe, before plugging the cord into a common wall outlet for a brief second. He removed cord and clips, and calmly punched in the pad a standard set of numbers for opening the safe, should its circuitry ever get shorted out. With an easy turn of the handle, Randolph swung the door open and looked inside the normal-sized wall safe.

Just inside the door, sat a jewelry box as the obvious first item to be extracted. This he moved carefully, sliding the box to the edge of the safe and leaving it there. Next he took out the pen light and moved a few feet to his left in order to cut out a piece of the paneling to slide the box out on, without exposing the bottom. With the booby trap resting on the paneling, Randolph transported the box out of the way, on to a book shelf.

Now that he could inspect the rest of the safe, Randolph heard Jill's chair creak as if someone stood. When he turned, lowering his arms, Jill was pulling off her shirt and approaching.

"What the hell are you doing?"

Jill dropped her shirt without regard of where they were, and reached out for him. "John, please hold me, love me, I need to feel your arms tight about my body, taste your lips on mine, feel the warmth of your passion on my skin."

"Jill? Now is not the time for this," he stressed, eyes wide to her behavior. "I've perhaps ten more minutes and we can go."

"But that's such a long time," she complained, her wide eyes and swollen lips exposing her desires. "Could you not spend a few moments and love me?"

"Control yourself!"

But in answer to his request, Jill took his head in her hands and forced her lips on his.

Randolph grabbed her shoulders to push her away, but she slid her arms around his neck, making it that much harder to dislodge her hungry mouth from his. At the same time she worked her leg up and down his.

Stunned and confused, Randolph got her lips off only to have her nuzzle his neck. Fearful of being found out, he took her head with considerable strength and pushed her away. "Will you stop it! We're going to be discovered!"

"I'm sorry. I can't control this, I need...I need so desperately to feel you deep inside, the rock hardness of you between my thighs, please, John, can't you tell I'm on fire for you?"

"Yes I can, but—"

"Then shut the hell up and screw me damn it, before I burst into flames!" she demanded loudly.

Wide-eyed and shocked that she said that with such volume, Randolph used all his strength to separate them and prepared to strike her to render her unconscious.

But before he accomplished that, the lights came on and a voice from the door said with amusement, "I really underestimated how well that stuff works."

Chapter Twenty-Three

Randolph blinked repeatedly, and snapped his head toward the doorway as Jill reapplied her body to his.

Still at the doorway, Mr. Hilden remarked further, "I must admit, I'm very impressed."

With their discovery, Jill whimpered in misery before she slid down Randolph's body to the floor at his feet, seemingly in immeasurable distress, still trying to unbuckle his pants with trembling fingers, which Randolph grabbed to keep her from accomplishing.

Feeling a lead weight pole-vault into the pit of his stomach, accepting these as his last minutes on earth, he still couldn't help but feel the fool inside as he asked, "What's wrong with her?"

The two men he'd seen earlier, accompanied by two other redundant guards, spread out about the room with pistols raised. Mr. Hilden remarked easily, "Nothing a man's dick won't solve."

Still puzzled, Randolph watched Mr. Hilden stroll confidently over to his desk, assured in Randolph's defenselessness, and lit an overpriced cigar. "You see, she's under the influence of a powerful drug I'd placed in the ventilation system earlier. This remarkable drug makes women horny as hell."

Ill-tempered at Jill's constant efforts in clawing at his belt, trying to get his pants off, Randolph slapped her hands away and kneed her to the floor as Mr. Hilden chuckled.

"It's an illegal drug, if you hadn't guessed. One that some of my associates request from time to time if their desires cannot be met by position or ego." Mr. Hilden ignited his cigar, and took several starter puffs as he strolled over to his open safe. He eyed Randolph's handiwork, made a face of disgust to the destruction of his paneling, and closed the safe.

With an amused look to Jill's half-naked, shaking body, Mr. Hilden explained, "The drug was originally designed to induce frigid women with the desire for sex. However," Mr. Hilden remarked, toeing Randolph's small bag of tools, "a lab assistant with a grasp of understanding in economics felt the black-market was a more profitable proposal for himself, and the rest is history."

By this time Jill's pain became very evident to Randolph as her tears rolled unchecked down her cheeks, and she pleaded for him to end her agony. But Randolph had more serious matters to consider as two of Mr. Hilden's men motioned him to turn to the wall, all the guards thus far totally ignoring Jill.

"Now, please don't be a bore, Mr. McCann, and do as my men direct. I give you my word I'll make your deaths relatively painless."

Before he capitulated, wishing nothing more than to stall, plead, or beg—anything to gain him time in considering other possibilities than receiving a laser burst through the brain pan, Randolph asked, "How did you know Jill would be with me?"

"An educated guess. Once an acquaintance passed over the video of your anti-climatic escape, I couldn't help but note how well Major Wander worked with you. And seeing as I'd set you up so Mr. Stanton could take out the rather bothersome Henderson family, I felt it a good bet you'd set aside your reputation this one time and accept her help in eradicating me."

"In truth, I had thought about it. Jill told me she could have taken you out more than once in her surveillance, but I wouldn't hear of it, unfortunately my principles are far stronger than you give me credit for."

The Paranoid Thief

Mr. Hilden waved his cigar in a dismissive gesture. "A weakness I dare say in your genetic make-up that made you useless to me, save for that one job."

"So why me? What was so detrimental to your empire you'd waste an entire family and servants over?" Randolph wished he could do something about Jill's whimpering, her hands still working to draw his pants down, which forced him to keep his own busy in keeping the pants in place.

Mr. Hilden tapped off the ashes of his cigar before drawing in a long lungful of flavored nicotine, then expelled the smoke Randolph's way. "I had no real choice. Their underage daughter was very persistent one evening at a party I was holding. A rather enticing prospect, I might say, had she been of age. However, as she wasn't, she received my negative response unwell and upon slipping me a Mickey, got her wish." He took another draw, and watched Jill's antics with normal male interest.

"Her desires were of course guided by her father, a rather embarrassing blackmail plot he concocted in his political ambitions to hold sway over me, or face arrest for statutory rape once I was proven the father of her growing child."

Not having turned around, Randolph began forming an ideal about what to do. But he still needed time to develop it out.

"So why the whole family? Why not simply take out the girl? And above all, why involve me in this?"

Mr. Hilden leaned back on his desk, eyes looking off into space a moment before returning them to Randolph, deciding to be gracious. "You really don't know the depths of the world you inject yourself into, do you?" He took another puff before signaling one of his guards to pour him a drink. "Disposing of the girl singularly would only dispose of future irritating expenditures on lawyers in family courts, while doing nothing in protecting my wealth and reputation from countless innuendos from Mr. Henderson, his family and servants. Thus my response was really none of my doing, but a pragmatic resolution in countering his ambitions. And as for you, well, let us say there are some very influential people I have gained monetary and positional gains from in disposing of a tiresome threat. A rather fortuitous side effect which made the whole episode acceptable."

While Mr. Hilden took a sip of his drink, Randolph sought one more stalling action. "So what tipped you off we were here? I know I hadn't missed any security system and even though Jill's outburst was loud, it wasn't enough to carry into your room."

"Knowing full well you could surpass any system you set your mind to, I bought a simple low-tech baby monitor and set it on my desk." Mr. Hilden moved his hand to indicate the simple black speaker box with his cigar. He took another sip of his drink, obviously enjoying the look of pain on Randolph's face.

To be out witted by a simple sound amplifier. Randolph scolded himself, losing his train of thought.

Though Randolph ranted within, he still saw Jill's apparent need for sexual release over-ride her repulsion of the men near at hand. Clawing her way up Randolph's body, she turned to the men in the room and unfastened her pants in a manor to draw all male eyes.

"Please, sir," Jill began, stepping out of her pants, dropping them behind her only after freeing up the two pistols from their concealment. "I can't take this burning desire any longer, I need a man! I'll die if I can't get a man inside me!"

The demanding tone in Jill's voice lent a certainty in Randolph's mind to whom of Jill's personalities now stood before him. Not a simple-minded average woman, or a doped-up female on pheromones, but a cold-blooded killer. One who expertly thumbed off the safeties to two pistols behind her back while Mr. Hilden and his men eyed her as nothing but a sexed-crazed woman in heat.

This mistake only registered on Mr. Hilden's face when Jill stretched out her arms to either side, leveling pistols and firing in a swiping motion, taking out the four guards with precision accuracy before aiming at Mr. Hilden, telling the man in deadly calmness,

"One move and I'll cut you in two."

Still unable to stare on her bare form without disbelief at such a personality, Randolph saw Mr. Hilden's forgotten cigar fall to the floor while Jill, standing stark naked without shame, ordered.

"Randolph! Quit gawking at my ass and make certain the bodyguards are dead."

Startled out of his amazement, Randolph noted how tense Jill's shoulder muscles were, and got the impression she was fighting something off with a tremendous force of will.

"Now damn it all, before I kill him," she ordered Randolph like a drill sergeant.

Goaded into motion, Randolph moved to the unmoving men and removed all guns while checking for pulses. His heart sank as he found not one. Although he hated the deaths, Randolph consoled his beliefs they aided Mr. Hilden in killing others. Removing the last of the hardware, Randolph told Jill solemnly, "They're beyond any-one's help."

"Good. Now tell me, do we really need this piece of garbage alive?"

Randolph took note of the quiver in her voice, but before he could answer, Mr. Hilden's clinched jaw, telegraphed his intent to Jill's military training. Jill deftly burned off his arms as they came up, and brought the gun handle down on his cranium as he passed, felling him in a wasted heap of unconscious flesh on the floor.

Randolph swallowed his heart. "Damn, Jill, I'm so glad you're back!" Wanting to hug Jill like never before, Randolph halted his approach when Jill turned, her face contorted in pain. Uncertain if she was in full control of her mind, Randolph backed away, raising his hands to show he was of no danger to her.

Jill dropped the guns on the closest chair and demanded in an angry screech, "Damn it Randolph! Quit backing away and drop your pants. I can't take much more of this!"

Before Randolph could react, she cleared off the desk with a swipe of her arm, grabbed his shirt, and jumped on the desk's edge, gathering him into her arms, wrapping her legs tightly about his torso before he could step out his pants.

Feverishly locking her lips on his own, with demanding force, Jill fused every inch of her skin with his, deftly stripping his clothes with fast moving hands.

In spite of the fact there were four dead men and one unconscious lying in the middle of the floor, Jill's expert manipulation of her body forced Randolph's mind into another world where she could work through her demanding need for sexual release with her chosen partner.

Chapter Twenty-Four

Randolph sat heavily in the desk chair when Jill's needs finally subsided enough to let him go. Collapsed like a rag doll, filling his lungs with great gulps of air to reintroduce oxygen into his blood, he barely noticed Jill did the same lying a-top the desk.

Only after Randolph was able to breathe semi-normally did he set to work reapplying his clothes before clearing out the safe. Though he was bothered by his performance with such carnage sprawled about him, Randolph was pragmatic enough to move around the bodies and help Jill into another chair so he could turn on Mr. Hilden's personal computer and hard wired unit.

Now is not the time to fall apart. And taking his own advice, he preceded to take advantage of this once in a life time opportunity. After cracking his fingers over the desk, Randolph dropped chip after chip into Mr. Hilden's private computer and saved file after file on his own disk, skimming each for what he was looking for.

Mean while, as Randolph involved himself in the computers, Jill stood and stretched out her lithe body in an effort to work out the soreness which would develop later before putting on her shirt. While doing so, she took notice of Mr. Hilden stirring, picked up one of her guns and sprayed him with a wide beam to keep him unconscious. After which she lower her arm in irritation at her inability in controlling her body's desires. In disgust with her action that could have gotten them both killed, Jill tossed the pistol into Randolph's bag and started pacing the floor without bothering to put on her pants.

While Jill paraded before him in agitation, Randolph located Mr. Hilden's assets, bank accounts and investments. Now able to work on the computer hooked up to the hard line, Randolph entered passwords, and moved right into the online broker and proceeded to make Mr. Hilden a pauper. With fingers flying, he sold off stocks, bonds and investments, switching next to online banking and initiating maximum loans on all properties, vehicles and registered insured valuables.

As each delivered payable credits, Randolph dumped all acquired funding into Mr. Hilden's bank account before transferring the credits into his own Switzerland account. After this, he remembered Mr. Hilden's company ties, and ignoring Jill's impatience, her eyes imploring him to finish up, he broke into the company's accounts and payrolls, dumping all funding into Mr. Hilden's bank account before rerouting to his own. Then only after leaving an electrical foot print in the accounts did Randolph refinance the building to its absolute maximum.

As for anything else possible, it would have to await another time, for when he glanced up at Jill, he saw her glaring at him to move it, or she was going to beat the shit out of him.

Acknowledging her need to leave, Randolph eliminated any foot prints of his own work and with Jill's help, rearranged the room to appear as if Mr. Hilden had an argument with his staff.

The ruse, of course, would fool no one, but as the over taxed courts liked things simple, he would aid them to follow the simple assumption.

Randolph then gathered up all chips and disks, dumped all in his bag, and pulled out his homemade DNA scrambler. Activating the timer while Jill reinserted herself back into her restricting clothing by force of will, he drew up his own remaining clothing and steered Jill to the security room. After disabling all active measures and eliminating all video feeds and sound files of their night's work, he made certain no one was about watching the place at five in the morning. Gaining the front porch, and gathering up Jill's little deterrents, they both heard Randolph's little toys go off throughout the home. Only then did the couple walk out the front gate, arm in arm, across the street and right on through the park, looking very much like any other loving couple out for an early morning stroll.

Upon clearing the city limits two hours later, driving a brand-new Arjentay air-car, the latest model with all luxuries included, Randolph had to smile, picturing Mr. Hilden's face when told by the hospital he held no insurance to cover the cost of reattaching his arms.

Still smiling with the knowledge he now held all the names of the people who screwed him and his brother, he remove his eyes from the road momentarily to admire how lovely Jill looked in the brand new dress she'd purchased while he paid for the car.

Jill saw him looking and smiled as well, but shortly became serious. "So how do we rescind the orders to have us killed?"

"That'll be handled on its own when the stock market opens in a few minutes." When Jill's face bore puzzlement, which was only natural for one uninformed with the financial world, Randolph went on to explain, "All the dealing I preformed a few hours ago will be tallied up in the accounting firms precisely at 8:00 a.m. when the markets open. You see, although all corporations work 24 hours a day, there's a down time between 3:00 a.m. and 6:00 a.m. every morning so all financial programs can tally up the day's activities for tax purposes. It was during this window of opportunity I sold off and hocked everything Mr. Hilden owns. Thus the programming will automatically tally all the activity to post on yesterday's board, this morning at 8:00 a.m."

"So how does that stop an assassin if he's already taken the job?"

A rather pertinent question unless you have knowledge of the beast, Randolph reminded himself before answering her. "If the man's a pro, he'll check the stock market at eight to make certain Mr. Hilden can pay the fee. If he's not, there's nothing I can do about it, save to say I tried." As Jill mulled this news over, Randolph decided it was time she remedied his concern of her antics back in Mr. Hilden's home. But being tactful, he asked her in a mild but curious tone, "Jill, I'm still puzzled over what happened to you in Mr. Hilden's home and why you let your other self out at such a time?"

Jill looked sideways at him as if debating whether to tell him or not, but after only a moment of silence, she said, "That jerk was right about those pheromones he used, and it hitting the black market." She bit her lip, as though remembering something awful. But then she took a deep breath and confided in him. "I was a sophomore in school when some rich joker put several bottles of that concoction in the air circulation unit one hot and rainy day. It wasn't till the trial I learned he was horny as hell for his history teacher and hoped it would make her horny enough to screw him. It also came out that he hadn't been given instructions on how much to use and had done no research into whether the unit moved air throughout the school."

"You don't mean?" Randolph asked in shock.

"Yep. Within a half hour, three thousand girls along with one hundred and sixty-two women teachers and supporting members were affected. And the closer they were to the originating source, the worse it was for both sexes."

"I take it you were in school that day?"

"I was in the same damn room as the teacher he wanted to screw," Jill admitted with remembered feelings, turning her head away, too embarrass to face Randolph while she bitterly recalled the event. "At that time, me and my other self were still working out our personalities, and as there was two of us within one skull feeling the effects, it took twice as much sex to alleviate the fire."

Jill sat awhile without talking, her shoulders shaking as if she were silently crying.

Believing it might help her to heal, Randolph prompted her gently, "And this happened all over the school?"

Jill glanced his way after wiping her eyes then busied her hands by brushing out her dress. "In verifying degrees, of course; there was hardly a boy or girl not affected in some way." Jill paused yet again and seemed to debate on continuing her tale that would reopen the old wound further, but then confessed, "Randolph, when you guessed I'd gone to see my family, I really went to see my daughter."

Randolph turned to look at her with an *Oh?* He wished he could have gathered her into his arms, but his mind and hands were needed to guide their air-car through the highway of daily commuters. Still, Randolph wanted to show her some support by words if nothing else, but before he could, Jill went on.

"It was for my daughter that I joined the corps. You see, Mother and I were on the poor side after Daddy ran off with his busty secretary. And not having the credits for an abortion, it was the only thing I could do to lower my mother's financial burdens for any hospital bills accrued in my birthing her."

"But, but surely the courts made the prankster's parents pay for all medical bills? After all, you did say he was rich."

"No, I said his parents were rich. Once the lawsuits started piling up in the courts, his parents disowned him, only spending enough credits on a high class lawyer to get him out of serving time, which the slick-talking bastard did," Jill said hotly.

Randolph heard the words law suits with a capital S. Sensing where this was going, he still asked the obvious. "You weren't the only one hurt…"

"Seventeen girls, one teacher and two boys committed suicide," Jill began, reciting the numbers as if it happened yesterday. "Two hundred and sixty-three girls, twenty-five teachers, six supporting faculty members and twenty-two boys were institutionalized, of which seventeen will never leave. Two hundred and five girls, twelve teachers and supporting members tested pregnant, along with a thousand or so miscellaneous medical bills for injuries and psychiatric treatments."

As the traffic thinned enough for Randolph to pull over, he pulled to the side and gathered Jill into his arms while her tears ran unashamed down her cheeks. After some minutes of her body heaving with pent-up emotions, Jill regained some control and pushed from Randolph's comforting embrace.

"My mother and daughter think I'm dead." Jill sniffed, with eyes downcast. "And as much as I want to hold Miranda in my arms, and ask for my mother's forgiveness, I know I could never do so without causing them both any more pain."

"Well, once I sort out some of these chips and disks, I'm sure we'll have enough for Senator Sterling to proceed on his promise of clearing your name."

Jill allowed a small smile to touch her lips, which seemed to slow her tears.

When it appeared she was in better control of herself, Randolph gave her a hug before shifting to get them back into the flow of traffic, and on their way.

"Randolph, as this unemployed prankster pays no money to anyone as the courts directed, and his parents pick up all his bills, keeping him in the luxury he was born into, do you think you could persuade them into making some amends for his deed?"

Randolph smiled, then chuckled, and gave her one more reassuring hug before moving out onto the road, promising, "My love, it would give me the greatest of pleasures to redirect all his parents' holding and liquid revenue into his name, so the court's can seize and disperse all credits obtained to all victims named in this deviants sexual adventures."

Upon hearing her lover's commitment to force this well-to-do family into making restitution to those whose lives had been forever changed by their pampered son, Jill leaned in and kissed Randolph's cheek before she snuggled up as close as the vehicle would allow. But before she allowed exhaustion to carry her away into the land of dreams, she curled her lips into a content smile, knowing full well her lovely paranoid thief was even now involved in running down the list of normal items they would both need for this new collaboration.

END

About the Author

Born in Tennessee and raised in California, Danny Estes graduated high school in 1977 and entered the working field with rudimentary skills in reading and writing. In 1978, Danny was introduced to fantasy role gaming, and enjoyed hours socializing with people whose imaginations needed more than the norm. These gamers acquainted Danny with his imaginative days of old.  With their inspiration, he began reading fantasy novels, and although his communication skills were barely adequate, he began writing fantasy stories. Then Word came to computers, and with this tool, Danny reinvented himself in writings.

Enjoying years of gaming and allowing his mind to run free, he met Patricia, a crafter of many arts with a passion to create. With her diligence in craftsmanship and urgings, Danny took the plunge and created full-fledged novels, developing stories to entertain in the science fiction and fantasy realms.

Between these stories, Danny has a normal domestic life and a regular mundane job in North Carolina. However, during off hours, Danny rubs his hands together, smiles maliciously, and settles before his computer to ventures forth into his mind and create fun and exciting adventures which he hopes will reacquaint you, the reader, with your own imagination.

You can email Danny with your questions and comments at dannyestes@wordbranch.com.

If you liked *The Paranoid Thief*, please leave feedback.

The Paranoid Thief is published by Word Branch Publishing, an independent publisher located in Marble, North Carolina. If you have a finished, or near-finished, book, we would like to hear about it. Word Branch Publishing believes that everyone has something important to say. http://wordbranch.com

See more of Word Branch Publishing's books at
http://wordbranch.com/book-shop.html

Made in the USA
Charleston, SC
05 April 2014